BOOK
FOUR
THE WEDDING·VOW

Never Love a Lord

REGINA SCOTT

*To the incomparable Jannie Meisberger, who brings my
stories to life in a whole new way, and to the Lord, who
gives me the stories to begin with.*

CHAPTER ONE

Chelsea Palace, England
Late August, 1825

PETUNIA BATEMAN MIGHT have been a commoner, but she was far from common.

Tuny took some pride in that fact as she followed her brother and sister-in-law through the crowds thronging the ornate reception room. How many other young ladies of her acquaintance were invited to a soiree at the palace being leased by the King of Batavaria and his sons outside London? Well, her dear friends Larissa and Callie were here, but they were betrothed to the crown prince and his brother, so they had a reason. So did their sister, Belle, who was also the daughter of a duke.

In fact, in a space filled with titled lords and ladies in fine clothes, Tuny, in her sunny yellow evening gown with the puffed sleeves, was probably the least notable.

But she did her best not to goggle.

It wasn't as if His Majesty was in attendance. The king was being very careful to distance himself from the Batavarian question, as the papers called Prince Otto Leopold's quest. The prince and his brother wanted King George to support their cause to see their ancestral lands restored. King George wanted little part of it.

Neither did the stunningly handsome fellow

approaching on their left. Panic threatened, and Tuny tugged at her sister-in-law's arm.

"Bit warm in here," she said when Charlotte looked at her askance, grey eyes wide and russet brows up in question. "I think I'll wander closer to the window."

"I'll come with you," Charlotte offered with a smile. She had no trouble blending in with present company. In her white silk gown embroidered with lilies, hair arranged in braids around her head, she looked her usual calm, composed self.

She patted the burly arm of Tuny's brother, and Matty promptly shouldered his way to where two tall windows overlooked the grounds. Her brother might once have been a pugilist, but she defied anyone looking at him now to see anything but a gentleman with his sable hair and elegantly tied cravat.

"Still avoiding Lord Ashforde, I see," Charlotte murmured, strategically placing her back to the gilded wall and nodding to the passing company.

Tuny drew in a breath of the perfumed air. "And will until I have a husband standing next to me."

"You might find it easier to attract a husband if you smile more often," Charlotte shot back.

Tuny smiled, but she wouldn't have been surprised if it looked more like a grimace.

She had had three Seasons, *three Seasons*! And she'd yet to attract a suitor she felt comfortable accepting. Larissa and Callie had been in nearly as dire straits before they'd met their true loves. That was likely why Belle had elicited a vow from her sisters and Tuny that they would all be married by harvest.

Tuny had lived her entire life in cities, so she had little knowledge of when farmers harvested their crops. But she had a feeling the time was drawing near. And not a suitor in sight.

"That Ashforde fellow seems determined," Matty said

with a tip of his chiseled chin toward the tall, ascetic gentleman who was once again strolling in their direction. "Should I speak with him, Tuny?"

"No!" The word came out forcefully, and the elderly matron promenading past stuck her nose in the air and plied her ostrich plume fan so quickly that Tuny felt the breeze.

"That is," Tuny said, tempering her volume, "there's no need for you to speak with him, Matty. He means nothing to me."

Something inside her informed her that statement was a lie. She forced down the thought. She'd been avoiding admiring his perfectly combed raven hair, deep blue eyes, high carriage, and graceful step for nearly three years now. What was one more night?

"May I have your attention, please?"

The words rang out over all other sounds, and heads turned toward the dais at the top of the room. In an old-fashioned powdered wig and green velvet coat with gold buttons the size of saucers, Mr. Lawrence, Lord Chamberlain for the Batavarian Court, stood tall and proud. His sharp gaze alone demanded that the buzz of conversation cease. Quiet settled on the room.

"Thank you," he said. "His Royal Highness, Prince Otto Leopold, has an announcement."

"It can't be his betrothal," Tuny whispered to Charlotte. "They announced that ages ago."

Charlotte patted her hand, gaze on the Lord Chamberlain.

Whose eyes were now trained on Tuny, as if he'd heard her murmur. She pasted on another smile.

Leo, as he was known to friends and family, rose from the throne and looked out on his guests. Resplendent in a scarlet tunic trimmed in gold, curly hair tamed into place, he was every inch the crown prince.

"On behalf of my father, King Frederick Augustus of

Batavaria, I would like to thank you for your kind support these last few weeks we have been in your beautiful country," he said, glancing around at his guests. "Your welcome, your offers of friendship, have touched our hearts. I would be remiss if I did not recognize those who have provided not only friendship, but material support. Their Graces, the Duke and Duchess of Wey, have been particularly helpful."

Across the room, Larissa's father inclined his head in acknowledgment, while her dark-haired mother beamed.

"We are also continually indebted to the keen mind and sage advice of Lord and Lady Belfort."

Meredith and Julian—more like aunt and uncle to her, Larissa, Callie, and Belle—offered smiles of appreciation. They had been given their titles by Leo's father, but they too wore them well.

"Sir Matthew Bateman and Lady Bateman have also given of their time most generously."

Now all gazes turned their way, and Matty tipped up his chin, smile hovering. Tuny couldn't help her grin.

"But tonight, I want to thank someone who went above and beyond to support our cause. She provided wise council to my brother and myself in matters of personal importance, and, when danger reared its head, she was among the first to step forward to help us combat it, at no small risk to her person and her reputation."

Was he talking about Larissa? Tuny craned her neck to catch sight of her friend, but Larissa didn't appear especially excited or honored. In fact, she was frowning as if she wasn't sure of the identity of this paragon either.

"Miss Petunia Bateman, step forward."

Tuny's head jerked to face Leo. His look was solemn, and he held out his hand, palm up, as if expecting her to walk over and put her fingers in his. Around her, she could see gazes turning, as the glittering company recognized her presence, perhaps for the first time.

"Go on," Charlotte whispered, giving her a nudge with her elbow.

Heart pounding in her ears, Tuny started forward. The crowd parted before her, leaving her a clear path to the dais. Every gaze was on her. She tried not to meet any of them. If she did, she might stumble to a halt. As it was, she barely managed to stop just short of taking Leo's hand.

It dropped to his side. Mr. Lawrence scurried forward to offer him a gold coronet surmounted by pearls.

"For services to the House of Archambault," Leo intoned, taking the coronet and raising it over his head, "I hereby award you the status of a baroness of Batavaria and the title Lady Moselle." He settled the coronet on Tuny's hair. "You have all my gratitude, your ladyship."

She must be dreaming. Her brother had been given the title of baronet when he'd saved the life of the then Prince Regent. Her oldest sister had earned the title of marchioness by marrying a widowed marquess to help him raise his baby daughter. She'd done nothing of such importance.

Yet the weight of the gold felt so real on her forehead. And was that… applause?

She turned, careful not to put her back to Leo. Thanks to Charlotte's tutelage, she knew that wasn't done, at least. All around the room, gloved hands clapped, and titled faces smiled.

"Huzzah!" Matty shouted.

From the back of the room, the Imperial Guards on duty shouted back, "Huzzah!" and clapped their fists to their black-clad chests in salute.

Tuny couldn't even find a nod in response. Any moment, she was going to wake up and discover herself tucked into her childhood room in Matty's house, just off Covent Garden. Girls whose fathers owned mills, much less worked in one as her father had, didn't become baronesses in their own right.

Leo linked his arm with hers. That too felt real. She clung to him, afraid she might fall over from shock otherwise!

"Will you join me for a moment of private conversation about your duties, Lady Moselle?" he asked solicitously.

She must have nodded, for the coronet slipped on her hair as if even the gold and pearls knew that they didn't really belong to her. She reached up a hand to right the coronet, nonetheless. Leo began strolling toward the tall doors that led out onto the gallery, nodding to this acquaintance and that friend. She felt the weight of their stares, heavier than the crown he'd put upon her head. Mr. Keller, a member of the Imperial Guards, held open one of the doors for her. Though she knew he was the shiest of the guards, his face broke into a grin as if he couldn't be more proud of her.

This must be real. She was a baroness. She had a title. The door closed behind them with a determined thud she felt to her bones.

She rounded on Leo, pulling away from him. "You've gone mad. There's no other explanation. Shall I call for a physician?"

Leo chuckled. Like that of his twin brother, Count Montalban, his curly blond hair just brushed the collar of his scarlet tunic. Larissa claimed his sharp blue eyes could look like diamonds. At the moment, Tuny believed her, for they were certainly sparkling.

"You earned that title," he assured her, voice colored by a complicated combination of accents from his time abroad. "I will not forget how you ventured out that night to make sure we could track our enemies to the source."

Earlier this month, she and the prince had attended a house party at Wey Castle, home of the Duke of Wey in Surrey. While there, enemies of Batavaria had attempted to stop the prince and his brother from cementing a place in King George's regard. Everyone had pitched in to help stop the villains. Tuny's part, to wait and watch with Matty, then shoot a flaming arrow into the sky to warn the others their enemy was on the move, had seemed small to her, but it had been exciting sneaking around in the dark, knowing she was part of making history.

"It was nothing," she told him. "No more than a lark."

Leo shook his head as if he disagreed. "Even before that, you gave me and Fritz sound advice."

"I gave you a piece of my mind, more like," Tuny reminded him. "And I ought to again. Me, a baroness? No one will believe that."

Leo drew himself up. "I am the representative of the King of Batavaria in England. I have his authority to grant honors and favors. I know of no one more deserving."

The door to the reception room opened, and Larissa and another of the Imperial Guards came out. Tuny recognized Mr. Huber, whom she had also met at the house party. He inclined his head in greeting, and the light from the chandelier made a halo on his straight, brunette hair.

"Tuny's elevation is the talk of the room, just as you'd hoped," Larissa said to Leo as she joined him, Mr. Huber staying at a discreet distance. Like Charlotte, Tuny's friend appeared right at home. Larissa could easily be a baroness, even a princess, with her artfully curled blond hair, wise blue eyes, and elegant demeanor.

"Have you told her yet?" she asked Leo.

Something hitched inside Tuny. She should have known being elevated couldn't be this easy.

"Told me what?" she asked, glancing from her friend to Leo.

"As a member of my court, you may be called upon from time to time to continue your support," Leo said.

Oh, was that all? She already provided support to the Society for the Prevention of Cruelty to Animals by arranging benefits and mailing literature. "Anything for a friend," Tuny said.

"You might not say that when you hear him out," Larissa warned with another look to Leo.

Leo squared his shoulders as if about to march into battle. "You are aware that King George has appointed a group of respected lords to advise him on whether to support our cause?"

Tuny nodded. "Lord Wellmanton, the Foreign Secretary Lord Canning, and others. It was in *The Times*."

"We are aware that Lord Wellmanton and Lord Canning are against the idea," Leo told her. "Some of the others are more supportive. Still, we have been told that they remain fairly evenly divided. The final decision may well depend on the advice of one lord."

"Lord Ashforde," Larissa said, as if determined that Tuny understand.

Her stomach sank. "Lord Ashforde?"

Leo nodded. "Given that you are known and respected by his lordship, we were hoping you could convince him to see things our way."

Once more panic approached, this time so swift and hard that Tuny took a step back.

"What you mean is that you want me to turn him up sweet!" she cried. "You really are mad!"

Lord Ashforde meandered about the reception hall, greeting acquaintances and pausing occasionally to chat. All the while he kept the doors through which Petunia Bateman had exited in view. Ever since returning from the house party given by the Duke of Wey, he had looked for opportunities to engage her in conversation. Perhaps, if he could manage a private word, he could apologize for the tension that now held them apart.

Especially because that tension was entirely his fault.

"Lady Moselle," Mrs. Richmond moaned aloud as he passed the white-haired matron. "As if that family needed another reason to gloat."

"Indeed," Ash said, pausing beside the woman who herself was once-removed from a banking family. "Intelligent, devoted to one another, contributors to their community. They are to be envied."

Mrs. Richmond drew herself up and stomped off, obviously looking for someone who would agree with her dismal assessment of the Bateman family's progress into Society.

She wasn't likely to find many, especially here. The prince and his brother were obviously admirers. And most of the Englishmen and women in the room would know the story of how Sir Matthew had earned his baronetcy.

Ash had been newly home from university when the Beast of Birmingham, a legendary pugilist, had saved the life of the Prince Regent and been made Sir Matthew Bateman. His marriage to Charlotte Worthington, sister to Viscount Worthington, had been reported in the gossip rags Ash's father had left lying about. But the marriage of Sir Matthew's oldest sister, Ivy, to the Marquess of Kendall had quickly eclipsed that news.

Since then, thanks to the auspices of Lord and Lady Belfort, the Batemans had become friends with the Duke and Duchess of Wey and were well known to the Earl and Countess of Carrolton. The family was fortunate indeed in its acquaintances.

And Petunia Bateman, now Lady Moselle, was no exception, even if she was exceptional.

That thought was not reflected in the cool smile he directed at the next group of people who sought conversation. For three years, he had been trying to convince himself, without success, that another lady on the *ton* must be Petunia's equal. He could name her attractions. With her sleek dark-blond hair and wide, warm brown eyes, she had a pleasing face. She was nearly tall enough to look him in the eye, and she wasn't afraid to do so. She had a comment for every occasion, a handy trait when having to converse with strangers ready to censor her for her family antecedents. She was unrelentingly loyal to those she called friends.

But the emotions she raised in him were nothing short of dangerous to his vision for the future. And so, he had told himself to look elsewhere for a bride. A decided shame that no other lady had yet to rise to her stature.

She hurried through the doors now, face white and steps unsteady. He was moving closer before he could stop himself.

"Miss Bateman, Lady Moselle, are you all right?" he asked, hand cupping her elbow.

She yanked back out of reach. "Fine. Perfect. Never better." Her smile was a ghastly parody of its usual warmth. "Enjoying the evening, my lord?"

Until this moment, immensely. There was something right and good about her being given her due. He could only applaud the prince for his decision to recognize her.

"A fine soiree," he assured her, careful to keep his voice level. "Allow me to offer you my congratulations on your elevation."

"My demotion, more like," she said with a glance back the way she had come.

Ash stiffened. "If His Royal Highness has in any way discomforted you, I would be happy to take him to task."

Where had that come from? The urge was rising again, to gather her close with one arm and brandish a sword at her foes with the other. He wasn't some barbarian! He was an English lord, one who prided himself on his composure, his logic.

She rallied. "No need to trouble the prince, my lord. I can take care of myself. Excuse me. I should find my family."

She hurried away, head down and coronet slipping.

That had been the longest conversation they'd had since the evening three years ago, when he'd told her he would not be making an offer for her hand. It had been the worst decision of his life, one he'd paid for with sleepless nights and endless days. This Season, he'd told himself to look closer, reconsider his decision. Perhaps it might be possible to rebuild the friendship they had once had. Such a friendship might lead to marriage. It was all very logical.

But something wasn't right with the new Lady Moselle. Even the night he had rejected her, she'd shown more spirit, more fire. The prince had said something to her that had caused her to pull even farther away from Ash.

He owed it to himself, and her, to discover the truth.

CHAPTER TWO

"AND THERE IT is in *The Times*," Meredith Mayes, Lady Belfort, remarked the next morning over breakfast. "'Miss Petunia Bateman, sister of Lady Kendall and Sir Matthew Bateman, was awarded an honorary title by the Batavarian court last night. One can only wonder what services she rendered to the crown.'" She made a noise that would have been better suited to the grey-coated cat curling around her lavender skirts, if her pet Fortune had been in a particularly angry mood.

Leveling her gaze on her husband across the table from her, she asked, "Did you know of the prince's plans?"

"No," Julian admitted, calmly applying apricot jam to his toast. The color was only a shade lighter than his red-gold hair, beard, and mustache. "But I can only applaud his good taste. About time someone recognized Tuny."

On the whole, she agreed. Petunia was like a daughter to her and her husband, as were Larissa, Callie, and Belle. Very likely it was because they were related to those she and Fortune had aided years ago, gentlewomen down on their luck like Jane, now Duchess of Wey, and Charlotte, Lady Bateman. But she liked to think her girls were endearing in their own rights. And she had noticed that, on occasion, Petunia seemed uncomfortable in such august company.

"It is not the positive recognition but the negative that concerns me," Meredith informed her husband now.

"This is going to thrust her onto the attention of the *ton* anew."

As if Fortune agreed, she hopped up onto her mistress's lap. Although Meredith never fed her from the table, she allowed the cat to consider the toast and tea, gently running a hand down the silky fur.

"We must be ready," she murmured to her pet. "We may find an unexpected number of gentlemen at her door."

"And a dab of danger," Julian said. "The prince and his family have been stalked and threatened to prevent them from claiming their ancestral rights. Any who align themselves with Batavaria may be targeted for similar treatment."

Meredith's mouth quirked. "I should like to see them take on Sir Matthew."

Julian grinned. "Yes, the former Beast of Birmingham might have something to say."

Fortune flicked her paw toward the toast, as if it were of only minor interest. Meredith picked her up and set her back on the floor. The cat cast her an arch look before disappearing under the table.

"She's headed your way," Meredith told her husband. "Don't."

Julian raised his brows. "Me? I assure you, madam, I am utterly immune to her pleas." Crumbling off a bit of toast, he dropped his hand under the damask tablecloth.

Meredith tsked. "You spoil her. And you spoil me. Was that a first edition of *Paradise Lost* on the desk in the library this morning?"

"Perhaps," Julian said, but he sent her a wink. "Lord Ashforde told me at the house party a couple of weeks ago that it might be coming on the market."

"Kind of him," Meredith allowed, returning to her perusal of the paper. "I take it he already had one?"

"And many other treasures in that library of his." He

was quiet a moment, and Meredith glanced up to find him watching her thoughtfully. "I still think he might be a good choice for Tuny."

"That," Meredith said with a snap of the paper, "is entirely up to Petunia. But I will feel better if we introduce Fortune to his lordship as soon as possible."

Petunia's reaction to the story in *The Times* was far less constrained.

"Services to the crown!" she sputtered as she perched on the sofa in her brother's sitting room, newspaper spread across her muslin skirts. "What do they think I did, muck out the royal stables?"

"Probably something more salacious than that," Charlotte remarked from beside her. Then she cast a quick look out the sitting room door as if to make sure her daughters, Daphne and Rose, were safely occupied upstairs with Mrs. Quince, their governess.

Tuny shook herself as she lowered the paper. "Well, they aren't far off, are they? Not with His Royal Highness' latest idea of services."

Charlotte's face tightened primly, warning Tuny that she was about to impart some knowledge. Funny how she recognized the look after seeing it for the first time more than a dozen years ago now, when Charlotte had first entered Matty's house. Aunt Meredith, who managed an employment agency for gentlemen and gentlewomen down on their luck, had introduced Charlotte as an etiquette teacher when Matty had been about to be elevated to the rank of baronet. It had been the first big change in their lives since her brother had removed his sisters from their stepmother's clutches and brought them to London to live with him. At least the second Mrs. Bateman had relocated to Ireland and had not troubled them in some years.

"From what you said, Prince Otto Leopold did not ask you to effect a seduction," Charlotte informed Tuny now. "He merely asked that you attempt to reason with Lord Ashforde about the Batavarian question. My previous interactions with his lordship tell me that he responds well to reason, and you know more about what Leo and Fritz hope to accomplish than most."

Put that way, it sounded quite logical. Only Leo didn't realize the depth of Lord Ashforde's antipathy toward her.

No one did. When you'd been crushed to your soul, you tended not to want to brag about it.

"Lord Ashforde is eminently reasonable," Tuny agreed. "But I'm not the right person to reason with him."

Charlotte reached out a hand to cover Tuny's in her lap. Those grey eyes were so understanding. "Will you tell me what he's done to so put you in a pucker, Tuny? You know Matthew and I will be at your side, no matter what."

That was precisely the problem. She could imagine her proper sister-in-law taking his lordship to task and her brash brother taking him out into the garden and pummeling him flat.

"I know," Tuny assured her. "But it is a mess of my own making, and I'd rather not talk about it. What I need now is to determine how I'm going to help Leo, without making Lord Ashforde think I'm attracted to him."

"A simple conversation will not do?" Charlotte suggested.

"No," Tuny said. "Believe me." She sighed. "I'll call at Weyfarer House. Larissa and Callie have more experience with dealing with diplomacy." And Belle had more experience in turning people up sweet. But Tuny would not say that fact aloud.

They thought her a seductress. Ash noticed the paper was crumpling in his fist and set it on the tablecloth beside his plate at the breakfast table in his townhouse. What was it about Petunia Bateman? Simply reading her name rattled his senses. He'd long ago decided she was entirely too upsetting to his equilibrium.

Yet he could not seem to get her out of his mind.

"More tea, my lord?" his butler asked. Peaves stood ready with the silver pot, look concerned. It was his habitual demeanor, long nose slightly wrinkled, narrow cheeks hollowed, as if he were holding his breath in anticipation of what Ash would say or do.

"No, thank you," Ash said, pushing back his chair and setting his servant to scuttling out of the way. "I have a meeting with His Majesty's advisors this morning. Have the carriage out in front by half past."

"Very good, my lord," Peaves said, inclining his head. His hair had been thick and black when Ash was a lad. Now it was silver and thinning, and Ash wasn't entirely sure age was the sole cause.

You have no right to look at me so disapprovingly, boy. I sired you, I pay them. I can do as I like. And what I like is to have a little fun.

Ash thrust his father's words from his mind as he strode down the corridor for the stairs. *Fun*—at least the sort of fun his father had indulged in—had never brought this family anything but sorrow. Calm consideration, proper planning, and advised action were the course of the day. That had been his approach to pulling the estate out of the hole his father had dug. That had been his approach to ordering his life. That had been his approach to selecting a baroness.

Until he'd met Petunia Bateman.

He climbed the stairs to the next story and entered his bedchamber. Cool blue walls, clean white linens, polished walnut furnishings. All belongings neatly organized. His valet, Theban, would have had it no other way, and neither would Ash. The older man, more slender now than when he'd first come to work in this house, moved forward. Hands trembling just the slightest, he helped Ash out of his banyan and into a proper coat—dove grey with tasteful silver buttons—and shoes—polished black leather with no ostentatious buckles.

Ash glanced in the Pier glass mirror. His hair was as dark as his father's, his eyes as deep a blue. But the red veining was missing from his nose, the bags from under his eyes. And he carried himself tall and confident, knowing himself in control.

Usually.

"There's a curl at my left temple," he observed.

Theban peered closer. "A curl, my lord?"

"There," Ash said, pointing at the offending lock of hair.

Theban made a conciliatory noise before locating the scissors and snipping off the impudent strand. "Better, my lord?"

Ash studied himself a moment more, then nodded. "Yes, thank you, Theban. I'll be out most of the day today, but I expect to dine in tonight."

"Very good, my lord," Theban said, inclining his head. His hair, Ash couldn't help noticing, was also turning silver.

Look at yourself! You walk like you have a stick up your…

Ash turned from the mirror and strode for the door.

Why was his father's voice dominating his thoughts this morning? He dwelled on the fellow less and less often these days. It had taken him the bulk of five years to undo all the wrongs his father had done. The properties now flourished. The family coffers overflowed. The title was unencumbered, free of any whiff of scandal, and respected again. He had been unable to retrieve the Ashforde rubies from whatever crony his father had given them to in payment of a debt, but he intended to keep trying to locate them. His goal now—aside from serving in the halls of Parliament and ensuring those who depended on him were well cared for—was to find himself a bride and continue the line to the next generation.

And now it wasn't his father's drunken face leering at him in his thoughts but the knowing smile of a dusky-haired blonde. As he settled back in the seat of the carriage, he allowed himself to remember.

A summer night. A garden. A cool breeze, welcome after the heat of the soiree. The loveliest of ladies strolling on his arm. Stopping near a climbing rose, the scent still hinting in the twilight. Her face turned up to his, sweet, expectant.

A longing that shook him to his core.

The words he had regretted ever since.

"I fear I have raised expectations, Miss Bateman. I should tell you right now that I have no intention of offering for you."

The shock crossing her face, swiftly followed by fury. "I never really thought you would, my lord. Good evening."

The pride in even the way the skirts of her satin evening gown twitched as she walked away.

He shook his head now. Fool! He'd worked so hard to eradicate the emotions that had caused his father to stray far from what a gentleman should be that when one of those emotions had dared to blossom, he'd snipped it faster than Theban had attacked that errant curl.

Marriage, he'd reasoned, should be about commonalities, companionship. He wasn't sure he had anything in common with Petunia Bateman, even if he enjoyed her companionship. And he refused to set foot on the path his father had dashed down so merrily. Admiration was one thing, adoration a slippery slope that led to heartache for all concerned.

The trouble was, no other lady held a candle to her.

This one lacked her intelligence. He doubted he had the patience to spend the next thirty or more years of his life explaining even the simplest of facts. That one refused to so much as squeak in his company, and nothing he had done had encouraged her to relax in his presence, despite or maybe because of her mother's urging. And another had had a petty streak. He had lived under judgment long enough.

And so, he was once again faced with the possibility of courting a lady who might bring out the worst in him.

The other lords he met in a private room at White's gentlemen's club had no idea of the thoughts swimming through his mind. He had enough composure to remember to remain aloof, to merely nod at their greetings, and to take a seat at the very edge of the deliberations, where he could observe his colleagues as they sat in the paneled room.

Canning, the Foreign Secretary, paced before the white marble hearth, chin nearly on his chest and balding head catching the light. The more corpulent Wellmanton filled one of the upholstered wingback chairs, smiling genially around at the others. Trelawney, the current favorite of the king, sat on the matching chair, attempting to appear bored even though his cold grey eyes swept the room. The brown-haired, brown-eyed Greville, Clerk to the Council, had taken his place at the center table, on which he had a quill and parchment at the ready. Apparently, he expected them to issue some profound statement in need of immortalizing.

"But are we agreed?" Canning demanded in his reedy voice. "Britain ought not to interfere in matters of state on the Continent."

Trelawney leaned back in his seat, short blond hair brushing the fabric. "Much the same way we have not interfered with matters of state in Ireland or South America."

Canning flushed. He'd been the architect of Britain's renewed relations with various now-independent countries in the southern hemisphere.

"Now, now," Wellmanton said. "Let us not argue, friends. I think we can agree that it is best not to unmake what Castlereagh so aptly wrought at the Congress of Vienna."

Canning stopped his pacing to shoot the older lord a look. Had Wellmanton forgotten that the late Lord Castlereagh had once fought Canning in a duel? His name was not conducive to facilitating agreement now.

"But Prince Otto Leopold is very persuasive," Greville put in with a swish of his quill. "We would not stand for a British lord to be stripped of his estates and left only with a title."

Canning rubbed his chin. "An extraordinary move, I grant you. But to take a stand against King William of Württemberg?" He glanced at Ash. "What say you, Ashforde?"

"I can see several sides to the argument," Ash answered. "King William's family is related by marriage to our king, so it would seem we owe him some allegiance. On the other hand, he neither conquered Batavaria nor married to achieve its throne, so I struggle to see what right he has to hold it, particularly when its ruling house is very much alive and willing to resume its leadership. And any change could well upset the fragile peace we have built."

Canning nodded. "Well spoken. I for one will be advising His Highness to refrain from taking up the cause."

"As will I," Wellmanton assured them all.

Greville wrinkled his nose. "I'm for the Batavarians."

"I find myself in agreement with Greville," Trelawney said.

They all looked to Ash.

"I am as yet undecided," he said. "But allow me to

consider the matter more fully, and I will give you my answer before the prince returns from Windsor in three weeks."

CHAPTER THREE

PETUNIA FULLY PLANNED to call on Larissa, Callie, and Belle as soon as the fashionable hour arrived, but she soon found herself besieged. The first person to arrive was Mr. Huber of the Imperial Guard. Their maid-of-all-work, Betsy, showed him into the sitting room just as Tuny and Charlotte were about to head upstairs and change for making calls.

Betsy had been with them for the last thirteen years, and there wasn't much she hadn't seen in that time, from an aging hound to a cruel stepmother to two bouncy little girls. But she stood in the sitting room doorway and gazed up at the guardsman worshipfully before a cough from Charlotte sent her on her way.

Mr. Huber tended to have that affect on women and children, Tuny had noticed. He'd been a great favorite in the schoolroom at Wey Castle during the house party earlier this month, winning the regard of her nieces, the duke's sons, and Miss Winchester, the temporary governess hired for the event. She wasn't sure if it was the golden-brown cast to his eyes, like looking into a piece of amber; his sun-bronzed skin; or the way he held himself, calm, steady, as if ready for anything.

He removed the fur shako on his head now, ruffling his hair, tucked the hat under one arm, then clapped his other fist to the chest of his black dress uniform. "Lady Moselle. I am here to protect you."

"Protect me?" Tuny asked with a frown. "From what?"

"Indeed, Mr. Huber," Charlotte put in. "What do you and the prince expect?"

"Lady Moselle has been identified as a friend to Batavaria," he said. "She has been given an important assignment. I am here to see that no one interferes."

"And just what do you see as interference?" Charlotte asked, both voice and gaze dancing with amusement. "Dinner? Sleep? Small children?"

Mr. Huber directed his own gaze over Tuny's left shoulder. "I am more concerned with the enemies of Batavaria. His Royal Highness has decreed that we will take shifts keeping her ladyship safe. I have this day. Keller will take the night. Roth and Tanner will switch tomorrow."

Well, if that wasn't the outside of enough! Tuny marched up to him and planted her hands on her hips. "Now, see here. This house isn't all that big. As it is, we've had to put the governess with the other servants when I moved home from staying with the Duke of Wey for the Season. You'll only be underfoot, constantly. Besides, Matty can guard me. He's a former pugilist, you know."

Mr. Huber's golden eyes glittered. "I have heard stories. But he is not a Batavarian."

"Neither," Tuny informed him, "am I."

His gaze finally came back to meet hers. "No disrespect intended, Baroness, but you are. Prince Otto Leopold made you Batavarian when he awarded you a title from our country. You are a member of the ruling class. I would give my life to protect you."

How was she to argue with such earnestness! Her hands fell, and she glanced at Charlotte for guidance. What exactly was the etiquette for thanking someone who wanted to die for you?

"Lady Moselle may be Batavarian," Charlotte put in smoothly, "but the rest of her family is not. Because this is our home too, I think we should have some say in who else is allowed through the door. If you'll excuse me, I'll have my husband join us."

Tuny nodded, and Charlotte left the room.

Mr. Huber remained standing between Tuny and the door, as if to make sure she could not leave.

She flounced back to the sofa and plunked down on the green of the upholstery. "Just who do you think is coming after me?"

"The enemies of Batavaria," he repeated, gaze once more on the wainscotting.

"Who are?" Tuny pressed.

"Wicked indeed."

She barely stopped herself from rolling her eyes. She hadn't spent much time with any of the Imperial Guards until Mr. Huber and the other three he had mentioned had attended the duke's house party. Then, they'd been guarding the prince and his brother, Count Montalban. That had turned out to be a good thing, as spies from Württemberg were camped in the area. She was very glad to have had a hand in stopping those spies, but surely she had no need for guards to protect her too!

Matty came stalking into the room, Charlotte right behind. He took up a stance Tuny recognized—one foot forward, one back, fists at the ready. He might look the part of genteel baronet with his tweed coat and chamois trousers, but the Beast of Birmingham still lurked inside. She had to hide her smile.

"What's this?" he barked. "Is my sister in danger?"

Mr. Huber saluted him, fist to chest. "Sir Matthew. Prince Otto Leopold was concerned that Lady Moselle's sudden elevation might draw her to the attention of our enemies. I am at your disposal to help protect her."

Help protect her. At least he acknowledged her brother could be of some use. It was a start.

Matty didn't look as ready to accept. His gaze traveled

from the guardsman's black boots to his brown hair. "Handy with your fives?"

Mr. Huber frowned. "My fives?"

"Your fists," Tuny supplied. "Can you box, Mr. Huber?"

His face cleared. "I have been trained in grappling and throwing."

Matty stuck out his lower lip. "Always was one for grappling."

Charlotte smiled as if she knew firsthand.

"What about weapons?" her brother continued. "Knives? Pistols?"

"The Captain of the Imperial Guard considers me an expert in both," Mr. Huber supplied. He patted the hilt on his right hip. "For this duty, we will be armed with long knives and short swords."

"How fast can you cut a man's legs out from under him?" Matty asked.

Tuny shoved to her feet. "That's enough! I don't need protection!"

Matty's gaze, the same shade of brown as her own, swung toward her. "You might. And I have to sleep or be out of the house at times. I say we let him stay."

"Mr. Huber is not a pup we discovered on the stoop," Tuny scolded.

Matty grinned at her. "You insisted that we keep enough of those over the years. What's one more?"

"But surely he has better things to do," Tuny argued.

Mr. Huber's impressive chin came up. "None more important than keeping you safe, your ladyship."

"It isn't just Mr. Huber," Charlotte put in. "I understand we are to have an Imperial Guardsman in the house around the clock."

Matty's frown gathered. Her brother's frown could curdle milk. Tuny drew a breath. Mr. Huber was in for it now.

"Are all of them as good as you?" her brother asked.

Tuny sighed.

A clatter on the stair announced the arrival of her nieces. Five-year-old Daphne came first, hands twisting her pinafore and grin as wide as her father's. "Mr. Huber! You came to see us!"

"That was very nice of you," seven-year-old Rose agreed, right behind her.

Their governess, Mrs. Quince, came puffing after them, white hair falling free of its pins and serviceable brown dress rumpled. "Sorry for the interruption, your ladyship. They were certain they were needed."

Mr. Huber went so far as to crouch down so that he was on a level with them. "Miss Bateman, Miss Daphne Bateman, I am pleased to see you again."

"Did you bring Miss Winchester with you?" Rose wanted to know.

"She's ever so nice," Daphne agreed.

The two girls had talked of little else since returning from the duke's schoolroom. Pretty, sweet Miss Winchester kept her charges in line with a honeyed smile and engaging topics. Poor Mrs. Quince, with her harried demeanor, lack of imagination, and strict adherence to schedule, had suffered in comparison.

"I have not seen Miss Winchester since leaving Surrey," Mr. Huber told the girls.

Rose sighed, one finger twirling a strand of her russet hair. "I miss her."

"Me too," Daphne said, face puckering under her sable mop.

"As do I," he assured them.

"That's enough, girls," Charlotte said, stepping forward to put an arm around each daughter's shoulders. "Thank you for bringing them down, Mrs. Quince. I'll help them back upstairs."

The governess sagged in obvious relief, then rallied and made her curtsey to Matty, Tuny, and Mr. Huber.

Charlotte ushered her daughters out of the room, Mrs. Quince following.

"So you miss Miss Winchester, too, do you?" Tuny couldn't help teasing the guardsman.

To her surprise, pink crept up into his sculptured cheeks as he stood. "Miss Winchester is as lovely as sunlight on a spring meadow. She is also educated and cultured. Nothing can come of my admiration. I have my duty."

Tuny raised a brow. "Which apparently includes taking care of me."

He fixed his gaze into the distance. "Yes, Lady Moselle."

Matty pointed to the wall beside the hearth. "Stand there. You can see out the window, through the doorway to the stairs, and through the other door there to the dining room."

Mr. Huber glanced in each direction as if confirming her brother's assessment. "Strategic. Very well." He went and put his back to the wall, standing as still as a statue.

"Matty," Tuny started in protest, but her new guard stiffened.

"A carriage just stopped in front of the house, your ladyship. Are you expecting visitors?"

"No," Tuny admitted, "but it's time for calls. I do have friends, you know."

He nodded, but the set of his face said he doubted they were coming to call just then.

A knock sounded on the door. Mr. Huber put his hand on the knife at his belt.

"I'll get it, Betsy," Matty called to prevent their maid from hurrying forward. He strode from the room.

Male voices echoed from the entry hall. One sent a chill up her spine.

Not now! She wasn't ready! Her hands flew to her hair. What had possessed her to throw it up into a haphazard knot? Why had she thought a muslin day dress, the hem already starting to fray, was suitable even for breakfast with family?

A moment later, and Lord Ashforde stood in the doorway. He offered her a bow. "Miss B—that is Lady Moselle."

Panic pushed the words from her mouth. "Mr. Huber, do your duty. Make this man leave at once."

Ash blinked even as the strapping fellow along the far wall raised himself to his full height, an inch or so taller than his own, if his assessment was correct. He recognized both the face and the uniform. What was a member of the Batavarian Imperial Guard doing here?

Before the fellow could make good on his gathering scowl, Ash turned to the lady he had come to see.

"Forgive me," he told Petunia, who stood with head high and eyes flashing beside a sofa patterned in green leaves. "I didn't realize you were entertaining the prince."

"I'm not entertaining anyone," she informed him. "I am not at home."

It was the thing people said when they were not receiving, but as it was perfectly clear she was at home, and her own brother had welcomed him into the house, he wasn't sure how to take the statement. Indeed, he had seldom seen her in such dishabille—filmy muslin gown barely skimming her shapely ankles, as if she had outgrown it some years past, rich blond hair piled up on her head with curls teasing her pinking cheeks. The look was equally disconcerting and delightful, and he wasn't entirely sure why.

"Lady Moselle," he tried again. "At your convenience, I would like to speak with you privately. I believe I owe you an apology."

Now she blinked her deep brown eyes, as if she'd

suddenly stepped into the sunlight. "Oh. Well." She rallied. "Now is definitely not convenient."

The guardsman turned his frown on her. "But is this not Lord Ashforde?"

Ash inclined his head. "You have me at a disadvantage, sir."

The fellow clapped a fist to his chest in what Ash had come to know as the Batavarian salute. "Finn Huber, of the Imperial Guard."

"Mr. Huber," Ash acknowledged. What was the guardsman doing here? He couldn't have been calling. No visitor stood so straight and so distant, as if he were no more than a stick of furniture. "Are the other members of the guard in residence as well?"

"Only Mr. Huber," Petunia explained. "His Royal Highness thinks I need protection. It's silly, really. And I must ask you to leave, my lord. I have an appointment."

"Ah." Ash took a step back.

Huber took a step forward. "But your ladyship, you have an assignment."

"Assignment, appointment," she said with a wave of her hand. The light in her eyes was almost manic. "I'm a very busy person. Another time, my lord."

"But your duty," the guard protested.

She jerked around. "Not. Now."

His frown only grew.

So did Ash's confusion. "Would you prefer that I escort Mr. Huber out, Lady Moselle?"

The guardsman took another step forward, as if prepared to fight for his place. Ash moved to block him. He might not have been armed, but he'd been trained by Gentleman Jackson, who was still a bruising boxer decades after having retired from the sport. Ash lifted his fists.

Petunia held out her hands, one toward the guard and one toward Ash. "Gentlemen. Stop. I have a headache."

She dropped her hands and fled past him for the stairs.

The Imperial Guardsman marched forward as well. Ash refused to give ground.

"She will speak to you soon," the fellow promised before going to take up a position in the entry hall, gaze on the stairs, like a spaniel waiting for his owner's return.

Sir Matthew wandered into the room and nodded at Ash. "Ashforde. What brings you around?"

The words should have been friendly, but there was a decided chill to the baronet's usual growl.

Ash dropped his fists. "I had thought to visit your sister, but she appears to be indisposed."

Her brother nodded. "Good day to you, then, my lord."

Left with no other choice, Ash could only nod farewell and take himself off.

As he once more settled into his coach, he tried to tell himself that it was all to the good. He didn't want to lay his heart at her feet. He was trying for a more congenial relationship.

But the more she pushed him away, the more he wanted to close the distance, draw her out, learn everything about her.

What a perverse person he was!

But he would be back tomorrow, and the day afterward, and the day after that, until he had apologized to Petunia Bateman. It was the least he owed her.

CHAPTER FOUR

TUNY WAITED ON the landing, listening to footsteps and the sound of the door. Had he gone? Was she safe?

Why did she keep panicking every time he was near? He'd never harmed her physically. She ought to have sealed her heart against him by now. But one look in those blue eyes, surprisingly warm for the cool color, and she melted into a puddle!

"Are you hiding too?" Rose asked.

Tuny turned to find her niece peering out from around the side of the credenza that stood at the top of the stairs.

"Left Mrs. Quince again, did you?" Tuny countered.

Rose wrinkled her nose. "She fell asleep."

Cold tiptoed down her spine. "Where's Daphne?"

They located her youngest niece sitting at Matty's desk, quill in one hand and ink strewn across the blotter. It took a bit to clean things up, then clean them up. Mrs. Quince stumbled into the corridor, wide-eyed, as Tuny was returning her nieces to the former bedchamber Charlotte had turned into a schoolroom of sorts. Mrs. Quince had been staying in Tuny's bedchamber next door, until Tuny had returned from the duke's house party. She had made no secret of the fact she found living in the attics with their cook and maid-of-all-work both inconvenient and demeaning. If only Tuny had found her perfect suitor and married…

Now the governess shook a bony finger at the girls. "There you are! I turn my back for one minute, and off you go!"

It had been considerably more than a minute, but Tuny held her tongue, for now. It would do the governess no good to be berated in front of her charges. "I'm sure Rose and Daphne are ready for lessons."

Mrs. Quince sniffed as if she highly doubted that, but she turned to allow the girls to precede her through the door. "Thank you, Lady Moselle, for locating them."

She made it sound as if the family lived in a massive country castle rather than a humble London townhouse. "It was no trouble. If they are fractious, you might take them down to the garden for calisthenics."

She stared at Tuny as if she'd suggested the governess boil her nieces in oil. Then, shaking her head, she returned to her charges.

Charlotte must have been downstairs with their cook, for Tuny met her on the stair.

"Everything all right?" she asked as if she'd noticed Tuny's frown.

"You might pop in on Mrs. Quince more often," Tuny suggested. "I'm not sure she's up to Rose's and Daphne's energy."

Charlotte made a face, reminding Tuny of Rose. "I'm not sure anyone is up to Rose's and Daphne's energy. I was going to accompany you to Weyfarer House, but perhaps I should stay here."

In the end, they agreed that Tuny would go, with Huber as escort.

"It's only a mile," she explained as they set off from the house, herself now gowned in one of her favorite outfits that featured a plaid scarf and sash over a white bodice and blue chambray skirts. "Charlotte and I have walked it dozens of times."

"When you were Miss Bateman," he pointed out, gaze

swinging from one side of the street to the other. "Lady Moselle may find it more dangerous."

"I sincerely doubt anyone notices the difference in me," she informed him, twitching her blue skirts around a loose cobble.

"The ones we must watch for notice," he told her.

Tuny shook her head.

Just to be certain, though, she kept her gaze moving as well. The tall houses, the crowded shops, were no strangers, and none of the people hurrying to and fro seemed particularly nefarious. Still, she had to own it was comforting to stride along with a presentable gentleman at her side. Ladies cast her glances. Footmen looked at Huber with awe and envy.

How much better would it be if Lord Ashforde was walking next to me?

Where had that thought come from? She wasn't willing to speak with the man. She hardly wanted his escort as she crossed London.

She made herself focus on the hubbub as they approached Piccadilly Circus. The traffic circle was filled with carriages, lorries, wagons, men on horseback, and the occasional vendor relocating a wheelbarrow of goods. Vehicles clattered, tack rattled, and voices shouted to give way. She always had to go carefully through the area to avoid being run over or trampled.

As they neared the end of the pavement, Huber stepped in front of her and held up a hand. The driver of the lorry trundling closer yanked on his reins and came to a breathtaking stop. Riders reined in. Dust sparkled in the air.

"It is safe now, your ladyship," Huber announced.

The drivers and riders craned their necks, as if they thought a princess royal was flouncing through their midst. Tuny smiled apologetically before raising her chin and following Huber across the circle of traffic.

Perhaps there was something to be said for traveling with an Imperial Guardsman after all.

"Is there a reason you did not wish to speak with the prince's advisor?" Huber asked as they followed Regent's Street around the curve, past shops with wide front windows full of all manner of goods.

"I am still determining my strategy," Tuny told him. "That's one of the reasons I want to speak with Lady Larissa, Lady Callie, and Lady Belle."

He nodded at the names of the three daughters of the Duke of Wey, who had been her best friends since childhood. Larissa and Callie were betrothed to the two men he normally served. And Belle had an understanding with Owen Canady, a gentleman Huber had met at the house party earlier this month.

"Determining strategy is wise," he allowed as they turned onto Vigo Street and the shops grew more crowded and less enticing again. "But action is better. We have little time before he gives the prince his thoughts."

They fell silent until they reached Clarendon Square, where the duke had a fine stone townhouse. Mr. Underhill, the dark-haired, polished butler, was quick to let Tuny inside, but he narrowed his eyes at Huber.

"I did not see the royal carriage," he mused as he shut the door behind them.

"Mr. Huber has been assigned to watch over me," Tuny explained.

The butler's brows went up before he carefully brought them down. "Very good, Miss Bateman."

"Lady Moselle," Huber ordered, hand once more on his knife hilt, as if he suspected Mr. Underhill of hiding a dagger under his black tailcoat.

The butler went so far as to bow to Tuny. "Forgive me, your ladyship. I had quite forgotten. May I be one of the first to congratulate you on your elevation? Well deserved."

Much more of this, and her face would be flaming. "Thank you, Mr. Underhill. Where might I find Larissa, Callie, and Belle this afternoon?"

"In the library, your ladyship. Shall I announce you?"

"No need. I know the way." She took a step, and Huber fell in beside her. Tuny jerked to a stop.

"Stay," she said, pointing at a corner of the entry hall. "There. I doubt anyone would trouble me in the home of a duke."

He seemed content with the thought as well, for he positioned himself in a corner of the entry hall where he could see the door, the corridor, and the stairs.

Tuny ventured down to the library. It was a cozy space, lined with bookcases and dotted with upholstered chairs that begged one to sit and read.

"The lady of the day!" Belle heralded from where she stood perusing the books, her pearly pink skirts eclipsing the dark wood shelves.

"Lady Moselle," Callie agreed with a grin from her spot at the desk, her green gown like a spot of grass in the room.

"Lady Annoyed, more like," Tuny said, dropping down on the chair closest to Larissa. "Truly, what was Leo thinking?"

"That you are a rare gem and worthy of acclaim," Larissa said, arranging her own blue plaid skirts.

Tuny snorted. "So worthy he assigns me to charm Lord Ashforde."

"Ooh!" Belle snapped shut the book she'd selected and ventured closer, golden curls bobbing. "I hadn't heard that part."

"I had," Callie said, surprising no one. She had an innate ability to remain unremarked in company, and people tended to say things in her presence they would have avoided otherwise.

"Leo is hoping Tuny can persuade Lord Ashforde to

see his side of things," Larissa explained as her two sisters seated themselves on the remaining chairs.

Belle frowned. "But you abhor Lord Ashforde."

She had lounged in these chairs any number of times and never found one so hard. "I don't abhor him. I'm just not comfortable with him. But I want to help Leo, and his father, regain their lands, so I must find a way to speak to Lord Ashforde. The question is, how?"

Larissa spread her hands. "Simply open the topic of conversation and present your case."

"And Leo can't do that?" Tuny demanded.

Larissa colored. "Leo has tried. Lord Ashforde is reticent."

"Lord Ashforde," Tuny said, "is always reticent."

Callie cocked her head, pale curl brushing one cheek. "But he favors you. Remember how he bid for that painting at our benefit for the Society for the Prevention of Cruelty to Animals?"

How could she forget? She and Callie had sponsored a dinner and art auction to raise funds for the society. Lord Ashforde and Owen Canady had fought fiercely over one particular painting, until his lordship had bid an outrageous amount. And he'd looked right at Tuny while doing so. It was as if he were throwing down a glove to challenge her to a duel.

"That doesn't mean he favors me," Tuny told her friend. "He likes getting his own way. That's all."

"Is it?" Belle asked, glancing among them. "He seemed attentive at the house party."

So much so that she'd had to pretend affection for Owen to keep him at bay.

"He was only being polite," Tuny insisted. "Who else was he to pursue when it became clear that Owen was in love with you, not me?"

Larissa was watching her. "Tuny, I know you are certain

he cannot care for you, but you've never explained why. I don't want to pry…"

"Then don't," Tuny said.

"It's all right," Callie said quietly. "We care about you, Tuny. If he's done something horrid, we'll be on your side."

"And if he's done something *particularly* horrid, I'm sure your brother can show him the error of his ways," Belle reminded her.

Tuny couldn't help her chuckle. "I keep thinking about that, too." She sobered. "I know I told you I fancied myself in love with Lord Ashforde, but I never shared the rest of the story with anyone."

Her dear friends waited patiently. So patiently. She drew in a breath. "It was my first Season, and he was the finest fellow I'd ever seen. You remember how surprised I was when he showed interest, Larissa."

Larissa smiled. "You said it must be your lucky day."

Callie glanced at her sister. "Oh, very good. I'm usually the one who remembers."

"He was hard to forget," Tuny said. "He was so attentive. And sometimes, when he looked at me, I thought I was the most beautiful girl in the room."

"Oh, Tuny," Belle said with a happy sigh.

"It wasn't true," Tuny told her, the pain crashing in on her anew. "It was all in my mind."

"But how can you be sure?" Belle persisted.

"Because he told me so in no uncertain terms. We were out in the garden at one of Lady Carrolton's soirees, and we stopped in the moonlight, and I was certain he was going to kiss me and propose. My hopes must have shown on my face, for he said he was sorry he'd given me expectations and he had no intention of offering for me."

"The dastard!" Belle cried, and Callie nodded.

Larissa reached out a hand to hers. "I'm so sorry, Tuny. That's cruel."

"It was honest," she said, hurt burning like a coal in her chest. "I wasn't good enough to be his baroness. Girls like me shouldn't fall in love with men like him. What lord wants a wife whose father worked in a mill and died drunk in a ditch?"

"Where your father worked and how he died has nothing to do with you," Larissa said, in such ringing tones that no one would have argued with her. "You have sterling qualities any husband should prize. Intelligence, kindness…"

"Practicality," Callie offered.

"Loyalty," Belle put in.

"I'm a paragon, I am," Tuny said.

"Yes, you are," Larissa said. "I had no idea that Lord Ashforde was so very dull-witted that he missed that, and I'm sorry Leo asked you to speak to him. I'll tell Leo to find another."

"Is there another?" Tuny asked hopefully.

Her friend smiled ruefully. "Likely not as well positioned as you. But I'm sure Leo will contrive."

Perhaps he could. And perhaps he couldn't. If Tuny's silence cost him his kingdom, how could she live with that? And Lord Ashforde had been more congenial lately.

"No," she said. "I'll do it. I merely have to determine a location and time that suits me. No more dark gardens and private walks. Not that I could have one with an Imperial Guardsman at my side."

Callie grimaced. "I told Fritz that wasn't necessary. He insisted, and Leo agreed. They don't want you in any danger because of this assignment. They might have assigned a guard to Lord Ashforde as well, but that might have made it appear as if they were trying to hold him hostage."

"I understand," Tuny said, "even if I don't like it much. And having a guard at my side will serve to keep Lord Ashforde at a respectable distance."

"What you need is a public location where you can bump into him and have a conversation," Belle mused, tapping her chin with one finger. "Unfortunately, I haven't seen him at many events."

"He's more like Father," Callie said. "A bit of a hermit. He may need an excuse to attend."

"Then we will give him one," Larissa said. "Mother and Father are hosting a ball on Saturday. I'll make sure he's on the guest list. We can work on him then."

Tuny sent her a look. "We?"

"Of course," Larissa said. "You didn't think we'd leave you alone on this assignment, did you?"

"What are friends for but to plot triumphs?" Belle agreed.

Tuny smiled all around, feeling pounds lighter than when she'd entered. "Thank you. I begin to hope we'll have some success after all. Lord Ashforde won't know what hit him."

"Is everything all right, my lord?" Peaves asked late Wednesday morning.

Ash kept his gaze on the shelf of books in front of him. Amazing how rearranging titles both calmed the nerves and inspired the spirit. He hadn't read Thomas Brown's *Lectures on the Philosophy of the Human Mind* for a while. He would have to remedy that. And how had he forgotten how much he enjoyed the Scotch novels? Surely the author had something new out. His favorite clerk at Hatchards Bookshop would know.

"Fine, Peaves," he told his butler. "Was there something you needed?"

"Well," his man said, and Ash heard tentative footsteps across the polished wood floor, "Mrs. Clowers is wondering whether you will be wanting tea. I understand she has a lovely seed cake she could serve with it."

"Tell her not to go to any trouble," Ash said, reaching up for a book. "I'm perfectly fine."

"Yes, my lord." Once more, his man sounded disappointed. The footsteps retreated.

They worried. They fretted. Many of his staff remembered the dark days of his father, when the former Lord Ashforde might not return home for days, and, when he did, he would be in no fit shape to deal with decisions. Truth be told, he hadn't been much use in making decisions even on the good days. For his father, life had been about pleasure, indulgence. Anything else was simply a waste of time.

At the moment, was he any better? He knew what must be done. And he stood in the library and sorted books.

The footsteps returned, firmer, with greater purpose.

"Yes?" Ash asked. "Has Mrs. Clowers remembered she has a fine Stilton cheese as well?"

"No, my lord," Peaves said. "Lord Wellmanton is here to see you. Where would you like to receive him?"

Not whether he wished to speak to the fellow but where. Still, Peaves was right. It wouldn't do to be, well, peevish. A smile tugged at his lips.

He flattened it and turned. "You may show him into the library, Peaves."

His butler's look was triumphant. "Very good, my lord."

Ash had just taken his seat behind the desk his father had never bothered to use when the older lord strolled in. Wellmanton always dressed his ample frame soberly, somberly, but his round face was forever beaming, and even the light grey of his well-combed hair seemed to gleam.

Ash nodded him into the chair in front of the desk. "Wellmanton. How might I be of assistance?"

"Assistance?" He paused in the act of sitting. "No, no, you mistake me, my boy. I'm here to offer *you* assistance."

Ash leaned back in the chair. "I wasn't aware I required any."

"Perhaps not yet," Wellmanton allowed, settling himself in the seat as if he planned to stay a while. "But you will soon. The Batavarians have ears everywhere." He glanced around the library as if expecting to find Prince Otto Leopold or his brother hiding behind a shelf.

"I can think of nothing I've said or done that would offend," Ash said.

"Of course not," Wellmanton agreed, smile once more affable. "You are well known for your sagacity, your tempered consideration. It is not in you to offend."

He could think of one he had offended all too well, but he wasn't about to mention her to the viscount. "Then why do you offer assistance?"

Wellmanton eased forward on the chair. "Because it is well known that you and I are among those chosen to advise His Majesty on this Batavarian question. Some will seek to influence us."

Ash shrugged. "They are welcome to try."

"And they will try," Wellmanton assured him. "Make no mistake. You may be offered honors, funds, to sway your decision."

Ash shook his head. "I have a title that suits me, and I am content with the funds I have."

"So it would seem," Wellmanton said with an envying look about the beautifully appointed room. "But there are other ways to convince you to speak their words. A Shakespearean First Folio, perhaps?"

Ash nodded across the room. "I have one."

"A Thoroughbred foal."

"I have two at my estate near Cheshunt."

Again Wellmanton inched forward. "The Ashforde rubies?"

Ash frowned. Prince Otto Leopold could not have laid his hands on the set of rubies Ash's father had sold to finance his lavish style. Even the Bow Street Runner Ash had hired to look into the matter had discovered few leads. Was this conversation about what the prince might offer him?

Or about what Wellmanton could offer him?

"As much as I would like to recover my family's jewels, I am unwilling to change my opinion," Ash told his visitor. "You may rest assured that no one will bribe me in that regard."

Wellmanton sat back at last. "Good to know, good to know. And what of the ladies? I am certain His Royal Highness would not be above sending a seductress to tempt you. I would not want you to be swayed by a pretty face any more than you were swayed by pretty words."

Ash offered him a smile. "You have no need to worry on that score. No lady exists that would prevent me from relying on logic to make a decision."

CHAPTER FIVE

TUNY WAS ALMOST glad that Mr. Roth was on duty during the day Wednesday. One of the more senior of the Imperial Guards, he had coal-black hair and steely grey eyes that could narrow to rapiers of suspicion. She had a feeling Lord Ashforde might finally have met his match when it came to arrogance.

But she returned from a brief stroll of Covent Garden market with Betsy to find that she had missed Lord Ashforde entirely, and she could not understand why that fact made the day seem less bright. She ought to be relieved that she didn't have to spend time looking at his handsome face, listening to his intelligent conversation, wondering if their hands might meet.

Oh!

Mr. Tanner was on evening duty. Of the members of the Imperial Guard, she had had the least contact with him, but she was pleased to see he was a presentable fellow with russet hair a shade darker than Charlotte's and a ready grin. If the Season had been in full swing, he would have had to accompany her to some soiree or ball. As it was, most of the fine lords and ladies were rusticating at their country estates and avoiding the last heat of summer in London. Only a few had begun trickling back because it was rumored the Prime Minister might bring up the Batavarian question during a special session, if the king's advisors could not ease his mind.

Daphne and Rose were delighted that Huber returned on Thursday. They must have been watching from the upstairs window, for they escaped Mrs. Quince again to come pelting down the stairs to welcome him.

"Really, your ladyship," Tuny heard the governess say to Charlotte when she must have noticed her charges' disappearance, "I do not see how I can keep working under these conditions. People coming and going at all hours. Tiny living quarters so far from my charges. Armed guards in the house. It's made me feel quite unwell."

Charlotte sighed. "Take the rest of the day off. Perhaps you'll feel better tomorrow."

Tuny resigned herself to helping her sister-in-law deal with the two little girls.

As Mrs. Quince toddled away with shaky steps, Huber rose from where he had crouched while speaking to Daphne and Rose.

"That woman is not good with children," he informed Charlotte. "Miss Winchester is seeking a permanent post. Hire her instead."

Charlotte's brows climbed. "I am unused to being ordered about by the Imperial Guard, sir."

He had the good sense to look abashed. "Forgive me. It was not my place. But your daughters are bright and adventurous. These are traits to be nurtured, not denigrated. I know Miss Winchester would agree."

"Very likely," Charlotte said. "I was much impressed with her at Castle Wey. Do you have her direction?"

"I will get it for you," he promised.

"Mr. Huber could be our governess," Rose said, twisting from side to side, brown eyes wide.

"We like him," Daphne agreed.

"I like you too," Huber told them. "But my duty is to protect your aunt."

"Why?" Daphne asked.

"Because Prince Otto Leopold told him to," Tuny put

in before the guardsman could start talking about hidden dangers. "And a member of the Imperial Guard always does what he is told."

"Perhaps I'll be a member of the Imperial Guard when I grow up," Rose said.

"Then perhaps you can also work on doing as you're told," her mother suggested. "For now, let's find your reading book and hear you practice."

Rose heaved a weary sigh and suffered herself to be led with Daphne from the room. But Tuny was more aware of the slump of Charlotte's shoulders. Her sister-in-law worked with Matty to solve mysteries brought their way by friends and acquaintances. She also sometimes consulted with her brother and his wife on scientific matters. Perhaps she'd had something planned for today.

"If you're going to be here," Tuny told the guardsman, "you might as well make yourself useful. Let's help Charlotte with the girls."

He did not argue as he followed her out.

The day passed so quickly and so busily, that it wasn't until dinner that Matty mentioned Lord Ashforde.

"That fellow called again," he told Tuny as he was carving the chicken their cook had served.

Her traitor heart would start beating faster. "That fellow?"

"Ashforde," Matty clarified, handing Charlotte her plate. "Seemed a bit down that you weren't available."

"Good," Charlotte said with a satisfied nod. "Perhaps he'll be more attentive to what Tuny has to say in future."

She couldn't help noticing that Huber was nodding in agreement.

But he took her to task before turning over his post to Keller for the evening.

"You must speak to him," he said. "How else will you fulfill your duty to the prince?"

"Lady Larissa, Lady Callie, Lady Belle, and I have a

plan," Tuny informed him. "Be so good as to allow us to achieve it our own way."

He did not look convinced, but he said no more. At least the quiet Keller merely took up his place in the entry hall and refrained from pointing out her shortcomings.

Unsurprisingly, Mrs. Quince gave notice on Friday, after Matty had already left for an appointment in the city. A shame it was Roth's day. He stood in a corner of the sitting room, arms crossed over his broad chest, and scowled at the little girls frolicking around the room. When the knocker sounded, he strode to answer the door.

"At least that's helpful," Tuny said to Charlotte.

Her sister-in-law nodded, even as she tucked a strand of auburn hair back into her bun with one hand and snagged Daphne's arm with the other.

"The sofa," she ordered her daughters. "Now."

Rose and Daphne scrambled up onto the fabric and waited expectantly, hands folded in the laps of their chambray dresses and eyes attentive.

And that's when Roth ushered in Lord Ashforde.

Oh, why was she always at a disadvantage with him? He looked top-of-the-trees in a navy coat and buff trousers tucked into boots with nary a speck of dust on them. When she'd learned the governess had quit, she'd donned one of her older dresses, a muslin whose once-sky-blue shade had faded to grey and the trim picked off for better use elsewhere.

"I know you!" Rose exclaimed. "You were at the party."

Daphne wiggled closer to the edge of the sofa, as if ready to drop down and run to him. He must have thought so as well, for his eyes widened.

Lord Ashforde, panicked? It couldn't be!

"Girls," Charlotte admonished. She cast him a quick glance, likely concerned about taking her eyes from her daughters for long. "Lord Ashforde. I'm afraid you've come at a bad time."

Rose edged closer to her sister.

"I beg your pardon, Lady Bateman," he said politely, as if he greeted harried mothers on a regular basis. "When might be convenient?"

"Lady Moselle can be ready in a half hour," Roth told him.

What! Oh, the rat. She could see Roth's eyes, narrowing at her, daring her to disagree with him.

"No, I cannot," Tuny said. "You may have a duty, Mr. Roth, but I have a duty to my family."

She turned to Lord Ashforde. "The governess abandoned ship. I'm needed to help."

"Alas, she is," Charlotte said before plunking down on the sofa and putting an arm about each girl, anchoring them in place. "Unless you're good with children, my lord, I suggest you flee while you can."

"Lady Bateman, Lady Moselle, another time," he said before bowing and escaping.

"Coward," Tuny muttered in his wake.

"Clever fellow," Charlotte countered. "Now, young ladies, we will have a talk about your behavior."

Tuny remembered that tone. It had brought instant attention from her and her oldest sister, Ivy. Her other sister, Daisy, had fought against Charlotte's instruction, but she'd been raised under the second Mrs. Bateman and her scheming ways, and she hadn't been willing to put up with much.

Rose and Daphne had been raised by loving parents, and they listened solemnly while Charlotte explained how their routines would change until another governess could be found.

"You will be with me or your father or Aunt Tuny," she told them. "We want to spend time with you, so it would be very rude to run and hide as I hear you've been doing with Mrs. Quince."

"She falls asleep," Rose said, lower lip trembling.

"I poke her," Daphne said helpfully.

"But she just says go away," Rose finished. "So we go."

Anger pulsed through Tuny. How dare the woman treat her nieces that way! She was supposed to be caring for them.

Face tightening in obvious regret, Charlotte gathered her daughters closer. "I'm so sorry to hear that, my sweets. If anyone else treats you so shabbily, you must tell me or your father. And I promise you, we will watch the next governess more carefully."

"Aunt Tuny could be our governess," Rose offered with a hopeful grin to Tuny.

"Thank you, Rose," Tuny said. "I love you and Daphne very much."

"Aunt Tuny has her own life to lead," Charlotte said, look brooking no argument.

"Why?" Daphne asked.

"Because that's what young ladies do," Charlotte said. "They find an occupation or a husband or both and move out on their own."

Tuny knew it was true, yet the fact stung all the same. She should have married or settled on a plan long since. Now Charlotte and Matty needed her room for the next governess. They would always love and support her, but it was time to go on with her life.

If only she knew what that entailed.

The guardsman showed Ash all the way to his waiting carriage, earning the fellow a frown from Ash's footman.

"Shouldn't you be seeing to your duty?" Ash demanded as the guardsman hesitated beside the coach as if fully intending to follow Ash inside.

Roth glanced back at the house. "It is only for a moment. She is safer than I am in their company. With boys, I could instruct in history or fighting. What do you do with girls?"

Ash frowned. "I never had a sister, but I would imagine girls enjoy some of the same things as boys—rousing stories, games, riding."

"Dolls," Roth muttered, and a shudder went through him.

"Are things truly so dire?" Ash asked. "They seem like charming young ladies to me."

Roth leaned closer. "They never stop moving. They never stop talking."

Ash chuckled. "The Batavarian Imperial Guard has faced more formidable foes, I'm sure. But perhaps you and Lady Moselle could use additional ammunition. I'll be back shortly."

He glanced up at the older man on the bench. His grey-haired, whip-thin coachman was trying hard to look as if he hadn't been listening avidly.

"Griffiths, where would I find things to entertain little girls?"

His blue eyes brightened. "I know just the place, my lord."

It turned out he did, for a shop not too far away specialized in hobby horses, tin soldiers, dolls, and doll houses made to order. A quick conversation and a large promissory note were exchanged, and within the hour, Ash was returning with his prize.

The maid answered the door this time. She too wore a harried look, cap askew and apron crooked.

"I'm sorry, sir, but the family is not at home," she told him.

He nodded to his footman, who was balancing the paper-wrapped parcel in front of him, with only his stocking-covered calves and buckled shoes showing below. "But I've come with gifts," Ash said.

Her eyes widened. "A moment, my lord."

She turned and climbed the stairs without bothering to shut the door or ask them in.

Ash stepped inside regardless. Roth moved out of the sitting room to block any further progress. But before the guard could speak, Petunia appeared on the landing.

"Lord Ashforde?"

She sounded shocked and a bit apprehensive, as if he'd brought a constable to investigate a complaint. Ash offered her a bow. "Lady Moselle. I thought perhaps this might help with your nieces." He waved his footman forward, and Jarls tottered into the sitting room and deposited the parcel on the carpet.

"What have you done?" she asked, coming down the stairs.

Her gown was more worn even than the one yesterday. His tenants had better. Yet none of them had ever brought a smile to his lips with one glance. Her skin glowed with health, her eyes with interest.

"See for yourself," he said, stepping aside to allow her room to follow Jarls.

Roth was standing over the package, arms at the ready, as if he expected a tiger to come leaping out. Petunia untied the string and folded back the paper. Then she straightened, fingers flying to her lips.

"A toy theatre!"

The delighted cry drew him to her side like the tug on a string of one of the puppets.

"I thought your nieces might enjoy it," he explained, feeling absurdly proud of the pleasure that pinked her cheeks. "The maker hadn't quite finished it, you see, so some of the scenery requires coloring. And the puppets could use some clothes." Belatedly it dawned on him that he might have just given her more work. What did he know about the capabilities or interests of little girls?

"Not that I expect you to paint or sew," he hurried to assure her. "Perhaps I should have someone do that first." He reached for the brown paper that had wrapped the box.

Her arm shot out to stop him. "No. It's perfect. Rose and Daphne will love using watercolors to finish the paper backgrounds, and Rose is learning her stitches, so she can help sew the costumes for the puppets. Between setting things up and deciding on stories to enact, this could keep them busy for hours. I cannot thank you enough!"

Before he could do more than bask in the glory of her approval, she turned and threw her arms about him.

CHAPTER SIX

TUNY HAD ON occasion hugged someone when she was happy. She hugged her brother after they'd exercised together. She had hugged Charlotte when her sister-in-law had embroidered a hem for her. She'd hugged Larissa, Callie, and Belle any number of times when they'd been triumphant.

Hugging her family and friends was nothing like hugging Lord Ashforde.

She had meant only to thank him for his thoughtful gift. But the moment her arms came around him, she was aware of his height, his lean strength, the way he held himself, as if ready to repel all boarders.

As if ready to repel her.

She jerked back, unable to meet his gaze. "It was very kind of you, my lord."

"It was my pleasure."

Warmth tempered the words. It heated his gaze too when she dared to raise her eyes to his. And that smile made it entirely too difficult to breathe, as if Betsy had pulled the corset strings too tight.

"Have you nothing else to say to Lord Ashforde, your ladyship?"

Roth. She'd forgotten about the guardsman! Tuny shot him a look before focusing on Lord Ashforde again.

"Yes. I hope to see you at the Duchess of Wey's ball tomorrow night."

He inclined his head. "I will look forward to it even more, knowing you will be there." As if he realized how that might sound, he quickly added. "You and your family, of course."

Of course. Wouldn't want to raise expectations.

Something thumped overhead, and Daphne's voice rose in a wail.

He stepped back. "I should leave you to your duty. Good day, Lady Moselle."

"My lord."

He saw himself out.

"Tactical error," Roth said. "You should have spoken to him."

"I have the matter in hand," Tuny gritted out. "Now, excuse me. My family needs me."

As Lord Ashforde had surmised, the toy theatre was a huge success. Once Charlotte showed the girls how it operated, they threw themselves into finishing the sets and costumes.

"Genius," Charlotte told Tuny, watching Daphne carefully brush paint over a sheet meant to be sky. "We must thank him."

"You can thank him at the ball," Tuny reminded her.

Her sister-in-law shook her head. "Until we find a nanny or governess, there will be no balls for me. Little work for Matthew on our cases either. Good thing we recently settled the one for the McAllisters."

"Monday, we'll put an ad in the paper," Tuny promised.

"Not yet," Charlotte hedged. "Mr. Huber gave me the name of the employment agency that places Miss Winchester. I thought I'd contact it first."

It was a good plan. Almost as good as her plan with her friends to speak to Lord Ashforde at the ball. Maybe it had been the hug—which persisted in repeating itself in her mind the rest of the day and into Saturday. Maybe it was the importance of her mission. Either way, by Saturday night, she felt as scattered as the leaves in autumn.

But she followed the plan anyway. She dressed in one of her favorite gowns, a figured peach with a deep orange satin ribbon at the high waist. The ribbon at her throat echoed the pattern in the overskirt. It was simple, but elegant.

Like her, or so she preferred to think.

Larissa's mother had chosen the Athenian Rooms off St. James's for the ball. Tuny and Callie had used the large, wood-paneled space for their dinner and art auction for the Society for the Prevention of Cruelty of Animals earlier this year. Now the polished wood floor gave back the reflection of dozens of shimmering ballgowns, and the light from the crystal chandeliers overhead sparkled on gemstones as the company strolled about in anticipation of dancing.

"You have the advantage," Larissa assured her, taking Tuny's arm and beginning a promenade of their own. "You know most everyone present: Aunt Meredith and Uncle Julian. Lord and Lady Carrolton, Lord and Lady Worthington, and that sort. Callie is keeping an eye out for Lord Ashforde and will signal us as soon as he arrives. Belle will see him brought to your side with all dispatch."

She knew it a wise course, yet still her fingers tingled inside her white silk evening gloves, as if wishing to seize a spot along the wall and hang on.

And still, he did not arrive.

Leo claimed Larissa for the first dance. Owen came for Belle. Callie retreated from her place near the door to join Tuny along the wall.

"Perhaps he changed his mind," Tuny said, regret and relief mingling.

"But he's always so proper," Callie protested. "And most of the other advisors are here. Mr. Greville is over by the refreshment table. Lord and Lady Wellmanton are about to join the set. They were very nice in the receiving line, but I heard her complain later about Mother's dress."

"Not fancy enough for her liking," Tuny guessed.

"Some just can't forget she was our governess first," Callie said. "Still, even Lord Trelawney came, and I heard he is very select in his entertainments." She nodded across the room.

Tuny eyed the fellow. His black evening coat and trousers were well cut, but traditional, yet his golden blond hair had a decided wave in it, as if it defied convention.

"How is he expected to vote?" she asked Callie.

"Fritz says he is on our side," her friend told her. Then she brightened as Count Montalban, her betrothed, strode up and bowed before them. That curly blond hair defied every sort of convention, but then, so did he. Tuny had to admit he looked rather fine in the scarlet of the royal house.

"Would you honor me?" he asked, holding out his hand, palm up.

"Of course," Callie said, placing her hand in his. He tucked it close and led her toward the line with a nod of respect toward Tuny.

Tuny sighed. Oh, to have someone look at her the way Fritz did Callie—all hope and joy and awe, as if she were the most precious person in the entire world.

Lord Ashforde had looked at her that way once.

No, no he hadn't. She'd been mistaken. For if he had gazed at her in such a way, nothing would have kept him from her side. She'd sought that look on the face of every fellow who had come calling in the last three years. Once in a while, she'd thought she seen something like it, but she'd been afraid to take the chance of being wrong again. And so, it seemed, she would soon be considered firmly on the shelf.

"You should not sit out."

Tuny turned to find Keller beside her. Firm cheeks beginning to redden as if he were amazed at his own audacity, he inclined his blond head and offered her his arm.

"Aren't you on duty?" she asked.

"I have just now taken over for Huber, who will be serving His Royal Highness," he told her with a nod to where her nieces' favorite guardsman was now stationed along one of the walls. "And I know of no better way to keep you safe than to have you on my arm."

"Cheeky," she said. But she accepted his offer.

He was a good dancer, surprisingly light on his feet. He sincerely seemed to enjoy partnering her. Her spirits couldn't help rising a little.

"I will be watching," he assured her as he escorted her back to where she had been standing. "If you have any need of me, you have only to signal, and I will be at your side in an instant."

"Thank you," Tuny said, dipping a curtsey, for all a lady shouldn't do so to a guard.

Keller clapped his fist to his chest in the Batavarian salute, then took himself off to a discrete distance. From the other wall, Huber sent her a wink.

Tuny smiled.

"Good evening, Lady Moselle."

That smile was hard to keep in place as she turned to face Lord Ashforde. He too wore the requisite evening black, with a grey-striped satin waistcoat and a simply tied cravat. Traditional to the inch. Yet he shifted from foot to foot, and one hand was fisting at his side. If she hadn't convinced herself she did not know his mind, she might have thought him nervous.

"Good evening, my lord," she said, stopping herself just short of curtseying to him. As a baroness in her own right, she was his equal now. "I did not see you arrive."

"I was late," he admitted. Another gentleman might

have drawled the fact, implying that he had far better things to do. He shifted on his feet again as if embarrassed by his tardiness. "I apologized to Her Grace."

"Trouble?" Tuny couldn't help asking.

"Only of the mind," he assured her. "Would you favor me with the next dance?"

A herd of Batavarian cattle rushed through her stomach. Larissa would advise her to agree. Leo would want her to accept. Then she heard the music starting.

"You might want to rethink that offer," she told him. "That's the Batavarian waltz."

He held out his arm. "I have been tutored in the steps."

So had she, by the crown prince of Batavaria himself. And she knew what those steps entailed—swirling and twirling and lifts in the gentleman's arms.

Did she dare dance the Batavarian waltz with Lord Ashforde?

She hesitated, and Ash willed himself not to beg her pardon for daring to trouble her. And when she gave him a shaky nod and placed her hand on his, it was all he could do not to strut out onto the dancefloor like a rooster owning his coop.

When he had decided to seek a bride, he had had a dance master come in at the beginning of each Season to teach him the latest steps. There was little he disliked more than appearing a fool. Perhaps appearing a lovesick fool. He made sure he looked like neither as he and Petunia took their places among the circle of couples.

The first part of the dance was a typical waltz. He kept one hand in hers and the other resting at her waist. Odd that both felt decidedly warm, as if he could sense her through his evening gloves and her clothing. She tilted her head so that she was looking over his left shoulder, which was just as well. Looking into her eyes might have cost him a step.

And then it came—the first lift. He dropped her hand, braced both of his on her waist, and lifted her. The scent of vanilla drifted past, as if he'd entered the kitchens and discovered his favorite biscuits baking. He barely remembered to lower her in time to the music. Their gazes touched.

Held.

A cough from Sir Matthew, who was passing with his wife, informed him he was falling out of step. He swung Petunia back into the rhythm.

Each lift was a little longer, and the fellow was expected to add flourishes like twirls and turns, to prove both his mastery of the dance and his prowess as a man. Count Montalban swirled past, his betrothed high, her eyes alight with glee. Ash squared his shoulders and lifted Petunia up, then spun on his heels.

Her giggle so astonished him he nearly tripped as he lowered her. She bit her lip as if to keep the next laugh inside, but her eyes were dancing too.

The third lift, he let go only for a moment to toss her higher, then caught her safely and brought her back into the circle of his arms. For a moment, she was in his embrace.

The light in her eyes deepened, beckoned to him. He forgot about the music, the dance, his vows to keep himself at a distance. He bent his head. She swayed closer.

Around them, applause broke out. The dance had ended, and the prince and his supporters were thanking the musicians. Gentlemen bowed to their ladies, who curtsied in response.

"My lord?" she murmured, straightening. "You can release me now."

His heart was pounding unaccountably loud. Worse, he could feel that longing rising again, to hold her, to kiss her, to promise her undying devotion when he knew that polite companionship was the right course.

As if she saw inside him, she flushed pink. "My lord?"

Ash let his arms fall and swept her a bow. "Lady Moselle, thank you for the dance."

She curtsied, then accepted his arm to move off the dancefloor.

"Perhaps," Ash suggested, "you would have a moment for private conversation."

She stumbled, and he caught her before she fell. She pushed off his hands, as if they had burned her. "I'm fine. Truly."

All at once, another fellow was at her side. She'd danced with him earlier, and Ash recognized the dress uniform of the Imperial Guards. This one had blond hair and a surprisingly hard line to his face.

"Is this man troubling you, Lady Moselle?" he asked, interposing himself between Ash and Petunia.

Ash drew himself up. "I am a gentleman, sirrah." He had not intended his voice to carry, but others were glancing their way, stopping their movements.

Petunia stepped around her guardian dragon. "It's all right, Mr. Keller. Lord Ashforde means me no harm. Do you, my lord?"

The guardsman started, then peered closer. As if recognizing Ash for the first time, he paled.

Ash offered Petunia another bow. "Never, Lady Moselle."

"Then I think a short conversation may be appropriate, so long as you allow me to dictate the topic."

He had intended to apologize, but the fact that she was willing to speak to him was at least a good start. "Of course."

"Walk with me," she said. She nodded to Keller, who took himself back to the wall. But Ash felt the guardsman's gaze on him as they began a slow promenade around the edge of the room.

"You must know that most people here support Prince Otto Leopold in his quest to see his lands restored," she said.

That was what she wished to talk about? Disappointment bit sharply. Why? He had wanted them to be companionable.

"I had gleaned as much by the company," he acknowledged.

"I am also a fervent supporter," she said, then she hesitated, as if waiting for him to argue.

"You are friends with Lady Larissa and Lady Calantha," he said. "I would expect you to support their betrotheds."

"I don't support Leo and Fritz just because they're engaged to my best friends," she informed him, chin coming up. "I support them because they are in the right. The Congress of Vienna had no call to portion out their lands without even discussing the matter with them. We do not rule other countries."

His Majesty might disagree with her there. In his mind, and in the mind of many in the House of Lords, England stood supreme.

"I can see your point," Ash said. "But the decision was made ten years ago now. Undoing it might have unintended consequences."

"Such as?" she challenged.

"Lands previously held by the crown may have been transferred to private ownership," he extemporized. "Businesses may have been built. How will those who bought in good faith be compensated?"

She frowned. "I hadn't thought of that. But it's hardly fair to expect Leo and his father to pay for the land that was theirs to begin with."

Lord Trelawney strolled up to meet them just then. His

smile glittered brighter than the pomade in his golden hair.

"Ashforde," he greeted. "Be a good chap, and make me known to the lovely lady on your arm."

Ash's grip tightened, pulling her closer. What was he doing? He had no right to keep Petunia to himself. He forced himself to relax.

"Lady Moselle," he said, "allow me to present Lord Trelawney, a good friend to our king."

Trelawney took her free hand and brought it to his lips for a kiss. "A pleasure, your ladyship."

Everything in him demanded that he call the fellow out for his temerity. How dare he touch her, kiss her, on first meeting?

She pulled away. "My lord. Thank you for your support to the Batavarian cause."

"Of course," he drawled. "The ruling class must be upheld. Anything else is anarchy. May I request the favor of a dance?"

She hesitated, and Ash wanted to crow in delight. Then she inclined her head. "Very well."

She turned to him. "Thank you for the dance and the discussion, my lord. If you'd be willing to take a turn around Hyde Park tomorrow after services, we could continue our conversation then under more congenial circumstances."

"Delighted," Ash said with a bow.

And if he spent the rest of the evening grinning like a fool, he could only hope no one else noticed.

CHAPTER SEVEN

MEREDITH WATCHED AS Petunia and Lord Ashforde promenaded around the edges of the crowded room. Their heads were close together, their expressions animated. Of course, not nearly as animated as when they'd danced the Batavarian waltz together. For a moment, she'd thought they might kiss right there on the dancefloor!

Julian had been right. The spark between them was undeniable. A shame she hadn't been able to bring Fortune with her tonight. Her dear Jane, the Duchess of Wey, would have been forgiving, but the press of company, and all those tantalizingly swinging silk skirts, would prove too much for her pet. And Fortune had already had one visitor to greet today. Her reaction could only be called tepid.

Herr von Mandelsloh, the Envoy for Württemberg, had bowed over Meredith's hand before joining her and Julian that afternoon in their sitting room. He was a short, slender fellow with sandy hair just covering his high forehead, and his smooth features appeared arranged so as to give no clue to his inner thoughts. Fortune, who had been watching sights out the window, considered him, tail swinging idly. He either did not notice her or did not think to acknowledge her.

"Lady Belfort, Lord Belfort," he said before flipping

back his navy coattails and taking a chair, "thank you for receiving me."

"You are most welcome," Julian assured him. "How might we be of assistance?"

He swiveled slightly to face her husband more fully. "I have attempted to speak to Prince Otto Leopold and his brother, but they seem disinclined to hear what their sovereign might think of their misguided efforts to regain their lands."

Julian, bless him, had worked with so many high-and-mighty lords over the years that his face also betrayed nothing, though he must be bristling as much as she was.

"Understandable, I suppose," he mused. "They consider their father their sovereign and their efforts justified."

One corner of the envoy's mouth twitched, as if he could not quite muster a smile. "As you say. Because you are representing them at the court of St. James's, I thought perhaps we might have a conversation instead. I'm sure your lady would find such matters tedious. Please know I will not in any way be offended if she chooses to leave us."

"She chooses to stay," Meredith answered. "And I would prefer not to be spoken of as if I were in another room, lacking in intelligence, or a piece of furniture."

Immediately, he inclined his head. "Forgive me, Lady Belfort. There are times I find your language challenging. I meant no offense."

As he spoke flawless English, she could only wonder at the truth of either statement. She smiled politely and wiggled her fingers at the side of her lavender skirts. Fortune perked up.

"I'm not sure what we have to say to each other," Julian allowed, leaning back on the sofa and cupping one black-trouser–clad knee with his hands. "The prince and Count Montalban have made their position clear. I can't imagine anything changing their minds."

"But I have heard you are a man gifted with the ability to change minds," the envoy said. "I am certain I can provide information and an incentive that would help you see the matter from a different perspective."

An incentive? Was he attempting to bribe her husband? Meredith scratched the fabric, and Fortune dropped down and padded closer.

"You would do better to speak to His Majesty's advisors," Julian said. "They are the ones most in need of information."

"I intend to speak to them," von Mandelsloh acknowledged. "But if you convince the prince to withdraw his request for support, there would be no need."

"You have a very high opinion of my abilities, sir," Julian said with a wry smile.

Fortune stopped in front of the envoy, then cocked her head, as if she couldn't quite understand his purpose. He ignored her, gaze fixed on Julian.

"I had heard you can solve any problem, for a price," he said.

Julian rose. "The price, sir, is generally friendship. As you and I can claim none, I fear I cannot help you. Allow me to see you to the door."

Fortune hopped up on the sofa and made herself comfortable. Her eyes were unblinking as Julian showed the envoy out.

"He certainly seems a villain," Meredith had ventured to her pet.

Fortune had yawned, teeth white and sharp. And that was all Meredith had been able to learn. She had relied on the cat's insights, especially when her own had been tainted by fear or worry. What was she to make of Fortune's response to the envoy now?

On Sunday, Ash kept his gaze on the vicar of St. George's Hanover Square as the man exhorted his flock to charity and other good works. He had always tried to do his best in both areas. He donated twenty-eight percent of his income, a point for each year of his life, to the church and such civic projects that seemed sensible. He made sure every one of his servants, here and at Lamote Hall, his estate north of London, had opportunities for advancement and leisure. He rewarded good service. He saw to the wellbeing of his tenants, draining areas that tended to flood, replacing aging roofs, and repairing crumbling foundations. Perhaps all that counted toward good works.

Meeting Petunia after church probably did not.

That didn't stop the eagerness that flooded him as he stepped down from the carriage at the edge of Hyde Park. The sky was a crystalline blue, and the welcome breeze rustled the long, jagged-edged leaves of the squat plane trees that clustered along Park Lane.

"Meet me at Hyde Park Corner in an hour," he told his coachman.

"Very good, my lord." The coach trundled off.

A man should be able to have a conversation about the Batavarian question and apologize in an hour's time, even given a stroll to and from the location of his groveling.

He started along the closest graveled path. Others must have had the same idea of strolling through the park, for he could see couples and families ahead and on the paths to either side. The only man walking alone cast him a glance and then disappeared behind a shrub as if he relished his privacy. Ash could have told him there was only one conversation he wished to have.

He came out near the great bronze statue of Achilles. The ladies of England had gathered funds to pay cannons from Waterloo to be melted down and cast as the eighteen-foot marvel that celebrated the great general's triumph over Napoleon. How did Wellington ever walk by it without seeing his face in the features?

How could Ash walk by it without seeing the lady whose natural beauty eclipsed any work of art?

She was standing in the sunlight on the other side of the massive statue. Her dress was as blue as the sky, with pleats running up from the hem to the ruffled collar. The matching ribbons on her broad-brimmed straw hat fluttered in the breeze. She was positively enchanting.

"Lady Moselle," he said as he joined her.

Her smile was soft, hesitant, quite unlike her usual openness. Could it be he wasn't the only one nervous about this meeting?

"Lord Ashforde," she acknowledged. "Thank you for meeting me. Shall we walk?"

He fell into step beside her as she turned toward the Serpentine. His hand reached down as if to take hers, and he curled his fingers behind his back instead.

"No guards today?" he felt compelled to ask.

She nodded toward a copse of trees, and, for the first time, he noticed the darker shadow gliding among them.

"Matty suggested that they position themselves strategically," she explained. "Apparently, Mr. Roth finds the shade strategic. Probably cooler too in that black uniform."

"Matty?" he asked as they came out next to the blue-green waters. He didn't recall meeting an Imperial Guardsman by that name, but not all of them had accompanied the prince and his brother to the duke's house party.

"My brother," she supplied. "Sir Matthew."

"Ah, of course. I should have guessed."

Her shoulder lifted in a shrug. "You haven't spent much time with my family. You couldn't be expected to know."

He could not help but think it a failing that he didn't know. If he intended to marry a woman, shouldn't he have met her family, her friends? They would be joining two lives after all. But three years ago, he'd been so intent on fixing all his father's failings he hadn't considered his own.

"And how does your brother feel about having a guard at your beck and call?" he asked as she paused by the waters. Others were out enjoying the day: sweethearts strolling arm in arm and gazing at each other adoringly, families walking with their children. One little boy was studiously throwing stones, sending ripples to ruffle the waters.

She chuckled, a warm sound that made him feel as if he'd cuddled under a blanket with a good book on a cold winter's day. "He's none too keen on having them underfoot, although he likes the fact they can hold their own in a fight."

Ash raised his brows, concern dissipating the warm feelings like smoke in the wind. "Have they had to fight for you?"

"Not for me," she clarified. "But they have that capability. So does Matty. He was the Beast of Birmingham, you know."

"Indeed," he said. "I saw him take on the Giant of Lancaster. No one could touch him."

Her smile, brighter than the sun, stunned him. "You have *that* right. And I wager he could still take on any comers, if he wanted."

His befogged brain informed him that Sir Matthew could likely take on the lord who thought himself good enough to win his sister.

"I hope as baronet he has fewer causes to use his fists," he said with heartfelt sincerity.

"He does that," she said with a sigh, as if she regretted the fact.

She turned for the path to the north, and once again Ash fell into step beside her.

"Shall we discuss the Batavarian question?" she asked as the shade from the trees on either side covered them like a parasol.

Time to make a clean breast of it. "Actually, I was hoping to address another matter first. As you know, I've been wanting to speak to you for some time."

She lifted her chin in a show of her usual bravado. "Sorry to have inconvenienced you, I'm sure."

He sighed inwardly. "That came out wrong. What I meant was, I have been regretting how we parted three years ago, and I've wanted to apologize ever since."

She stopped and stared at him. "Truly?"

"Truly," he assured her, stopping as well and encouraged by the hope ringing in her voice. "I was unconscionably curt with you when you deserved nothing less than my respect and admiration. At the time, I had concluded that we would not suit, but there were far better ways to explain that."

She started walking again, this time faster, as if she could distance herself from the memory. "Apology accepted. We needn't dwell on the matter."

"Unfortunately, I find myself dwelling entirely too much," he told her, pacing her as they came abreast of the stone Keeper's Lodge with its tall pillars. "Against my better judgment, I cannot seem to stop thinking of you as a potential bride."

Once more she jerked to a stop, this time face flaming. "Oh! Against your better judgment? How very kind you are, my lord. I'm sure every girl longs to hear just such a statement from her *potential groom*!"

There were a number of statements he regretted over the years, but he had a feeling the one he'd just made would haunt him the rest of his life.

The minister at St. Paul's Covent Garden had spoken this morning about forgiving wrongs, but Petunia was certain that if the fellow had had the misfortune of meeting Lord Ashforde, he might have made an exception. *Against his better judgment?* As if she was something tantalizing he knew was terribly, terribly bad, like eating all the Christmas pudding before the family came down for dinner.

"Please, Miss Bateman, Lady Moselle," he said, hands behind his back as if they had been tied there. "I find it difficult to speak well in front of you."

"Balderdash," Tuny said. "You're a member of Parliament. You must have made speeches any number of times, in front of dozens of powerful lords."

"You are hardly a powerful lord."

And didn't she know it. "No. I suspect that's part of the problem."

He rubbed a hand against the back of his neck. His valet would likely have fainted in despair if he'd seen the mess his lordship was making of that perfectly tied cravat. "It is entirely the problem," he protested. "I have no vested interest in a speech before Parliament other than seeing the best outcome for the nation. Now, I'm attempting to speak to the one woman who ever captured my heart. That alone ties my tongue."

Captured his heart? Oh, could he be any more cruel?

"I doubt I ever captured your heart," Tuny retorted. "At times, I've wondered whether you have one."

He winced. "Justified. Please, may we start over?"

She could not seem to stop the words from pouring out of her. "How far back would you like to go? The first time we met, when you asked Larissa and Callie to dance before you considered me? The second time we met, when you spoke to Larissa during dinner while completely ignoring me farther down the table? What about when you decided I might be tolerable enough for a dance or two, a walk or two, only to tell me to my face that you were sorry if you raised expectations? Or just now, when you admitted your judgment must be addled for even thinking of me at all?"

"For all those occasions," he said, "and any other moment when I might have hurt you, I am deeply sorry."

She looked him straight in the eye. Pain was etched in the lovely blue. It dragged down the corners of his mouth. Even his voice held a throbbing note of sorrow. His shoulders, always carried so high and proud, were slumping, his breath coming slow and heavy.

Nothing about him suggested he was a good actor. In fact, she had never known him to show himself as less than perfect. Could he truly regret his actions?

"Lady Belle is one of my dearest friends," she told him. "She made some poor choices at the duke's house party. When she realized she'd hurt me by them, she apologized profusely. I'll say to you what I said to her. I accept your apology, but I expect it to be accompanied by a change in behavior."

He sighed as if she had set him a task worthy of that Greek fellow, Hercules, Charlotte had told them about. "I can but try to do better."

She nodded slowly. "Very well. You can start by answering two questions."

"Anything," he vowed.

He might regret that promise. "First," Tuny said, "why this change of heart?"

She was certain he would say that it was because she had been elevated into his sphere. Why else would she suddenly become interesting?

He rubbed his neck again. "I'm not sure it's a change of heart," he said as if heedless of the material wilting down his neck. "More of a realization. After three years on the *ton*, I can safely say there is no woman your equal."

Her equal? A shame she didn't believe him, or he might have set her to blushing.

And to dreaming of things she knew were impossible.

"That's true enough," she said. "Most young ladies making their debut don't live in Covent Garden."

"Or have your forthright nature, intelligence, and beauty."

Oh, he was piling it on thick. Tuny peered closer and took a surreptitious sniff. "Are you feeling the thing? Or did you perhaps overindulge in wine for luncheon?"

His back straightened to its usual upright stance. "I do not overindulge."

That, she could have wagered on and won.

"Then let us turn to the other matter," she said, moving past the Keeper's Lodge. He fell in beside her again. Beyond him, she sighted Roth moving from tree to tree.

"I told you last night that I support the full restoration of Prince Otto Leopold's lands and titles."

"So you did," he said, voice returning to normal with the change in subject. "And I explained there are more sides that must be considered."

"I am willing to concede that. So long as you are willing to listen to my side of the matter."

"Of course."

Now came the hard part. "But in having that conversation, you must know that I am not attempting a courtship or even a friendship. I simply hope to bring you around to my way of thinking, as a favor to my true friends. So, I must ask: are you willing to entertain the notion I might be right?"

He paused on the path and cast her a glance out of the corners of his eyes. She counted off the seconds, hoping.

Then he leaned closer, until his lips were only inches away. Once she'd wanted so much for those lips to meet hers. She was shocked by how much she still wanted it.

"Convince me," he said.

CHAPTER EIGHT

TUNY REARED BACK. "Convince you? What are you suggesting, sir?"

Lord Ashforde straightened with a calm she was beginning to find maddening. "You have apparently given the matter more thought than I have. Tell me what you have learned."

Well, that wasn't as untoward as she'd feared. For a moment, she'd had visions of enticing him with honeyed words and smoldering glances.

Not that those would work, but still.

On the other hand, she wasn't entirely sure what she'd learned about the Batavarian question. She liked Leo and Fritz and appreciated the way they included her in activities that would normally have been reserved for those with more august lineages. It seemed wrong for them to have been forced from their home through no fault of their own. But did it follow they should return to Batavaria and resume ruling now?

Suddenly, she was only sure of one thing: he was standing entirely too close.

She took a step back. "Challenge accepted. I'll put my arguments together. Meet me here again at three on Tuesday."

He inclined his head graciously. "I look forward to it. May I escort you to your carriage?"

"I don't have a carriage," Tuny told him. "I walked."

She thought that might be enough to deter him. It certainly reminded her of the gulf in their stations, for all her fancy new title. Besides, another minute in his company, and she could be blurting out her admiration from three years ago. Silly, silly, silly, but there it was. The fellow was simply no good for her equilibrium.

He sent a look toward the guardsman waiting under the trees. "If the prince believes you require a guard, I cannot think walking about London safe. Allow me to drive you home."

Alone in a closed carriage with him? That didn't sound wise. What might she say? What might she do?

As if he had seen Lord Ashforde's look, Roth loped out from under the trees and headed their direction. Ah! She wouldn't be alone with Lord Ashforde. Her faithful guard would be at her side. And it was warm. Nice to be driven home instead of walking.

"Very well," she said. She motioned to the guardsman to join them.

"Lord Ashforde has offered us a ride home, Mr. Roth," she explained.

Roth inclined his dark head. "My lord."

"Sir," Lord Ashforde returned. She would have thought it a cool greeting, but, then again, all his greetings were rather on the colder side. But he offered her his arm, and she lay her hand on his. A tingle ran up her.

Having Roth there was such a blessing.

Still, she'd wondered how it might feel to be promenading with Lord Ashforde rather than one of the Imperial Guards. Now she knew. He had a confidence in his stride, as if he knew he owned the very ground, though he slowed his steps to match them to hers. Gentlemen approaching inclined their heads or bowed outright, as if they knew they were meeting someone impressive. Ladies simpered at him. Even the little children watched him pass, wide-eyed.

"That's Lord Ashforde," someone whispered, voice caught on the breeze. "You seldom see him out in public."

"Who's that with him?"

Tuny tensed, waiting for the criticism.

"I don't know," came the puzzled answer. "But she's a very lucky woman."

At the moment, she almost agreed.

They reached his carriage, a lacquered black affair with silver appointments, and Roth stepped in front of them even as a footman jumped down. As the servant watched with a frown, Roth opened the door and made a show of peering inside.

"Safe, your ladyship," he told her, as if he had suspected a convention of highwaymen might have gathered inside.

"Thank you, Mr. Roth," Tuny said.

The footman offered her his hand to help her inside.

"Covent Garden," Lord Ashforde called up to his coachman. "Off the northeast corner of the square."

He remembered where she lived? Well, of course he remembered. He'd called several times in the last week. But he must have remembered from before as well, even though he hadn't called more than a few times then. She glanced his way as he sat beside her, but he merely offered her a smile. With a last look about the area, Roth joined them, sitting on the rear-facing seat.

She resisted the urge to bounce on the padding as the carriage started forward. Her family borrowed Viscount Worthington's carriage when needed—Charlotte's brother was ever-so accommodating—but even his did not boast such splendor. She'd never seen so much tufted upholstery in her life—figured satin and creamy white, as if nothing would ever spill or splatter despite bumpy roads or inclement weather. Even the window shades were satin, tastefully edged in braid.

She wanted to tell him she approved. But Charlotte had explained that a lady did not comment on the things others had as if tallying them for a sale. One might remark on a new painting or bonnet, but carriages and furnishings were to go as unnoticed as the servants. They simply existed in the luxurious world of the aristocracy.

A world in which she'd never felt entirely comfortable. She kept expecting someone to point her toward the servants' quarters.

"And how are your brother and sister-in-law faring with the defection of the governess?" Lord Ashforde asked.

"Much better, thanks to that toy theatre you brought," Tuny said with a smile. "Charlotte says it was a stroke of genius. How did you know? Did you have one as a child?"

"Alas, no," he admitted. "Toy soldiers were more the order of the day." He paused, frown slipping into place. "Perhaps I should have purchased those instead."

"They would only get underfoot," Tuny said. "No, the theatre was inspired. The girls are planning their first performance."

He dropped his gaze to his flexing fingers. "Perhaps they might extend me an invitation."

Tuny blinked. "Do you really want one?"

"Of course. I'd like to see my investment bear fruit. That is, to see them enjoy it." He snapped his lips shut, as if realizing he was stumbling again.

"I'll be sure to mention it to Charlotte," Tuny promised, taking pity on him.

"Your sister takes an active role in raising them. Is that what you'd prefer for your children as well?"

It was probably the most intimate question he'd ever asked her, but she found the answer easy. "Yes. I know many in the aristocracy hire nannies and governesses and tutors for their children, but I was raised by my older sister, for the most part. I can't imagine willingly turning over my children to others, except for limited roles. I certainly can't claim any skill at teaching, so a governess at least part of the time would be wise when the girls are old enough. And I know boys are expected to go off to school at some point."

"Eton," he said. "At eight."

So young? "You must have missed home terribly," Tuny said.

"I enjoyed the library," he said, and a smile touched his mouth.

"I remember the first time I saw the library at Wey Castle," she told him. "So many books! I couldn't imagine anyone reading them all. His Grace confessed he's still trying."

"And still adding to the collection. He and I have run into each other a few times in bidding on a choice title."

"People bid on titles? For charity, like at the auction?"

"For acquisition, I fear," he admitted. "When it comes to some of the most ancient titles, only a few copies exist in the entire world. When one comes on the market, the bidding is fierce."

Tuny smiled at him. "But you're good at bidding. I've seen you. If you want something, you don't stop until it's won."

He met her gaze, and once more warmth shimmered in the blue. "You're right. I don't."

She tore her gaze from his and glanced out the window. "Unseasonably warm, even for the end of August, isn't it?"

"Decidedly so," Roth put in across from them, but his smile was amused.

She'd completely forgotten about the fellow again! So much for not feeling alone with Lord Ashforde.

She managed to keep the conversation more general until the carriage pulled up before the house. The Imperial Guardsman jumped down first and glanced around the area as if checking for bandits, then handed her down himself.

"I will see you on Tuesday at three by the Wellington monument," Lord Ashforde promised. "And I greatly look forward to our discussion."

Tuny nodded, and the carriage swung back onto the street, but her smile faded as the vehicle disappeared around the corner.

"Your talk did not go as you wanted," Roth said, gaze still roaming.

"That obvious, am I?" she asked, pivoting on her heels to head for the door.

"Obvious enough," Roth allowed. "He resists your attractions."

Tuny cast him a narrow-eyed look as she reached the step. "My attractions aren't involved in this."

He raised a dark brow in question.

"They shouldn't be," she insisted, but he reached around her and opened the door for her.

Shrieks of laughter sounded from the back of the house, along with a deep growl. Roth's hand went to his knife.

"That's Matty," Tuny informed him. "He's playing the Great Bear with the girls. He used to do that with us when we were little. Come into the sitting room. I'd like to talk with you."

Roth dropped his hand, but he followed her inside. She took a seat on the sofa. He put his back to the wall.

Tuny sighed. "You don't sit in Batavaria?"

"Not while on duty," he said.

"Huber sits," she told him. "He plays with the girls as well."

His look darkened. "Thank you for letting me know. I will see that he is disciplined."

Tuny shot to her feet. "Don't you dare! He's a very nice fellow. And each of you has every right to behave like the rest of us."

"Agreed," he said. "When we are not on duty."

Tuny shook her head. "What do you think is going to happen? A rifle shot through the glass? You wouldn't reach my side fast enough to prevent the bullet from hitting me. A brigand run through the rear door? Matty would flatten him before he took three steps. Someone climb down the chimney? He wouldn't be worth much once he reached the bottom. I could probably take him out myself."

He chuckled. It was a surprisingly gentle sound. "You probably could talk him to death."

Well! Tuny was ready to take him to task, but his mouth was turning up.

"Yes," she said, resuming her seat with a swish of her skirts. "Yes, I could. See that you remember that."

"I promise," he said. "Now, what did you wish to speak of?"

She puffed out a sigh. "I need help gathering my arguments to present to Lord Ashforde. Why should Leo and his father be given back their kingdom?"

He started, and his hand was on his knife again, as if she had impugned the honor of his beloved rulers. "Because it is their right," he said, voice sharpening.

"Is it?" she pressed. "Other people decided the right should go to Württemberg."

"Without the consent of the Batavarian people," he assured her. "We were happy, secure, and prosperous under King Frederick's rule. I do not know the same can be said of the King of Württemberg."

"You do not know." Tuny seized on the words. "Why don't you know? Hasn't your family written to tell you how they're doing?"

Now his face hardened as well. "I am an orphan. I have no family."

How awful! She had been raised surrounded by family, and now she often felt Larissa, Callie, and Belle were her family too. Tuny rose, closed the distance, and grabbed his hand. He resisted the pull.

"Come on, Roth," she said. "You're here to protect me. That means you're under my orders."

He nodded slowly. "In the absence of my prince and the captain of the guard, yes. But you must not countermand their orders."

"Wouldn't dream of it," Tuny told him. "But I'm going to spend the rest of the afternoon with my family, and I order you to take part. Sunday afternoons Charlotte reads to us from an adventure novel. I'm sure you wouldn't want to miss that."

Ash savored the memories of his recent interactions with Petunia the rest of Sunday and into Monday. The delight on her face when he'd delivered the toy theatre for her nieces. The feel of her against him, warm and supple, when she'd hugged him in thanks. The fire in her eyes when he'd challenged her to convince him of her point of view about the Batavarian question.

From the first time he'd met her, something about Petunia Bateman had drawn him closer. That sense had deepened in the intervening years. Now he could only admire the way the sunlight caught in her hair, turning the dark blonde to bronze. She moved with a confidence few ladies seemed to manage. When she glanced at him from the corners of her eyes, smile playing about her rosy lips, she seemed equally confident that he was going to say something marvelous.

Even if he seldom managed to form a coherent sentence in her presence!

She was right. He had spoken before Parliament. He had stood up to thank staff and tenants for their service at the annual harvest festival. He knew how to share his thoughts with precision, logic, even command.

And one look at her, and he was that small boy gazing up at the moon and knowing it forever beyond his reach.

Yet, was a courtship, a marriage, with Petunia truly beyond him? He had blundered badly three years ago, but at moments, he thought perhaps she still cared. Marriage to him certainly held advantages. He could give her a bigger house in London, an estate, and the clothing and jewels that she so deserved. The last few high sticklers who sneered at her family's antecedents might finally open their doors to her.

Yes, he could give her a great deal, but he still feared to give her the one thing she most likely would demand from a marriage.

His heart.

Always it came down to that, no matter how he turned the situation around in his mind. Some marriages were based on cool detachment and no expectation of love. Petunia Bateman had every right to hope for something more, something better. Could he keep himself and give it to her?

He had reached no conclusions when Peaves announced a visitor early Monday afternoon.

"Herr von Mandelsloh, the Envoy for Württemberg," his butler volunteered. "I took the liberty of placing him in the sitting room."

Peaves only put those he didn't approve of in the sitting room. Though it was suitably furnished in crimson and bronze, it overlooked the street, with the attendant noise from passing vehicles.

"I'll meet with him," Ash said, rising from his favorite chair in the library.

The envoy bowed to him when Ash stepped into the room. Ash had met him at various events associated with the diplomatic corps. Now the fellow offered him a hesitant smile as nonthreatening as his navy coat and fawn trousers.

"Lord Ashforde, I am honored to see you again."

"To what do I owe this pleasure?" Ash asked, going to take a seat on one of the chairs.

Herr von Mandelsloh returned to his own seat. "It is my understanding that you have undertaken the daunting task of advising your king on the Batavarian issue."

Not question, as everyone else called the matter. For Württemberg, it seemed, the matter was more of a problem than an uncertainty.

"Along with Lords Wellmanton, Canning, and Trelawney as well as Mr. Greville," Ash allowed.

"I have met with each of them. I apologize for coming to you so late. My secretary was recently returned home, so I have had to function alone."

He'd heard about the secretary. Gruber von Grub had been sent home in disgrace after attempting to ruin Count Montalban's reputation and poison King George against Prince Otto Leopold and his family. Since then, he'd managed to send back another spy, who had also been apprehended. The envoy had disavowed all knowledge of the plots.

"No doubt you're doing your best for your king," Ash said.

"I can but try," von Mandelsloh replied. "I'm sure you must have questions about how we are managing the lands that were once Batavaria. Allow me to answer them."

Ash leaned back and crossed one booted foot over the other. "I have more questions about the people of Batavaria. Are they safe? Do they thrive?"

The envoy spread his long-fingered hands. "But of course. King William would have it no other way."

"Would their representative in the Württemberg legislature agree?" he asked.

Herr von Mandelsloh's smile seemed to be glued to his face. "Our legislature is made up of members from many of the most prestigious families in the land. They see to the well-being of all our citizens."

Or at least to their own interests. "And do the Batavarians acknowledge William as their king?"

"Those who do not are dealt with, just as you would deal with anyone who does not acknowledge George as your king."

His words answered more questions than he knew. Ash rose.

"Thank you for coming to see me, Envoy. I assure you, I will be giving the Batavarian question considerable thought, but I cannot promise King William will like my conclusions."

Herr von Mandelsloh rose as well. "I hope you can bring yourself to see the right of it, my lord. I would hate to find a rift growing between our kingdoms. Wars have been fought for less."

Ash frowned. "Are you saying Württemberg is willing to go to war to preserve its rule over Batavaria?"

"I would never wish to state such a claim publicly," the envoy said. "I merely mention the possibility, as a contribution to your deliberations. Good day, my lord."

He bowed, and Ash inclined his head. And the fellow quit the room, leaving a shadow of darkness behind.

CHAPTER NINE

MONDAY, KELLER WAS on duty. He was content to stand quietly in the entry hall at Weyfarer House where Tuny had retreated for help.

This Season, she'd been staying at the duke's townhouse. Charlotte had thought attending events with the duchess's daughters might bring Tuny to the attention of more suitable gentlemen. She'd had her share of attention, but what she enjoyed most were these moments when she and her friends could share confidences, plot strategy, or at least commiserate. A shame Belle was out in Hyde Park this morning with her betrothed. She and Owen enjoyed riding too much to remain indoors on such a lovely summer's day.

"So, the story is that Württemberg cannot have Batavaria's best interest in mind," Tuny said, pacing the pretty withdrawing room, her blue chambray skirts snapping. "And Leo and King Frederick will do a far better job of taking care of their people."

"Exactly," Larissa said approvingly from her place on the sofa, her own blue lustring skirts arranged properly. "And I think we have ample proof of the fact."

"Forced labor in mines," Callie, in her signature pink, put in from her chair. "Lack of representation in the Württemberg parliament."

Tuny nodded. "Taxation without representation. If that was a good enough excuse for the American colonies, I would think it would stand for Batavaria too."

"The American colonies and England ended up in a war," Larissa reminded her. "We don't want that for Batavaria and Württemberg. Leo and his father merely want to ensure the security and prosperity of their people."

Roth had said something similar. Security and prosperity. Who didn't long for such?

"That will give me something to argue about, in any event," Tuny said, plopping down beside Larissa.

"Is it an argument?" Callie asked, brow puckered in concern.

"Depends on what you call an argument," Tuny said. "I can't imagine Lord Ashforde raising his voice to make a point. I always thought him the perfect English gentleman, but I'm beginning to wonder whether he's too perfect."

Larissa nodded. "We should be able to answer that question shortly. Mother returned to Wey Castle this morning with Thal and Peter to prepare for Michaelmas term at school. Aunt Meredith will be chaperoning us again, which means we'll have ample access to Fortune."

Relief coursed through her. Her aunt's cat, Fortune, was a creature of legend. If she approved of you, you were of high character indeed. If she did not, you had best reconsider your choices. She had matched every member of the duke's family since the current duchess as well as Charlotte and Matty and Tuny's sister Ivy and her marquess, Kendall. Tuny might struggle to understand Lord Ashforde, but Fortune would see right through him.

But did she really want Fortune to confirm her worst fears? At moments—in the park, in his carriage—she'd thought he truly cared. Still, what if she was mistaken again?

She and Keller had just returned home later that afternoon when the knocker sounded. Whether to spare

Betsy or to protect Tuny, who was taking a moment to read in the sitting room, Keller answered it.

"What do you want?" he demanded.

The quiet Keller? Who could have raised such a reaction? She was on her feet and moving toward the door before the visitor answered.

"I am here to speak to Miss Bateman."

The accent sounded a great deal like Keller's or any of the Batavarian contingent, but she didn't recognize the voice.

"Lady Moselle," Keller growled as Tuny stepped into the entry hall.

An older man, impeccably dressed, looked beyond him to Tuny. "Would you be so good as to locate your mistress?"

Wouldn't be the first time she'd been mistaken for the help. Tuny moved to Keller's side.

"I am Lady Moselle," she said, for the first time relishing the sound of the haughty name. "I do not believe we have been introduced."

The man looked to Keller, brows up in challenge.

She thought she heard the guard grind his teeth before turning to her. "Lady Moselle, this is the Envoy to England for Württemberg."

Ah, so that was the problem. The Batavarians would likely consider him the enemy, even though he had disavowed involvement for any troubles coming from Württemberg thus far this Season.

"Luther von Mandelsloh," he said, inclining his head and clicking his heels together. "A pleasure."

The way Keller's eyes remained narrowed, she could not return the compliment. She also didn't have to let him in the house.

"How might I help you, sir?" she asked.

A slight frown beetled his brow. "A moment of conversation."

A squeal and a bump came from upstairs, followed by Charlotte's voice. "Daphne! Give your sister back her doll immediately!"

"A moment is all I have," Tuny told him.

Something crossed his face. "Then I will be brief. It is my understanding that you are a special friend of one of King George's advisors on the Batavarian problem, Lord Ashforde."

She wasn't sure she liked being called a special friend. The fellow almost implied something untoward. "I am acquainted with Lord Ashforde," she corrected him.

"I had hoped you might be able to help him see that it is in his best interests to consider the position of Württemberg in his deliberations. I can provide more details at your convenience."

Keller's hand dropped to his sword.

Tuny shook her head. "I don't see how thinking about your interests helps Lord Ashforde. Besides, I was just made a lady of Batavaria, and you can see I have a loyal guardsman at my side. My dearest friends are about to marry into Batavarian royalty. You, sir, have come to the wrong house. Good day."

By the grin on his face, Keller took great pleasure in shutting the door on the envoy. Then he turned and saluted her. "A triumph, Lady Moselle."

"That's me," Tuny said, turning for the stairs. "Vanquishing pesky envoys and busy little girls." But she couldn't help her smile as she went up the stairs to assist Charlotte.

Tanner accompanied her to the meeting with Lord Ashforde on Tuesday. So as to avoid having to spend time with his lordship in his carriage again, Tuny had asked Charlotte to borrow her brother's carriage. Viscount Worthington—Worth to family and friends—lived with his wife, Lydia, on Clarendon Square not far from Weyfarer House and the home of Aunt Meredith and Uncle Julian. Charlotte's brother and sister-in-law were natural philosophers and often spent their time in remote locations studying the science of ballooning.

"Off to the Scottish Highlands this time," their coachman confided in Tuny when he pulled up in front of the house. "Apparently there's a unique air current in the area they want to try." He shook his head in what appeared to be equal parts amazement and amusement.

"What interesting people you know," Tanner said as he rode with her to the park.

"You know a prince and a count," Tuny pointed out. "Not to mention a king."

"But none of them have been up in a balloon or won a prizefight," he said with a grin. "If ever Lord and Lady Worthington need a guard, please keep me in mind."

"Why, Mr. Tanner, I thought you forever loyal to the Batavarian cause," Tuny teased.

His grin slipped the slightest. "I hope your work earns the prince and his brother back their kingdom, your ladyship, but I fear I may never see the mountains of Batavaria again." He winked at her. "Unless of course I cross them by balloon."

She felt as if a balloon were rising inside her as she stepped down from the coach on Tanner's hand and spotted Lord Ashforde waiting near the great bronze statue. Funny how his body looked as lithe and powerful in his dove grey coat and buff trousers. She had to keep her steps steady, or she likely would have run to meet him.

He must not have noticed her until she was nearly upon him, for he appeared to be studying another man down by the Serpentine. The fellow didn't look familiar, but he hurried off as if he'd been uncomfortable with his lordship's scrutiny. Or Tanner's.

"Lady Moselle," Lord Ashforde said, bowing. "A pleasure, as always. I see you brought reinforcements again."

Tanner clapped his fist to his chest in salute. "Kristof Tanner, my lord. Call if you have need of me." He waited for them to set off, then fell in behind them a good few feet back.

Once more, they strolled through the park. The day was warm, and few enough people had come out as yet that she could hear birds trilling in the trees. The musty scent of the Serpentine drifted on the air. She could almost imagine they had nothing more pressing to discuss than the next ball.

But, as Tanner had reminded her and the envoy from Württemberg had implied, the fate of Batavaria was in her hands. She drew in a breath.

"Thank you for agreeing to meet me again," she told Lord Ashforde. "I have carefully considered my arguments and am prepared to lay them out."

"Very wise," he said appreciatively. "I'm listening."

And he was. She could feel him lean ever so slightly closer, his gaze brushing hers, as if she were about to impart the secret to a satisfying life. He had the longest lashes, thick and dark, brushing across the blue like a raven's wing against the sky.

She forced her gaze out over the park ahead. "First, the House of Archambault has been the ruling house of Batavaria for ten generations. Tradition would seem to demand a continuation."

"Ruling houses change on occasion," he countered as they came out closer to the water. "Lines die out, princesses marry kings from other countries, a kingdom loses in a war."

"Ah, but none of that is true of Batavaria," Tuny said. "No one died or married, and they didn't lose a war. France lost, and the remaining countries on the

Continent apportioned her holdings. Batavaria was never a French holding. They fought against Napoleon, the same as Britain."

"But Württemberg fought against Napoleon as well," he pointed out as they followed the curve of the water. "In fact, if memory serves, they switched sides, giving the Coalition forces enough power to overthrow Napoleon. They were awarded Batavaria in thanks."

"And if a friend of yours had done the king a service, would he award your friend *your* estates?"

He chuckled. "Point taken. Still, Württemberg has ruled well these last ten years, by all accounts."

"Not by all accounts," Tuny told him. "There are reports of Batavarians being forced to mine silver from veins King Frederick refused to open because of the dangerous conditions."

He stopped to watch a little boy kneeling beside the waters. The child had brought a toy sailboat, which he slipped ever so carefully into the Serpentine. His father knelt beside him, smiling encouragement.

"I've seen nothing in *The Times* or through diplomatic channels," Lord Ashford said. "Where did you hear these reports?"

He didn't sound condemning, merely curious.

"Larissa and Callie had them from Leo and Fritz," she admitted.

"Ah, so those most interested in the outcome of the decision are providing input to that decision."

He said it softly, but she bristled nonetheless. "I'm sure they wouldn't lie."

"Perhaps not," he agreed. "But their longing for home might color the way they see things. I have heard that the Batavarian silver mines are unusually rich. A number here have invested in them."

Tuny frowned at him. "Have you?"

"No."

"But you're an interested party in your own finances. How can I believe anything you say about them?"

He smiled, and she wanted to prance up the path with pride that she'd had something to do with it. "Well done. Your point, again."

"Points?" Tuny asked, cocking her head. "Is this a game to you, then?"

He turned from the boy and met her gaze directly. "No. This is far more important. I promise you I am giving it my full attention."

Tuny straightened. "And I appreciate that, my lord."

"Your servant, Lady Moselle," he said.

Tuny wrinkled her nose. "I cannot accustom myself to that title."

He cast her a quick glance as they set off around the water at a good pace. "I cannot call you Miss Bateman. It would be disrespectful." He hesitated a moment. "Would you, perhaps, allow me to use your first name?"

Well, that was progress, though she wasn't sure in which direction, Batavarian restoration or courtship. Both seemed equally gratifying at the moment.

"Very well, my lord. You may call me Petunia."

He inclined his head as if cognizant of the honor. "And I would be honored if you would call me Ash."

"Ash?" She regarded him. "Surely that's a nickname. You don't have a first name?"

"I prefer Ash," he said.

She wasn't sure it suited him. Ash was something you cleaned from the hearth on occasion or the speckles left on the carpet after Matty had smoked a rare cigar. Ash was what remained after a fire had died.

Had his fire died? Was that why he seemed so cool at times? What could possibly have happened to him?

How fervent she was. She had obviously given the question of Batavarian restoration much consideration, and he could appreciate her points. But it seemed to him the question was not so easily resolved.

"Petunia," he said, pleased by the sound of the name he had called her in his mind for months, "have you considered the way that government has changed? France will crown a new king this December, but it has a legislative branch now as well. Our Parliament has, in effect, as much or more power than His Majesty when it comes to making laws and seeing to the good of the people. Württemberg has a Parliament for such a purpose. Batavaria never had."

The breeze had tugged free a lock of her dusky blond hair, and he had to hold himself tight to keep from reaching out to tuck it back. "I imagine Prince Otto Leopold could be persuaded to add one," she mused. "He's very forward thinking."

"But who knows how long His Royal Highness will be a prince instead of the king? His father is in remarkably good health, and he is, I believe, a traditionalist."

She nodded. "I've only met him a few times, but I'd have to agree. Still, it seems wrong to deny the prince his birthright because his father's an old stick in the mud."

He loved the way she spoke, forthright, using vivid images. "On that I agree as well. Yet we must face facts. King Frederick will be the one who steps back on the throne if the country is restored to its former status. Will he be a good ruler?"

"Will he be a better ruler than King William, a hundred miles away?" she argued. "Surely King Frederick knows his people."

"He *knew* his people," Ash corrected her. "He hasn't been allowed to set foot in the country in ten years. Much will have changed."

"Little that can't be changed back, I warrant."

"And some that *shouldn't* be changed back."

She blew out a breath and stopped. They had circled the Serpentine and come out where her carriage waited. He recognized the crest on the door: Worthington, her sister-in-law's family. It seemed she'd rather borrow from a near relative than accept a ride from him.

"Are we at an impasse, then?" she asked, gazing up at him.

He couldn't allow it to come to that. If he told her he was done, she might well walk away, and he would have no reason to see her again. And he truly wasn't ready to give in to her arguments.

"Perhaps what we need is a better setting to continue our discussion," he suggested. "Would you be willing to join me for dinner on Thursday evening, you and your family?"

She eyed him. "My whole family?"

"With the exception of your nieces," he caveated. "I doubt my staff is ready for them."

"I doubt *you're* ready for them," she said with a laugh. "But I also doubt they'd have much fun at a formal dinner. Still, with no governess in the house, we might find leaving difficult. I'll tell Matty and Charlotte about your invitation and send word whether we can accept. For now, I should go."

"Of course."

He bowed, and she curtsied, and Mr. Tanner escorted her back to the carriage.

And Ash spent the rest of the afternoon waiting for a knock on the door. When it came, he sat up higher on the upholstered chair just inside the withdrawing room. But instead of a card accepting or declining his invitation, Peaves ushered in Mr. Tanner of the Imperial Guard.

Ash was on his feet. "Has something happened to Petunia?"

Mr. Tanner went so far as to smile at him, as if consoling

an old friend. "Have no concerns, my lord. The Imperial Guards on duty will ensure her ladyship's safety. I have been relieved for the afternoon and was heading back to the Chelsea Palace, so she asked me to relay a message."

"A message he did not see fit to entrust to me," Peaves put in with a huff and a dark look at the russet-haired guardsman.

"That will be all, Peaves," Ash said, and his man stiffened his shoulders and marched from the room as smartly as any member of the guard.

"And the message?" he asked Tanner in the quiet that followed.

"I have one from Lady Moselle," he said, "and one from the Imperial Guard."

Ash could not imagine what the guards could have to say to him, but he nodded. "Proceed."

"First, Lady Moselle, her brother, and her sister-in-law would be delighted to join you for dinner on Thursday," he reported.

The air tasted sweeter. "Excellent."

Tanner took a step closer. "Second, the four of us who are guarding her ladyship have become very fond of her. We have all noticed that you are attempting to court her. And doing it badly."

Ash stared at him. "Now see here, sirrah…"

Tanner held up a hand. "We have no quarrel with you, my lord. We have asked around, and you are widely respected. You have much to offer her. But if you wish to win this war for her affections, you must change your tactics. If you will listen, I can tell you our ideas on how to go about that."

CHAPTER TEN

"DINNER WITH LORD Ashforde," Charlotte marveled, not for the first time since Tuny had ventured the question about joining Ash at his home. She and Charlotte were returning from Covent Garden, baskets loaded with peaches, apples, sweet potatoes, and artichokes. Their housekeeper and cook often shopped the market, but Charlotte had wanted to take her daughters away from the house to give Matty a moment of peace. Tuny had come along to help. The trip had been uneventful, though at one point, she'd wondered whether she might have seen the same man who had been in the park the other day. But when she'd looked again, he'd disappeared.

Now Charlotte had ahold of Daphne, and Tuny was helping Rose along, while Keller, the guardsman on duty, kept his distance. It might have been to allow a wider vantage point, but Tuny had a feeling he wasn't entirely sure how to deal with her nieces. Both girls loved the bustle and color of the market, still they tended to tire by the end of the trip. Daphne at least might take a nap when they reached home, and Rose might be content to draw pictures or read.

Then they all might have a moment to breathe!

"Yes, dinner," Tuny said because Charlotte seemed to expect a response. In truth, Tuny had thought of little else except Ash's invitation. He'd suggested it, he'd said, as a better location to continue their discussions about Batavaria. But surely a gentleman didn't request a lady's family to dine unless he had some idea about furthering an acquaintance.

Her stomach fluttered at the thought, and she tightened her grip on the basket handle.

As if Charlotte had reached the same conclusion, she edged closer and lowered her voice. "I take it this means you've forgiven him for whatever he did to hurt you."

"Who hurt you, Aunt Tuny?" Rose, ever the sharp-eared, demanded. "Father will not stand for it."

"Will he sit for it?" Daphne wanted to know.

Keller took a step closer as if he needed to hear the answer as well.

"I'm fine," Tuny told both her nieces, with a stern look to the guardsman, who dropped back, cheeks reddening. "No reason for you or your father to be concerned."

"Let's get the girls settled," Charlotte murmured as they neared the house. "Then we'll talk."

It took a good half hour to make sure the girls were occupied—Daphne resting as Tuny had hoped and Rose playing with a doll at Matty's feet in the study—before Tuny and her sister-in-law could slip away. With Keller stationed in the entry hall, Charlotte collapsed on the sofa in the sitting room and fanned herself with one hand as Tuny dropped onto the closest chair.

"Any word from Miss Winchester?" Tuny asked.

Charlotte leaned her russet head back against the fabric of the sofa, squashing her bun. "The director of the employment agency reported she was on another temporary assignment, and they did not expect her back for some days yet. If they don't send word soon, we may have no choice but to begin looking for someone else to replace Mrs. Quince."

She glanced out the door, then looked to Tuny. "So, have you forgiven Lord Ashforde?"

"I believe so," Tuny said, though the fingers pleating her skirts belied the comment. She shook out her hands and continued. "He made a very pretty apology. And then he invited us all to dinner."

"That would seem significant," Charlotte allowed.

"I can't help thinking as much," Tuny said. "But how can I trust his attentions? He played the devoted suitor before, only to inform me that he did not intend to be a suitor at all. He never explained what caused the change then. I don't understand what changed now."

Charlotte nodded. "Trust must be earned. Perhaps this dinner can be a start."

"Perhaps," Tuny said, but once more hope was rising.

"Would you mind very much removing yourself to the library, my lord?" Peaves asked in an aggrieved tone Wednesday afternoon from the drawing room doorway.

Ash had spent the morning with his man of affairs in the city and had only just returned to the house to find it in something of an uproar. Footmen thundered up and down the stairs with chairs and rugs as if he had invited dozens instead of three extra. Maids bustled from one room to the other with feather dusters, mops, and cleaning rags, as if the place wasn't always kept spotless already.

He rose, folded the newspaper he'd been reading, and tucked it under his arm. "Happy to oblige, Peaves, but I must ask. Why the consternation? It's only a dinner party, and a pitifully small one at that."

Peaves drew himself up. "We have not entertained in years, my lord. A great deal must be done, with a lamentably short time in which to accomplish it. Mr. Theban is ransacking your closet for something suitable. Mrs. Clowers is in tears at the thought of letting you down."

"Mrs. Clowers has never disappointed me in my life," Ash said. "I only made a few suggestions as to the menu. Shall I go down to the kitchens and apologize?"

Peaves clutched his chest so tightly he crushed the figured silk of his waistcoat. "Certainly not! I doubt she would ever recover." He dropped his hand and smoothed it down the cream-colored fabric. "But if you could just see fit to find an out-of-the-way place to sit, my lord, we will endeavor to do you proud."

"The library will be fine," Ash assured him. "I don't intend to show it off tomorrow."

"No?" Peaves' hand paused, and he seemed to decide against clutching his chest anew. "But my lord, if I may say so, it is a testimony to your intelligence and acumen. Surely the young lady should know of its existence."

The young lady. So, that was what this was about. It wasn't the prospect of entertaining that had them in a fluster. They thought he was courting, and they wanted to give Petunia no reason to refuse.

Neither did he.

"Excellent suggestion," he told his butler. "See that it's been thoroughly cleaned as well. Do we need to hire additional staff?"

Peaves heaved an audible sigh. "No, my lord. We are sufficient. Might I suggest luncheon at your club this afternoon?"

"Call for the coach," Ash said. "Are you certain you don't want more help?"

Peaves raised his chin. "Before I became a footman and butler, I served in the army, my lord. I remember how to prepare a camp for battle."

Battle. He hadn't thought about courtship that way. The Imperial Guards certainly had. He still couldn't believe they'd laid out his campaign for him.

"Lady Moselle is no delicate creature," Tanner had said to him yesterday when he'd brought the message from

Petunia agreeing to have dinner with him. "She is fiery, determined. She will not thank you for treating her as less."

"I'm sure I have ever only treated her with respect," Ash had said.

"Respect is fine," Tanner allowed, "for aged dowagers and learned lords. This is the woman you intend to wed. You must show her you are utterly devoted."

The very idea set up a discord inside him, as if cymbals had clashed in the middle of a waltz. It seemed some part of him found utter devotion only her due. And another part squirmed at the idea of so much emotion.

"And what," Ash said cautiously, "will she see as utter devotion?"

"Compliment her," Tanner urged. "Not just on her looks, which I agree are stellar, but on her intellect, her capability. Learn what she enjoys, and learn to enjoy it yourself. Share what you enjoy, and find commonalities. Offer her a hand when she slips, applause when she soars."

Ash had stared at him. "You seem to have given this considerable thought, Mr. Tanner."

He had grinned. "A man has to do something standing along the wall for hours at a time."

So it seemed. Perhaps he should look through his library. He was certain he had a book with all one hundred and fifty-four of Shakespeare's sonnets. Surely reciting one or two would make him appear utterly devoted.

So long as he did not allow that devotion to color his life.

But the maids were already attacking his library with flying dusters and swishing cloths, leaving him no peace to be had even as he waited for the coach. It pulled in front of the house in a remarkably short time, as if even Griffiths wanted him gone. He ended up retreating to a quiet corner of White's with the paper and a nice cup of tea. That's where Lord Wellmanton found him a few hours later.

"Good to see you out and about, my lad," the viscount said, as if Ash had been ill for some time. Unbidden, he lowered himself into the opposite wingback chair. "Do I take it this means you've made up your mind about the Batavarian question?"

He was at the point where the next person who mentioned Batavaria was likely to get an earful. "I am still taking the matter under consideration."

Wellmanton tsked. "You haven't much time. The king will return from Windsor in less than a fortnight. I expect he will want us to give him a consensus answer."

"Then perhaps you should be speaking to Trelawney and Greville," Ash said. "You may be able to persuade one of them to see your side. I see any number of sides, and I cannot yet judge between them."

Wellmanton shook his head, jowls quivering. "You cannot remain neutral. Too much is at stake."

Ash peered closer. Was that a drop of moisture along the viscount's pale hair? Another on his upper lip?

"What, exactly, is at stake for you?" he asked.

Wellmanton sat back, both hands resting on the arms of the chair. "For me? Oh, nothing, my boy, nothing of any import. I am a disinterested party."

No, he wasn't. Ash was certain of it. "Even in the Batavarian silver mines?" he guessed.

Wellmanton wagged a thick finger at him. "Ah, you have been speaking with Count Montalban, I fear. The fellow is a rebel, a rascal. You cannot believe anything he says."

"Then you have no interest in the mines," Ash pressed.

"I cannot say for certain," Wellmanton allowed, moving his hands to fold them over his bulging gut. "My man of affairs takes care of my investments. Silver may be involved, but whether it comes from Batavaria or the

African continent, it matters not to me, so long as it turns a handsome profit."

That, Ash could believe. "But others in England are invested in these mines. That much is true."

"I believe some may have been so foolhardy as to invest," Wellmanton agreed. "But that has nothing to do with the problem. Württemberg has been managing the lands that once composed Batavaria for ten years. The citizens there are content. We should not disrupt their lives with selfish politics and posturing."

"On that, we quite agree," Ash said.

Wellmanton beamed. "Good, good. I'm glad to hear you are thinking matters through. By the by, I heard a rumor that a fellow from Italy may be in possession of the Ashforde rubies. I could look into the matter, once this issue is settled."

Ash cocked his head. "Are you attempting to bribe me, Wellmanton?"

The viscount heaved himself to his feet. "Certainly not. Merely attempting to do a favor for an old friend. Let me know when you have made your decision. I have a feeling we will have much to celebrate."

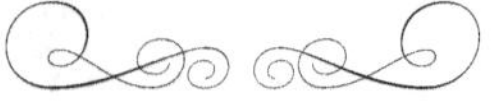

By Thursday evening, Tuny was ready for dinner with Ash. She wore her ice blue lustring dinner dress with the silver braid running from the high waist in two swags down to the hem. The pearls Ivy had given her for Christmas adorned her neck, with a bracelet around her white silk evening gloves. Belle would likely have added an ostrich plume, but Tuny had never been particularly pleased with plumage, so she crimped her hair in tight curls around her face and piled the rest at the top and back.

She glanced at the coronet, sitting on her dressing table because it was entirely too large to fit in her jewelry box.

Charlotte had said it was only worn on state occasions, which meant it would likely never be worn again. It wasn't as if the king would invite her to dine.

Although Ash had.

Remaining calm and cool was easier with Charlotte beside her in the coach and Matty across, next to Roth, who was on duty that evening. Her sister-in-law had borrowed the Worthington coach again, so they rode the mile or so from Covent Garden to the northern edge of Mayfair, where Lord Ashforde had a townhouse.

A very tall, stately townhouse without a smudge of soot to mar the white stone or grey trim. Of course.

A footman in navy livery with silver buttons pressed with a crest that must belong to the Ashforde family was standing outside. He hurried to open the door for them as the coach drew to a stop. Roth eyed him as if suspecting treachery. The footman's pristine cravat was so starched it didn't bob, but Tuny would have wagered he'd swallowed.

Another footman held wide the silvery-grey front door. He didn't wilt under the guard's scrutiny. But inside, a butler in an impeccable black tailcoat stood with his nose in the air, as if he'd smelled something he shouldn't.

"Lady Moselle, Sir Matthew Bateman, and Lady Bateman have come to dine with Lord Ashforde," Roth informed him. "Is this house secure?"

It certainly looked secure. The black-and-white marble floor—again spotless—ran from the door down the corridor. The walls were paneled in lacquered white with a few tasteful gold sconces for lighting. The stairs, with white curved balusters and a newel post topped with mahogany, marched smartly up the wall to the landing.

The butler sent Roth a dark look. "Lord Ashforde would never stand for anything less than the utmost security and propriety, I assure you."

Of course not.

"This is Mr. Roth, of the Batavarian Imperial Guard," Matty told the butler. "He's with us. You'll get used to it."

Charlotte smiled apologetically. She'd dressed in silver grey that looked right at home in this house. And she had an ostrich plume.

"A guard was expected," the butler acknowledged. "He will be served dinner in the servants' hall."

Roth's jaw tightened, and Tuny thought he might argue. Instead, he inclined his head. "Very well."

The butler's shoulders came down just the slightest.

"Once I have assured myself of the security of this house," he finished.

The butler drew in a sharp breath, but he stepped aside. "Do what you must. In the meantime, your ladyships, Sir Matthew, allow me to show you to the withdrawing room."

Roth followed right behind him as the butler led them up the stairs.

Lord Ashforde's townhouse was larger than most, with four rooms on each floor. The withdrawing room was off the landing on the next floor up. It was done in shades of tan and grey. Though all the materials were fine, Tuny could only feel it a bit colorless.

Not so the painting over the marble hearth. Charlotte went to it immediately and gazed up at the portrait of a woman with dark hair who was nearly eclipsed by a set of rubies in silver, complete with tiara, pendant, earrings, and cuffs.

"The Ashforde rubies," Charlotte said as if she'd noticed Tuny looking as well. "Lord Ashforde's mother managed to carry them off."

His mother. She could see the resemblance in the high, arched brows and the cool coloring. But where Ash tended to look contemplative, his mother looked resigned, as if she had come to terms with an unpleasant life, despite her wealth and beauty.

"Good evening," Ash said, and Tuny turned for the door.

He also looked right at home in the space, in a black evening jacket tailored to his lean frame and gold-shot cream-colored waistcoat. "Thank you for joining me," he said, smiling around at them all.

Roth pushed past him to bow to Tuny. "The house is secure, your ladyship. I will leave you to your dinner."

"Thank you, Mr. Roth," Tuny told him. "We'll send word when we're ready to return home."

Ash eyed him as he pressed his fist to his chest and marched out.

"Still under guard, I see," he mused as his look returned to her.

"It's nonsense," Tuny assured him. "I don't know why Prince Otto Leopold bothers. No one is going to care what I do or where I go. I'm simply not that important."

"On that opinion," he said, "we differ."

She wasn't sure whether he meant he thought she was in danger, or that she was more important than she expected. Her cheeks heated nonetheless.

He turned smoothly to Charlotte and Matty. "A pleasure to see you again, Lady Bateman, Sir Matthew. How are your daughters, Rose and Daphne?"

Charlotte looked impressed that he would remember. "Bright, active, and incorrigible, much like their father," she told him.

Matty chuckled. "Handfuls, they are, but I wouldn't have it any other way."

"I have noticed that forthright ladies run in your family," Ash observed. "As does beauty."

Much more of this, and she'd be fanning herself. "Charlotte mentioned your mother, my lord," she said. "Will she be joining us tonight?"

His face shuttered. "Alas, she passed away some years ago now." He nodded to Charlotte. "Though I'm certain she would be pleased you remembered her, Lady Bateman."

"She was a gentle soul," Charlotte said, gaze returning to the portrait. "And sorely missed, I'm sure."

"No doubt," he replied, voice as contained as his look.

Did he think they would judge him if he showed a modicum of sorrow? Because his mother had passed away years ago, he had to have been a child. Her mother had died when she was born, and Ivy had been the one who'd raised her. If anything had happened to her sister, Tuny probably wouldn't have stopped crying for years.

The butler appeared in the doorway. "Dinner, my lord, is served."

"Thank you, Peaves."

Peaves. It suited him. The thought had no sooner crossed her mind then Ash turned to her and offered his arm. Why should he escort her? Tuny glanced to Charlotte.

"Thank you for escorting our new baroness, Lord Ashforde," Charlotte said with a smile.

Oh, right. For the first time in her life, Tuny outranked her brother and even her illustrious sister-in-law, who was the daughter of a viscount.

And, though she would admit it to no one but herself, she'd have far rather walked in to dinner with Ash than any other man.

Tuny put her hand on his, and he led her forward.

CHAPTER ELEVEN

ONCE AGAIN, TUNY had to struggle to keep from gawking as Ash led her into the dining room. All of the walls were paneled in a warm, reddish wood nearly the shade of Charlotte's hair, and someone must have had a fondness for grapes, for clusters were either etched or carved over each panel and the lintel of the doors.

The table draped in white could have seated more than a dozen, but places had been set near the top with fine white porcelain edged in gold. Ash ushered Tuny to his right, with Charlotte on his left and Matty just beyond her. Footmen began bringing in all manner of delicacies. There was baked sole simmering in butter and spices, stewed tart cucumbers, and a scrumptious meat pie with the flakiest crust.

"All your favorites," her brother joked to her.

But he was right. The only item missing was her sister Ivy's famous cinnamon buns, and Ash could hardly have sent to Surrey for them, if he had even known to do so.

She turned to Ash. "What made you choose these dishes?"

He took a sip from his goblet before answering. He'd chosen a lovely mulled cider rather than wine. "Some, like the sole, are personal favorites," he said. "But I have noticed at events you tend to prefer the pies and cucumbers."

He'd watched her eat? It was both gratifying and a little

disconcerting. "Very kind of you," she said before applying herself to the pie before something more incriminating popped out of her mouth.

Charlotte must have noticed, or at least expected, Tuny's state of nerves, for she steered the conversation back to Ash and his family.

"I couldn't help noticing the Ashforde rubies on the portrait of your mother," she said. "They have a particularly romantic origin, if memory serves."

"My mother found the story charming," he said in a way that implied he didn't. When Charlotte raised a brow and Tuny looked at him askance, he set down his fork and continued.

"In the twelfth century, a knight vowed to win a certain lady of noble birth. Her father did not favor the match, but he agreed to allow them to wed if the knight could prove he was capable of caring for her in the style her father expected."

"Bit high-handed," Tuny said.

"Not at all," Matty insisted. "A fellow wants to know those he loves will be well cared for." He sent Ash a considering look.

Ash returned to his story undaunted. "He certainly tried. Valiant deeds won him acclaim, recognition, even a more exalted title and his own lands, but still the father refused."

"I hope his sweetheart had some say in the matter," Tuny put in.

Ash smiled. "She did. You see, the knight had the stones set in silver stones and presented them to her, claiming each ruby a piece of his heart he wanted only her to have, whatever her father's decision. She told her father her own heart would be shattered in as many pieces if he did not allow them to wed. Seeing her love, her father consented."

Tuny clapped her hands. "Oh, well done."

"A shame he didn't just ride up on a prancing steed and carry her off to Gretna Green," Matty said. "Might have saved him time and money."

Charlotte shook her head.

"Matty," Tuny scolded before turning to Ash. "That's a wonderful story about true love triumphing. Thank you for sharing it."

"Then you appreciate true love, Lady Moselle," he said.

He'd asked to use her first name, but perhaps he didn't want to set expectations again by using it in front of her family.

"I do, Lord Ashforde," she said, just as formally. "Mind you, I know true love doesn't blossom overnight for many people. It's more likely to grow from acquaintance. But that doesn't mean it's as rare as your rubies."

"Mine no longer, alas," he said, retrieving his fork. "They were sold before I reached my majority. I've tried to determine who holds them now, with little luck."

How sad. Yet how odd that they had been sold. From what she'd seen, the aristocracy prized its possessions and generally tried to add more.

Charlotte, however, perked up. "Sir Matthew and I might be able to help you there, my lord. You may have heard that we occasionally investigate mysteries."

"I had not heard that," he allowed, pushing his fork into the pie with considerably more care than the movement required. "But if you'd like, I can show you the information I've gathered so far."

Matty stuck out his lower lip. "Sounds like an interesting problem to solve. Count us in, my lord."

"They're very good," Tuny confessed to Ash. "If anyone can locate the rubies, they can."

Charlotte blushed. "Thank you, Tuny, but I wouldn't want to raise Lord Ashforde's hopes. After we've looked at the information, we may be able to suggest next steps."

"I'd appreciate any help you can provide," he said,

inclining his head. He lifted his glass and held it up in toast. "To new beginnings."

"To new beginnings," they all chorused.

His gaze brushed hers, and her spirits rose higher than their glasses.

It was going well. Better than he'd feared. He had only to look at the light in Petunia's eyes to know. He couldn't remember feeling so pleased.

They adjourned to the withdrawing room together after dinner. Peaves looked the slightest bit concerned about the matter. Very likely he had expected Ash to entertain Sir Matthew while the ladies withdrew, but it seemed rather rude to exclude Petunia and her sister-in-law. And he was eager to see what they would make of his search for the rubies.

Lady Bateman and Sir Matthew sat on the sofa, and Ash had Peaves bring in the portfolio of information.

"It's arranged chronologically," he explained as he spread the leather case open on Sir Matthew's lap. "There never was a bill of sale, but you can see a copy of the notation from the page from White's where it mentions that my father's debt to a Lord P. was discharged in full. We found the rubies missing shortly afterward, so I assume that was what he used."

He waited for someone to question why a peer of the realm with wealth at his fingertips would be so in debt he needed to offer one of his family's most cherished possessions, but Sir Matthew and his wife merely bowed their heads over the materials as if they found them fascinating.

All at once, watching them dig into his father's indiscretions wasn't nearly as fascinating. Indeed, he rather felt as if a noose had tightened around his neck.

He turned to Petunia. "Perhaps a walk about the house

while we wait for their verdict, Lady Moselle?"

"Delighted," she said, and he made sure his steps out of the room were no more than a stroll.

"They won't surface for some time," she predicted as he led her back down the stairs. "They're very dedicated to their work."

He ought to take comfort in that. Putting aside the frustration that always rose at the thought of his father's actions, he focused on the present. What would she make of the library? He hadn't been sure what to think when Peaves had first suggested the idea that Ash show it to her. Once more, emotions threatened. Why was he so jittery? He hardly needed her approval.

He opened the door and let her in.

She took two steps on the carpet, then stopped and stared. "Oh, my."

Those two breathless words couldn't help but inflate his chest. He would have sworn Peaves had lit an extra lamp or two, so bright did the room appear.

She turned in a circle as if taking it all in, then looked to him, eyes shining. "I'll ask you the same question I asked the duke when I first saw his library. Have you read them all?"

He grinned. "Yes."

Her eyes widened, until he could see the candlelight reflected in them. "Which is your favorite?"

He chuckled. "Oh, there are too many to count. I've always enjoyed works of philosophy, and any of the bard's comedies is sure to leave me smiling."

"The stories published by a lady?" she pressed. "*Pride and Prejudice? Sense and Sensibility?* And what of the Scotch novels?"

"Every book, in first edition."

"Horace Walpole?"

He glanced out the door before taking a step closer and lowering his voice. "I didn't sleep well for a week after reading *The Castle of Otranto*. And I have a copy from the first printing of Mary Shelley's *Frankenstein*."

She shivered. "I've heard that one can be chilling."

"Would you care to borrow it?"

She nodded so quickly the enchanting curls beside her face danced. "Love to! Oh, and do you have anything on Greek mythology? Ever since Lady Belle had me play Athena in her tableau of the Judgement of Paris at the house party, I've wanted to know more about that whole story."

And ever since, he'd kept remembering how she'd looked in that tableau. He'd arrived late to the house party, just as the three groups had set up their *tableau vivants*, scenes staged of famous allegorical, mythical, or historical events. The duchess and some of the guests had enacted King Alfred defeating the Norsemen. The duke and other guests had portrayed the legend of Robin Hood. Lady Belle, Lady Bateman, Owen Canady, and Petunia had presented the judgment of Paris, a mortal choosing the most beautiful of the Greek goddesses. The sight of Petunia draped in white silk, face aglow, had stopped him in his tracks.

"You made a very good Athena," he said, "goddess of wisdom."

She snorted. "Better than the alternative. Belle wanted me to play Aphrodite. Who would have believed me as the goddess of love and beauty?"

"I would."

The words were out before he could think better of them.

She cocked her head as if trying to see his point. "Next to Belle?"

"Next to any lady of my acquaintance."

What was wrong with him tonight? Where was his composure, his poise? His heart jerked in his chest, and the desire to kiss her would not be denied.

He leaned closer. If she hesitated in any way, he vowed to retreat immediately. But her gaze darted from his eyes to his lips, and she leaned closer too.

He ignored the voice warning of danger and pressed his lips to hers.

Coming from a man so very in control of himself, Ash's kiss was soft, gentle, tender. It raised such a response inside her that she grabbed his lapels and held him to her. His arms encircled her, pulling her closer, even as the kiss deepened, became something more urgent.

She was drowning in him, and she never wanted to come up for air.

Voices down the corridor recalled her to another world. Blinking, she pulled away and let her hands fall.

He held himself with his usual stillness, but she could almost feel the kiss reverberating through him. He pressed one hand to his lips, as if he sensed it even now.

"What was that?" Tuny demanded.

He lowered his hand. "That was why I decided against offering for you three years ago."

Hurt and anger collided inside her. "Well, then, you must be glad to have your concerns confirmed. Excuse me." She stalked for the door, the floor as firm and unyielding as her convictions.

He caught up to her before she could climb the stairs. "Petunia, wait."

The footmen must have been still clearing after dinner, and Roth must be patrolling elsewhere, for there was no one in the entry hall. Ash's very presence made it feel crowded.

Tuny put her back to the wall and raised her chin. "I won't apologize."

"I wouldn't ask you to. That kiss was, quite frankly, magnificent."

The word rolled off his tongue with gusto, as if she were a fine wine or the latest first edition he'd acquired.

"It was uncalled for, that was what it was," she insisted. "You don't have any proper feelings for me."

He bent closer. "Believe me, Petunia. When I look at you, propriety is the last thing on my mind. That is entirely the problem."

She crossed her arms over her chest. "Matty might find that a problem as well."

He glanced up the stairs as if expecting her brother to come pelting down at any moment. Then he looked to her. "Would you give me a little more time? I promise to explain further. We could move into the sitting room, just there."

Farther down the corridor, a door opened, and Roth stepped into view. Finishing another round of the house, no doubt. She wouldn't actually be alone with Ash.

Which was a good thing at the moment.

"Very well," she said.

He led her into a sitting room where everything looked as stiff as his carriage, from the harp-backed chairs, to the horsehair sofa and wood-wrapped hearth. She positioned herself on the sofa and spread her skirts, leaving him little room to join her, if that had been his intent. He took the chair opposite her.

"My father," he said without preamble, "was a drunkard and a wastrel. His self-centered ways broke my mother's heart and nearly ruined the family. I vowed never to be like him."

With someone else, she might have offered a hug in commiseration. Tuny settled for a nod. "Makes sense."

He cocked his head. "This history doesn't trouble you?"

"Why should it?" she asked with a shrug. "He's gone, or you wouldn't be the baron."

"True," he allowed. "But what I saw in him caused me to become who I am today. He was ruled by his passions, and they drove him to do things beneath the dignity of a gentleman. I have never let my passions overcome my good sense. Until I met you."

Wonderful. Once again, he implied he liked her despite of who she was. Defeat marched in and took up camp in her chest.

"Of course," Tuny said. "Wouldn't want the little common girl mucking things up, would we?"

He frowned. "It wouldn't have mattered if you were the heir to the British throne. It wasn't your background that concerned me. It was my reaction to you. You're like fine wine to my system, Petunia. Delightful in small doses, but dangerous when overindulged."

A laugh forced its way up. "Oh, that's me all right. As dangerous as they come."

"It is a danger I am finding I cannot live without."

Though the words were said in his usual measured tone, heat lay beneath them. She met his gaze. Those blue eyes begged for understanding, for acceptance.

For love?

She dropped her gaze. "Ash, I don't know what to say."

He rose and went down on one knee in front of her. She wanted to lean closer and rear back at the same time.

"Say you'll allow me to court you," he urged. "Say I stand a chance of winning you. If you find we will not suit, I promise I will not bother you again."

He was so fervent, so earnest. She should tell him to cease trying. She could not bear it if he changed his mind again. Like that of his lady ancestor, her heart would shatter, and there would be no one to put the pieces back together again.

But her head had other ideas, for it was nodding rather eagerly. He started up, lips nearing hers once more. She closed her eyes in anticipation.

"Your family seeks your advice, Lady Moselle," Roth said.

Tuny opened her eyes to find her guard in the doorway, gaze on Ash.

Ash pulled back.

"I'll be right there," she assured Roth, rising.

Ash followed her up and stood at her elbow as if ready to protect as well.

Roth didn't move until she approached him. Then he let her past and squeezed in behind her.

"You are not following the plan we laid out," he murmured.

She shot him a glare, only to see that he was focused on Ash beside her.

Ash was frowning at the guard. "I'm doing my best," he gritted out.

Wait, wasn't she the one with the assignment from Leo?

Her tumultuous emotions must not have been evident on her face as they entered the withdrawing room upstairs, for Charlotte merely beckoned her and Ash closer.

"Your investigation is painstakingly documented," she praised him, as Ash seated himself not far from Tuny, and Roth took up his stance along the wall. "Matthew and I have one suggestion. Our friend, Lord Belfort, has worked with a jeweler in the city, Mortimer Hollingsworth. His daughter married the Earl of Danning some years ago. Mr. Hollingsworth may be able to learn who has your rubies now. We'd be happy to approach him, if you'd like."

Ash nodded. "I'd be indebted to you, Lady Bateman."

Matty slapped his hands down on his trousers. "That's settled then. We'll be in touch. Ready to go, Tuny?"

Not in the slightest. Her mind was still spinning. But time alone might be the best thing at the moment.

"Yes," Tuny said. "Thank you, Lord Ashforde for… an enlightening evening."

He rose and bowed to her. "Thank you, Petunia, for your understanding."

Matty looked to Charlotte in question. Her sister-in-law shook her head ever so slightly. Then she and Matty thanked Ash as well. It wasn't until they were all in the carriage with Roth that Charlotte spoke up.

"Care to share what happened between you and Lord Ashforde while we were starting the trail?" she asked, russet brows up in question.

Roth's frown was nothing to the one on Matty's face.

"Something happened between you and his lordship?" her brother growled.

She would not tell them about the kiss. Besides, her decision afterward was far more momentous, in the scheme of things.

"Lord Ashforde asked to court me," she said. "And apparently I agreed."

"Apparently?" Matty's frown only grew. "Did he insist on it? I've half a mind…"

"And entirely too much character to run off half-cocked," Charlotte finished for him. "Still, Tuny, I think you should explain."

Roth crossed his arms over his chest, bumping into her brother in the process. "As do I."

Tuny pointed a finger at him. "You are here to guard my person. You don't get a say in who courts me."

His arms fell. "Forgive my presumption, Lady Moselle. I had thought we were becoming friends."

"Friends support each other," she said, then she looked to her sister-in-law and brother in turn. "So does family. I haven't agreed to marry the fellow, just to see if there's possibly some reason why I should."

"And what of your promise to Prince Otto Leopold?" Roth pressed.

Her promise! Ash had said they'd talk about the Batavarian question tonight, and they'd talked of everything but!

Matty reacted just as strongly, for he rounded on Roth.

"I've had just about enough of you. My sister can do as she likes."

"Your sister," Tuny informed him, "and the woman he's guarding does not require a gentleman to come riding to the rescue. In answer to your question, Roth, Lord Ashforde has indicated that he is willing to consider the Batavarian question from my point of view. That's all I can ask."

Both her brother and Roth nodded thoughtfully.

"So," Charlotte ventured from beside her, "what do you plan to do next?"

"Invite Lord Ashforde to tea," Tuny said. "And invite Aunt Meredith and Fortune as well."

Charlotte smiled.

CHAPTER TWELVE

"AND MAY I inquire as to whether your guests were satisfied with the evening, my lord?" Peaves asked from the library doorway.

The remains of dinner had long ago been packed away, and his butler was no doubt making the rounds to lock up the house for the night. He'd seemed surprised to find Ash still in the library, feet to the fire and books piled around him. Greek history, English adaptations of the plays of Sophocles and Euripides, Ovid's Greek mythology. Which would Petunia enjoy most?

Petunia, who'd agreed with a tremulous nod to allow him to court her, as if she had been as overcome by the moment as he had been.

Peaves cleared his throat. It seemed his man expected an answer.

"I heard no complaints," Ash said.

"And the young lady was appreciative of the honor?" Peaves crept closer, face turned slightly as if he hoped to hear a particular answer.

"It wasn't the young lady who was honored," Ash corrected him. "I was the one honored to have her in my house."

Delight brightened Peaves' face a moment before he snuffed out the light. "Will you be going out tomorrow, my lord?"

Ash lifted one of the volumes and weighed it in one

hand. "Yes, I believe I will, Peaves. Don't expect me until dinner."

"Very good, my lord."

He had intended to wait until an appropriate time the next day to call on Petunia, even if a part of him demanded that he rush over at first light. He had let his emotions get the better of him last night. He could not regret the outcome, but today, calmer heads must prevail. She had been understanding itself when he'd confessed his father's shortcomings. He refused to compound them by his own actions.

But a card arrived before he could call for the carriage.

"Bad news?" Peaves asked, hovering at Ash's elbow as he sat in the library.

"Excellent news," Ash replied. He set the card down on the arm of the chair. "Lady Bateman invites me to tea this afternoon with Lady Moselle."

"Another honor," his butler mused.

"Indeed." Ash rose. "Tell Jarls to take an acceptance, and tell Theban to meet me upstairs. I think I will change."

"Of course, my lord. At once, my lord."

Tuny had been busy that morning. That alone was a blessing. If she had stayed home, she would likely have spent the time staring into space, reliving the moment Ash's lips had touched hers and the look on his face when he'd begged to court her. She wouldn't have been surprised if her brother hadn't called her moony rather than Tuny!

But she had a goal, and she knew just how to achieve it.

"Then you'll all come to tea this afternoon?" she confirmed after she'd met with Aunt Meredith, Larissa, Callie, and Belle at Weyfarer House. Thank goodness her aunt and friends did not stand on ceremony. Few ladies would have accepted callers at the unreasonable hour Tuny had arrived. Even Keller, stationed now in the entry hall, had seemed surprised.

"Certainly," Aunt Meredith said.

Fortune, patrolling the room like one of the Imperial Guards, sent Tuny a glance from her copper-colored eyes as if agreeing as well.

"Of course," Larissa said with a look to her sisters. Callie nodded.

"Do you wish Owen as well?" Belle asked, beaming. "He tends to temper Lord Ashforde's reticence."

"He brings out the worst in him, you mean," Tuny said with a grin. "And no, I won't ask Owen to intercede just yet. I'd like Fortune to be able to focus her attentions."

"And she will," Aunt Meredith promised. "I've been hoping for just such an opportunity for her and his lordship to meet."

Fortune must have decided who to favor at the moment, for she hopped up onto the sofa beside Tuny, then took possession of her lap.

"I'm counting on you," Tuny told her, running a hand along the sleek fur.

"Do you doubt him still?" her aunt asked.

"I don't want to," Tuny said, gaze on the cat curled up on her muslin skirts. "There was a time when I would have given everything to hear him say he wants to court me." She chuckled. "There was a time when I thought he *was* courting me! But I was wrong then, and I fear to be wrong now."

"Surely he would not have asked to court you if he wasn't serious," Larissa said.

Tuny glanced up to find her friends and aunt nodding support.

"And if he cannot value you, then he isn't worth your time," Aunt Meredith said, as if that was that.

It was a sobering thought, but the day still seemed

brighter as she headed home. Keller kept pace with her as she crossed Mayfair.

"So Lord Ashforde has declared his intentions to court you," he ventured as they came out on Regent Street. "The others will be pleased."

"Others?" she asked with a frown. "Who's in your pocket, Keller?"

Red rose into his cheeks, like rosebuds opening to the sun. "The four of us who have been your guards noticed he favored you. We offered some suggestions."

Tuny stopped so quickly, the fellow exiting the haberdashery they were passing had to detour around her with a puzzled look. "What do you mean, you offered suggestions?"

He must have heard the anger in her tone, for he grimaced. "We only want what's best for you."

She poked his black-clad chest with one finger. "I decide what's best for me. And what I decide about his lordship is between him and me."

Keller attempted to look conciliatory, blue eyes dipping down at the corners. "We only ask to be kept apprised."

"Why?" Tuny demanded.

"If I find you in his arms, it would be good to know if he is kissing you or attempting to kill you," he pointed out.

Tuny shuddered. "I'll be sure to let you know."

"He seems a good man," Keller ventured as they set off once more.

"He does indeed," Tuny replied. Still, some part of her kept wondering.

What if Fortune proved Ash was not to be trusted after all?

By the time Ash left the house that afternoon, he was assured—by Theban and Peaves and even his footman,

Jarls—that he looked quite the thing. The forest green coat had always seemed a bit overdone to him, with its double-breasted front and cutaway sides, but at least it had simple cloth buttons. And the cream-colored trousers tucked well into his Moroccan leather boots. The maid who answered the door at Sir Matthew's home goggled at him. The Imperial Guard on duty, Mr. Keller, nodded slowly, as if impressed. Lady Bateman smiled particularly warmly when he bowed over her hand.

But the smile from Petunia was all the more gratifying. Her whole countenance brightened as she accepted the books he'd brought her.

"Ovid is accounted one of the best Greek writers," he explained. "This translation is particularly true to his voice. And Homer will give you more details about Paris and the aftermath of his poor judgment. Keep the candle burning while reading *Frankenstein.*"

"I can't wait," she assured him. She set them almost reverently on the hall table, then wrapped her muslin-clad arm in his and tugged him toward the sitting room.

Where an army waited.

Lady Abelona was closest to the door, a vision in frilly pink. Her next oldest sister, Lady Calantha, was on the chair beside hers, radiant in tailored yellow. Nearer to the hearth sat Lady Larissa in a cool blue gown with braided trim. A sweet chorus heralded his bow, "Good afternoon, Lord Ashforde."

"Ladies," he said, straightening.

Petunia went to sit on the sofa and eyed him expectantly.

"And Lady Belfort as well," Lady Bateman said with a nod toward the door to the dining room before he could join Petunia.

A dark-haired older woman in lavender strolled into the room, a cat up in her arms. The cat's tail was lashing, as if she felt trapped.

Ash could commiserate.

"Lady Belfort, a pleasure to see you again," he said with another bow in her direction.

The cat watched him with eyes as bright as copper pennies. Her dove grey fur reminded Ash of a gentleman's morning coat, the ruff of white around her throat and down her belly a cravat.

"That's Fortune," Petunia said, and there was a tone in her voice he didn't recognize. "Fortune, come meet Lord Ashforde."

He could not recall being introduced to a pet before. He wasn't entirely sure how to respond as Lady Belfort bent to release her cat onto the carpet. He'd never been the kind to speak to kitty or pup. He wasn't even sure whether a smile was warranted.

The cat padded toward him, only to stop a few feet away and regard him as if she weren't any more certain of him.

"Why don't you have a seat, Lord Ashforde?" Lady Bateman asked. Her voice held a lilt, as if she was trying not to laugh.

He went to sit beside Petunia, and Fortune followed him. Now every woman in the room was watching the cat. She was a lovely creature, but it seemed they all knew her. Why such avid interest?

No sooner had he settled himself than Fortune jumped up into his lap and commenced rubbing her face against the satin stripe of his waistcoat. Ash leaned back, but her purr vibrated against his chest.

"Well," Lady Belfort said, moving closer. "Isn't that lovely?"

"Quite," Petunia's sister-in-law said, voice nearly a purr itself.

Lady Abelona went so far as to clap her hands. The cat cuddled closer to him.

"You can pet her," Petunia suggested.

There was something about Fortune. He was sure of it.

It was as if he had passed a test of some sort. Slowly, he raised his hand and ran it along the fur. Fortune arched her back against his touch and began to knead his trousers. He'd never been so happy for thick English wool.

"Allow me," Petunia said with a smile. She reached out and pulled the cat into her arms. Bending her head, she murmured against the grey ear.

She likely thought no one could hear her, but Ash caught the words.

"Thank you, Fortune. I hoped he was a good fellow, but you've eased my mind."

"Ah, here comes tea," Lady Bateman said.

The maid brought in a tray with all the accoutrements, and another older woman, likely the cook, brought in another tray with biscuits of various sorts. And all the ladies began talking.

"Have you been able to enjoy the opera this year, Lord Ashforde?"

"I understand you have an extensive library, my lord. What prompted you to start it?"

"Your estate is in Herefordshire, I believe. Do you spend much time there?"

"I saw you at St. George's Hanover Square last Sunday, if I'm not mistaken. Isn't the vicar a marvelous speaker?"

He fielded one question after another, from all directions. Lady Bateman, who insisted he call her Charlotte, poured from as fine a China pot as any duchess, and the pekoe tea was better than what his cook procured. But he was aware of Petunia beside him, smile still broad and body more relaxed than he recalled in his company.

"I understand you have yet to decide your stance on the Batavarian question," Lady Belfort said after he'd managed his second sip of tea.

Ash lowered the cup. "I am attempting to understand the situation from all sides."

Petunia nodded approvingly. Through the door to the

entry hall, he saw the Imperial Guardsman reposition himself as if to take note of the discussion.

"Very wise," Charlotte said.

"How many sides do you find there are?" Lady Abelona put in, her sisters watching with the same interest.

Ash set down his cup and ticked them off on his fingers. "First, the Batavarian court's. King Frederick and Crown Prince Otto Leopold are understandably determined to regain the lands and position that have been their family's for generations."

"It is their right," Lady Larissa held, and Lady Calantha nodded.

"The Congress of Vienna was shockingly high-handed in reapportioning Europe," Lady Belfort agreed. Her cat, who had returned to her skirts for a time, wandered closer. Petunia reached down for a pet. He could imagine those fingers sliding through his hair as easily.

What was the topic of conversation again?

"Second," Ash said, rallying, "the court of Württemberg. King William has, by many accounts, ruled fairly and justly, working to knit together a single kingdom from the pieces he was given."

"Pieces that should not have been his to begin with," Lady Larissa argued. Now the Imperial Guardsman nodded.

Ash inclined his head. "Third, the British court. King William has been an ally for some years, and we thrive when there is peace on the Continent."

"Some might say we thrive when there is a war somewhere," Charlotte said. "I don't see that as a reason to go looking for one."

"Finally," Ash said with a glance to Petunia, "the people of Batavaria. Are they content to be citizens of Württemberg, or do they long for a different future? And does that future involve the return of their previous rulers?"

"You're one of the few who's mentioned the people," Petunia said. "I'm glad they're part of your considerations."

So was he, especially if the fact caused her to smile at him that way.

Something thumped on the stairs, and the Imperial Guardsman's gaze snapped forward again.

Charlotte's jaw tightened, and she turned purposely toward Lady Belfort. "More tea, Meredith?"

"Yes, please," the lady replied, holding out her cup.

Another thump, this one closer to the door of the sitting room. The guardsman jerked his head toward the stairs, as if urging someone to climb back up them.

"Unseasonably warm weather we've been having," Charlotte said loudly, reaching for the plate of biscuits. "More, Lord Ashforde?"

"No, thank you."

A giggle pealed. Lady Abelona put her hand to her lips, but he was certain she hadn't made the sound. Fortune dove behind Lady Belfort's skirts again.

"You cannot deny them, Charlotte," Petunia said, setting down her cup. "If they've escaped Matty, you might as well invite them in."

Charlotte closed her eyes a moment and heaved a sigh. Then she opened her eyes and looked toward the door. "Come in, girls."

The Imperial Guardsman shook his head as Petunia's nieces scampered into the sitting room, only to stop and stare at the other guests. They both wore blue cotton gowns today, covered in white pinafores that had a decided wrinkle to them, as if they had been crawling about only moments before.

"What do you do when presented to company?" Charlotte asked them.

Rose, who had her mother's coloring, bobbed a wobbly curtsey. "How do you do?"

Her little sister, who favored their father, copied her, wobble and all. "How do?"

The duke's daughters smiled at them.

"Very well, thank you," Lady Belfort said. "And you?"

"Hungry," the youngest said, venturing closer. "May I have a biscuit, Mama?"

"Young ladies who sneak downstairs are generally not rewarded with biscuits," her mother informed her.

She frowned. "Why?"

"Because we're supposed to be upstairs with Papa," her older sister told her. "He fell asleep, Mama, and Daphne didn't want to nap. I'm too old to nap," she added with a look Ash's direction.

"I find naps invigorating," he told her.

She frowned as if she thought that very odd indeed.

Daphne wandered closer to him, peering up at him with a similar fascination to the cat's. "You gave us a present."

"That's right," her sister said. "Thank you, Lord Ashforde. It's ever so nice."

"Lord Ashforde provided a toy theatre for Rose and Daphne," Petunia supplied, glancing around at the others. "It's been a source of great amusement."

"What a thoughtful gift," Lady Belfort said.

Daphne was still regarding Ash as if she couldn't understand him. "You're funny," she announced.

That was the first time anyone had thought as much. "Am I?" Ash asked. "Why?"

"You didn't drink your tea," she said, pointing to his brimming cup.

"I'll tell you a secret," he said, beckoning her closer. She leaned forward, eyes bright. "I'm having so much fun talking with your aunt and mother and their friends, I forgot to drink it."

She straightened. "I'll help you."

"No, thank you, Daphne," her mother said firmly.

At that moment, Fortune peeked out from behind Lady Belfort's skirts.

"Kitty!" Daphne shrieked before rushing forward.

Fortune darted toward the sofa and squeezed herself under it. Petunia twitched her skirts as if to hide her. Ash positioned his boots to prevent access from that side.

Daphne stopped, lower lip trembling. "I'll be nice to the kitty."

"I'm sure you would," Ash told her. "But I don't think the kitty wants to play just now."

Something bumped his boot as if to thank him.

"That's enough visiting for today," their mother told her and her sister. "Make your curtseys, girls, and go wake up your father."

He thought they might argue, but, once again, they bobbed, this time a little more surely, then hurried for the door. Mr. Keller smiled at them as they passed.

"Thank you for your understanding, my lord," Charlotte said in the quiet that followed. "We are having a little trouble locating staff at the moment."

"Still nothing from Miss Winchester?" Lady Belfort asked.

Charlotte shook her head. "We'll have to find someone else. Either that, or give up entertaining at all."

"They are delightful young ladies," Ash assured her. "Your true friends won't mind if they join you."

"Certainly not," Lady Larissa said with a pleased nod in his direction.

"I'm glad to hear you say that," Petunia told him. "Perhaps you and I can help my brother with them for a while this afternoon, my lord, so Charlotte can continue visiting."

CHAPTER THIRTEEN

IT HAD BEEN a calculated comment. Fortune had been approving, and Ash had humored her nieces. Tuny had a sudden longing to see how well he'd fare under forced proximity. Every lord seemed determined to have an heir, but, unlike the duke, many of the aristocracy she'd met had only one child. She certainly hoped for more. She'd grown up with two sisters and a brother, after all. She knew the love that could abound.

With every gaze on him, he might well have demurred, claiming the need to stay with the other guests, or a pressing engagement elsewhere. He didn't hesitate. "I'd be delighted."

"We can help as well," Belle offered.

So kind, that Belle. But having her friends along wouldn't help Tuny know Ash's mind.

As if she thought as much, Larissa stood, head held high, forcing Ash to his feet as well.

"Actually, it's time we took our leave," her friend declared. "Thank you so much, Charlotte, for the lovely tea. Aunt Meredith, may we see you home?"

Their aunt coaxed Fortune out from under the sofa. "That would be delightful. Thank you for having us, Charlotte."

"Thank *you*," Charlotte said. "And Fortune."

Fortune turned her head to eye Tuny before suffering herself to be carried to the door.

Larissa squeezed Tuny's hand in passing, and Callie patted her shoulder.

Belle leaned closer. "I knew he'd pass muster." She winked at Tuny before strolling after her sisters, pink skirts swaying.

"What is it about Fortune?" Ash murmured.

Tuny started, heat flushing up her. Then she lifted her chin. "Fortune has an uncanny ability to know a person's worth."

"I see." He glanced after the retreating line of skirts. "Then should I take it every lady in this room doubted mine?"

"No!" Tuny waited for him to sit beside her, then swiveled to face him. "I'm sure none of us doubted you are a gentleman of the highest order. But it's more than that. It's kindness and honesty and valor and…"

"Trust," he said.

She nodded. "Yes, trust."

"And you trust the opinion of a cat more than my word."

If it had been any other cat, she would have sounded mad indeed. But it was Fortune, who had never been mistaken. Though she had changed her mind, on occasion…

Tuny shook off the thought. "I trust Fortune implicitly, my lord. She approved of the Duke of Wey for his duchess, Matty for Charlotte. Why, she's matched the Earl and Countess of Carrolton, Lord and Lady Worthington, and my sister and Lord Kendall. She certainly approved of Prince Otto Leopold, though I will own she took her time warming up to Count Montalban and Owen Canady."

A chuckle popped out of him. "Then I suppose I am in good company."

"Excellent company," Tuny assured him.

Charlotte returned just then. "There. All settled. Are

you certain you want to spend time with my daughters, my lord?"

"Very," he said, rising. He held out his hand to Tuny. "Shall we?"

Relieved, Tuny nodded and took his arm.

Keller stood at attention as they came into the entry hall. "Lady Moselle. Do you require assistance?"

"No, thank you," she told him, starting up the stairs. "There's only so much room. If we need anything, you'll hear of it."

Though Ash had called on her years ago, she did not remember him ever going beyond the sitting room. As they came out on the landing, she couldn't help thinking he must be comparing. Carpet ran down the floor, clean, but well-worn. The wainscotting was dented or scratched here and there. She'd added a few marks in her day chasing after Rufus, the elderly hound she'd rescued, who'd lived to the impressive age of fifteen. Unlike Ash's townhouse, no precious vases or sculptures were in evidence. They wouldn't have lasted a fortnight.

Voices were coming from Matty's study, so Petunia led Ash to the door. Bookshelves might have lined two of the walls, but the room would have fit in a corner of Ash's library. Her brother had both girls at his desk and was attempting to help them copy their letters.

He glanced up at Tuny. "Sorry. I only closed my eyes a moment."

Mrs. Quince had said the same. "A moment is all it takes," Tuny sympathized, venturing into the room. "Ash and I thought we might be able to help."

Matty glanced at Ash, head cocked, as if seeing him from a different angle. "Have you experience with little ones, my lord?"

"None whatsoever," Ash said. "But I like to think I learn quickly."

"You'll need to," Matty said with a chuckle. He looked

to Tuny. "Can you keep them busy for an hour? That's all I need."

"Done," Tuny said, moving up to take his place at the desk. "Go."

Matty clapped Ash on the shoulder, nearly oversetting him, and strode from the room.

"Do you like A?" Daphne asked, waving a pencil enthusiastically.

"Very much," Ash assured her, pulling up another chair at her side. "It's the first letter in my name."

"I like D," she said. She bent over the foolscap and made a line, tongue protruding from one corner of her mouth.

"D for Daphne," he said.

She glanced up with a frown. "D for dog."

"Ah," he said.

"No," she insisted. "Deeeeee."

"Look, Aunt Tuny," Rose said, forcing Tuny's gaze away from the pair. "I wrote your name too."

Tuny glanced down and felt her face flame. Toonee Ashfourd was written in bold lettering.

"It's your *new* name," Rose whispered, loud enough that her father might have heard her in the other room. "Mama said so."

"It's not my new name yet," Tuny said, taking the paper and folding it carefully. "Let's work on writing *your* name."

To her surprise, the hour flew by. When the girls started bickering about pencils and writing, Ash suggested reading. He pulled a book from the shelf and showed the girls how the letters they were writing could form a story.

"D!" Daphne cried, pointing a chubby finger at a letter.

"Very good," Ash said. "That word is duke. Duke also starts with d, like Daphne and dog."

"Where's an R?" Rose asked. And he showed her words with that letter.

When that cloyed, he suggested they brief him on their progress on the toy theatre, and he oohed and aahed over the bits of scenery and the puppets' new clothes.

"Would you like to hear a story?" Daphne asked, eyes wide in hope.

"I can't think of anything I'd like better," Ash assured her.

Tuny winked at him. "This might take a bit."

"I am all ears," he promised.

She helped the girls position the little paper scenery around the box, then settled herself back on the floor beside Ash as her nieces took up their positions behind the theatre.

"Once upon a time," Rose said, using her hands to move a little girl puppet into a scene of a forest, "there lived a beautiful princess."

"All good stories start with once upon a time," Daphne said, clearly for Ash's benefit.

He nodded, but Tuny saw the twitch of his mouth.

"Everyone loved her," Rose continued with a look to her sister. "Except the wicked witch."

Daphne promptly marched a shriveled doll onto the scene. "I will eat you!" she told the princess.

Rose stared at her. "She isn't going to eat her! Bears eat people. People don't eat people."

"Then she's a bear," Daphne said. She shook the doll at the princess. "Grr! Grr!"

"Bad bear!" Rose the princess scolded, knocking her puppet against Daphne's. "I am a princess. You go home!"

The bear slunk off the scene.

"The princess was so brave and smart, that the prince decided to marry her," Rose said. She looked to her sister, who promptly walked a boy puppet onto the stage. The two puppets once more bumped into each other.

"They're kissing," Rose explained. "People in love kiss."

"Ah," Ash said, though pink was climbing in his cheeks.

Tuny's cheeks felt hot as well.

"And so they married and had two daughters, and they all lived happily ever after," Rose said.

"And that's how good stories end," Daphne said with great satisfaction.

Ash clapped his hands, and Tuny joined in.

"Well done," he said. "An enduring story for the ages."

"Take your bows," Tuny told them.

Rose and Daphne dropped the puppets. Rose curtseyed, and Daphne clapped her fist to her chest in the Batavarian salute.

"Come tomorrow," Daphne told Ash as Matty appeared in the doorway to relieve them.

Rose frowned at her before looking to Ash too. "That is, it would be very good if you could visit again tomorrow, Lord Ashforde."

Ash bowed to them both. "I will see if my schedule allows such, ladies."

"You were amazing," Tuny told him as they started down the stairs. "It's not easy keeping one step ahead of them."

"I imagine it's not that hard for an hour," he said.

"You'd be surprised."

At the door, he bowed to her. "Perhaps you would allow me to escort you to services on Sunday."

"You attend St. George's Hanover Square?" Tuny confirmed, though she was fairly sure of the answer.

"I do. For some years now."

Of course. All the nobs attended the church a block off Bond Street.

"We go to St. Paul's Covent Garden," she said, hearing the challenge in her voice again. "Services start at ten. If you arrive at half past, you can walk with us."

He did not argue, but merely inclined his head. "Your servant, madam."

Keller went so far as to open the door to see him out.

"Still, he thinks," he mused as he shut the door. "But he has not decided against us yet. That is your doing."

"I wouldn't be so sure about that," Tuny told him. "He seems to be one who must think through every decision before acting. Sometimes for years."

Keller's face tightened. "We do not have years. His Royal Highness says your king will return to London in ten days' time. He will want an answer then."

"Let's hope his lordship can reach a decision," Tuny said.

She found Charlotte in the sitting room with her head back and her hand on her forehead. Concerned, she dropped down beside her sister-in-law. "Are you all right?"

Charlotte lowered her hand as she straightened. "Fine. Just tired. Thank you for the hour, Tuny. I was able to work in the garden, then talk to Mrs. Prescott about meals for the next week uninterrupted. I was never so thankful for a moment to breathe, but I ask myself why this is so difficult. I managed my brother's household and much of his correspondence. I conducted my own experiments! And I am finding it particularly galling that I cannot seem to manage my own daughters."

Tuny patted Charlotte's skirts. "They are dears. They'll learn. We did, and I daresay we were far less civilized when you first came to this house."

"Not all that uncivilized," she said with a fond smile. "And it's been a long time since I was called upon to play etiquette teacher." She sat taller, returning to her usual composure. "Now, to business. I haven't forgotten our promise to Lord Ashforde. Either Matthew or I will watch the girls with you tomorrow so the other can visit Mr. Hollingsworth."

"About the Ashforde rubies," Tuny remembered. "I hope you can find them. It seems sad he lost them, through no fault of his own."

"His father wasn't the most attentive," Charlotte admitted. "To his duties or his son, it seems. Still, it sounded as if you and his lordship were enjoying yourselves upstairs."

She smiled. "You know I always enjoy Rose and Daphne's company."

"And Lord Ashforde's," Charlotte said wisely. "Though, if he is to call me Charlotte, I suppose I should call him Ash, as you do. Though most would call him by his title, I suppose he started going by Ash to friends to avoid confusion with his father."

"Did they share a name?" Tuny asked.

"Thomas, if memory serves. Your Lord Ashforde would be the third in a row to bear that first name."

Tuny glanced down at her fingers. "He doesn't seem to think highly of his father."

"I can understand. Not that the former Lord Ashforde was a bad sort. In fact, he could be quite charming. But he could never say no to another drink, a hand of cards, a wager, or a lady."

Tuny grimaced. "Unlike Ash."

"Very unlike him. I was delighted to see how much Fortune approved of him."

"Yes, she was enthusiastic," Tuny allowed.

Charlotte frowned. "You don't sound pleased."

"Oh, I am," Tuny hurried to assure her. "But she's changed her mind before. She didn't like Count Montalban at first, then later approved of him after he behaved well toward Callie. Fortune was even cool to Belle recently when she was acting high-handed. Perhaps she wouldn't have been so approving of Ash the year he broke my heart."

"Likely not," Charlotte said.

Tuny met her gaze. "And what happens if he decides to break my heart again?"

Charlotte dropped her arm about her shoulder. "Love

is a risk, Tuny. Only you can decide if you're ready to take it. But I can tell you from experience that, for the right man, it's worth any cost."

Her life was pandemonium. Friends coming and going. A guard watchful. Her nieces stampeding through the house with joyful noise. Ash had never lived in such a house. Could that be his future?

It did not seem as daunting as it once might have. In fact, it sounded delightful.

"I take it tea was a success, my lord?" Peaves asked as Ash came through the front door.

Jarls hurried to close it behind him. Mrs. Clowers was peering out the door down to the kitchens, and Ash spotted Theban on the first-floor landing. Even his maids seemed to find it necessary to dust the sitting room, quite close to the entry hall door, as if they hadn't scoured the place only the day before.

"Tea went quite well," Ash allowed, handing his hat to his footman. "I will be escorting Lady Moselle to church on Sunday."

Mrs. Clowers clapped her hands, but a look from Peaves sent her ducking back into the stairwell. Theban stalked off as if intending to determine the appropriate outfit even now.

"You will want the carriage in time to fetch her for St. George's," Peaves said.

"We'll be attending St. Paul's," he replied, heading for his library. He expected the quiet to welcome him as it usually did, but now it sounded entirely too still, the dark almost funereal. He shook off the feeling.

"St. Paul's Cathedral is impressive," Peaves said, following him. "But it is quite the drive, my lord."

"Not the cathedral," Ash said, sinking into his favorite chair. "St. Paul's Covent Garden." Ah, that was more the thing. The chair was wide, heavy, and thickly padded. Plenty of room for one.

Or two. He had a sudden image of Petunia seated in his lap as they read together. Now, that would be heaven!

He reined in his thoughts. Today had been highly successful, but he should not allow his feelings to override good sense. That way lay madness.

Peaves coughed, reminding Ash he was not alone.

"Something else?" Ash asked.

"St. Paul's Covent Garden, my lord?" his butler asked, face scrunched up as if Ash had suggested taking Tuny to watch the horses eat in the stables.

"That is where Lady Moselle and her family attend services," Ash said. "That is where I intend to be on Sunday. Now, will you ask Mrs. Clowers when dinner might be served? I seem to have developed quite an appetite."

"You will be pleased to hear that Fortune approved of Lord Ashforde," Meredith told Julian when he returned home from his offices that afternoon.

"Well," her husband said, coming to join her on the sofa in their sunny yellow withdrawing room. "That is good news. I'm glad you agreed with me, Fortune." He scratched the cat between her ears.

Fortune allowed the touch a moment before slipping down and padding toward the window.

"Quite in agreement," Meredith said. "I have seldom seen such an enthusiastic response."

"From Fortune or Petunia?" he teased.

"Fortune," she said. "Petunia seemed more surprised and relieved."

"As well she might. I'm sure any young lady of the *ton* would welcome that sort of certainty about a suitor's character."

One of the things she loved about Julian was his unqualified faith in her pet, and her. Now she leaned against him, and he put his arm about her shoulders.

"That will make all our girls settled," she murmured with a satisfied sigh.

Julian said nothing.

Meredith straightened away from him to meet his gaze. "Julian, is something wrong? Is one of these matches in jeopardy?"

"Perhaps not the matches," he allowed in his diplomatic voice. "But if the king should decide not to involve himself in the Batavarian question or, worse, come down on the side of Württemberg, it's possible Leo and Fritz and all their staff will be asked to leave England. I don't like thinking what that would mean for Larissa and Callie."

"Or Petunia, if Lord Ashforde advises the king in that direction," Meredith realized.

"Or us," he said. "I have been a noted member of the Batavarian court, particularly after King Frederick saw fit to give me this title."

"A title King George should have awarded himself," she said primly. "For your many services to his court over the years."

He inclined his head. "He will never admit as much. And there's more."

Her shoulders tightened. "What?"

"I've heard rumors von Grub sent another agent to England. Unfortunately, no one seems to know who or where. Canning even suggested assigning someone to keep an eye on Lord Ashforde, just in case there's trouble."

She did not question how he knew something apparently not even Lord Ashforde was privy to. Julian had made any number of friends in his career, at all levels of government and power. And she had unwavering faith in him too.

She settled back into his arms. "Between her guards and his shadow, they would be tripping over each other."

"So I told Canning. He has desisted, for now."

"But is there nothing more that can be done to protect them?" she asked.

"Not until Ashforde makes up his mind and shares his thoughts with the king," Julian said. "That decision could well change all our futures."

CHAPTER FOURTEEN

ASH WASN'T SURE what to expect of St. Paul's Covent Garden, particularly after Peaves' response to the location. The elegant stone church with its four tall columns at the false front dated from the seventeenth century, but much had changed in the area since the famous architect Inigo Jones had constructed it. While once surrounded by homes of the wealthy, now the area welcomed merchants, shopkeepers, and a few rather shadier sorts that were visited only at night.

Then too, the liturgy of the Church of England might be the same here and at St. George's Hanover Square, but the people responded differently. Where he was used to seeing gazes darting about as if seeking attention, these gazes focused on the rector and the elegant altar behind him.

Not that Ash spent his time observing the architecture and congregants. He was here to worship, after all. He listened to the readings and the rector's sermon, considered their application to his life. And if his attention strayed to the lady at his side more often than it should, that was only to be expected.

Petunia was dressed in a color between copper and bronze, the overskirt figured with clusters of flowers. They matched the flowers on her straw bonnet. She too seemed to focus on the service, but twice when he glanced her way, her gaze met his, and, for a moment, all other sound ceased.

"A very fine church," he said as he escorted her out the brick front of the building. Her brother and sister-in-law were just ahead, each firmly gripping the hand of a daughter, and Mr. Huber, the Imperial Guard for the day, was just behind him and Petunia. "Still the most prominent edifice on the square."

"You should see the area when the market is open," she said as they came around the building. "It's mostly closed today because of the laws, but during the rest of the week you can't see from one side to the other for the crowds."

The law forbid selling on a Sunday, but a few hardy souls had ventured to their stalls and waved passersby over to view their wares.

"Apples!" Daphne cried, tugging her mother to one side.

Sir Matthew hurried to keep pace.

"Still energetic, I see," Ash mused as Charlotte steered her daughter toward the far end of the market square.

"Always," Petunia said. "Do you recall Miss Winchester from the duke's house party?"

He had only seen the woman in passing, but he nodded.

"Charlotte had hoped to engage her, but she seems to have gone missing."

Huber took a step closer. "Missing?"

Petunia swiveled to glance his way. "Yes. The agency cannot seem to reach her at her new position. Charlotte has asked them to send other candidates."

His face was tight, but he resumed his usual distance.

"Are Mr. Huber and Miss Winchester acquainted?" Ash couldn't help asking.

"They met at the house party," she explained as they crossed the street at the base of the market, her brother effectively stopping traffic. "Mr. Huber spent a great deal of time in the schoolroom, but so did Prince Otto

Leopold. However, I'm beginning to think it wasn't just guarding the prince that held his interest."

Suddenly, the very guard was nearly pressed against his back. Ash started to turn, but Mr. Huber put a hand on his shoulder.

"Take the baroness home," he urged. "Stay there until I return."

Ash glanced back in time to see the guardsman dash off down a side street.

"What could that be about?" she asked.

Ash took her elbow. "I don't know, but I intend to do exactly as he suggested."

"Not much of a suggestion," she protested as he urged her toward the house. Why had he never noticed how narrow the road was, how many windows looked down on the cobblestones? Enemies could be anywhere. He nearly shoved her through the door ahead of him.

Petunia frowned at him, then turned her attention to helping her sister-in-law remove the girls' bonnets before they could be crushed.

"Something wrong?" Sir Matthew asked, moving closer to Ash. "What happened to Huber?"

Ash shook his head. "I don't know, but he wanted Petunia inside for now."

Sir Matthew scowled at the door as if warning off any interlopers. "Go up to my study, then. I'll see to Charlotte and the girls."

Petunia turned to Ash. "Will you stay for luncheon?"

"Delighted," he assured her. "Your brother suggested we might be more comfortable in his study. I believe it's this way."

She fell in beside him as he climbed the stairs. "You and Matty think there's something wrong."

"Well, I doubt Mr. Huber would go harrying off if he wasn't concerned," Ash admitted as they entered the room. Her brother's study was paneled in warm wood, with bookshelves on either side, a desk near the window, several spindle-backed chairs, and two upholstered chairs facing the hearth. Ash waited until she'd seated herself on one before taking the other.

"I'm sure we won't have to wait long," he told her.

By the way her skirts were swinging, she didn't like waiting at all.

He made a show of leaning back in the chair, as if the matter didn't concern him. "Did you have a chance to read Ovid?"

Her eyes lit. "Yes. It was a bit dense at first, but once I noticed the pattern, I found it fascinating. Did he write anything else?"

"A number of things," Ash said. "*Metamorphoses, Amores, Ars Amatoria.*"

"Perhaps you'd feel comfortable loaning me those, then," she suggested.

"Of course," he said. "I own the first two, but I'm still seeking *Ars Amatoria.* That means *The Art of Love.*"

She raised her brows, and he found himself studying her brother's bookshelves.

"Perhaps," she said, "we should both read that one."

His face felt unaccountably hot. He almost welcomed the thumps from downstairs.

A high-pitched voice whined. "But Mama, Lord Ashforde is ever so nice. Why can't we go see him?"

Tuny giggled. "You've made a conquest."

"Only one?" he asked.

She blushed and dropped her gaze, fingers pleating at her skirts. "Perhaps more than one." She glanced up. "Daphne adores you too."

He pressed a hand to his heart. "Ah, how am I ever to choose between them?"

"I wouldn't," she warned. "They're rather competitive. If you intend to bring a treat, make sure to bring two."

"I'll remember that," he promised. "Hatchards has

some beautifully illustrated copies of *Aesop's Fables*. Do you think they'd each like one?"

Once more her eyes brightened. "Oh, Ash, that's so thoughtful! I'm sure they'd be delighted."

And wasn't he the most brilliant, kind-hearted fellow in Britain? He was leaning toward her before he thought better of it.

A sharp rap on the front door jerked him upright. Her gaze darted toward the stair. Sir Matthew must have thought it prudent to check any visitors himself, for Ash heard his gruff voice a moment before boots thudded on the stair.

Mr. Huber paused in the doorway to salute Petunia with his fist to his chest. "Lady Moselle."

"Come in, Mr. Huber," she said with a tilt of her head. "What happened?"

With a respectful nod to Ash, he ventured deeper into the room. "A man followed you from the church."

Petunia shook her head. "I imagine a great number of people were walking in the same direction we were. Most everyone in the area attends St. Paul's."

"He was not in the service," the guardsman insisted. "He appeared behind us after we exited and kept pace across the square and down the streets. I did not like the way he watched you. So, I went after him to ask him his business."

She huffed. "You cannot accost every British citizen who happens to look my direction."

Huber raised his clean-shaven chin. "It is my duty to protect you."

"What did the fellow say when you caught up with him, Mr. Huber?" Ash asked even as her eyes narrowed.

The guardsman glanced his direction. "I could not catch him. He ran, and I lost him among this warren of streets. But I heard one exclamation before he escaped me. From that word, I have no doubt he was from Württemberg."

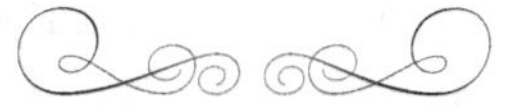

Tuny saw the change in Ash at the guardsman's words. His shoulders stiffened, and he seemed to have grown taller in the chair.

"We must inform His Royal Highness," he told the guard.

"Prince Otto Leopold and Count Montalban are worshiping with the duke's family today," Huber reported. "I will send word immediately."

Tuny held up her hand. "Stop. There's no need to worry Leo and Fritz. Just because someone who followed us from church may have spoken in the language of Württemberg doesn't mean I'm in any kind of danger."

"If they watch you, they want something from you," Huber predicted.

"I have to agree with your guard," Ash put in. "I wouldn't want anything to happen to you, Petunia."

Her name, said so softly, warmed her. "I don't want anything to happen to me either. But I'm surrounded by capable gentlemen, day and night. I'm not worried."

"Forgive me," Huber said, inclining his head, "but although I am sworn to protect you, my allegiance is first to my king and prince. I will wait to report to the captain of the guard when I go off duty this evening, but I must tell him what I saw."

"Very well," Tuny allowed. "But I won't have him assigning more guards. This household is crowded enough."

Neither of them seemed to agree, for Ash stayed long past luncheon, until even Charlotte was making polite suggestions.

Matty finally stood. "Let me see you to the door, my lord."

Given no other choice, Ash had bowed to them all. "Thank you for a delightful day. I believe the weather will hold favorable tomorrow. Would you accompany me on a drive through Hyde Park, Petunia?"

At least he was willing to let her out the door. And use her first name in front of her family.

"Certainly," she told him. "Would three be convenient?"

"Perfect." He bowed again and took himself off.

Huber made sure to tell Tuny he was leaving when Keller came to relieve him that evening. He must have let Keller know about the incident, for the quieter guardsman took up his place in the corner of whatever room Tuny happened to be in instead of remaining in his usual spot in the entry hall.

"Do you expect armed invaders to come riding through the door?" she asked him when he showed every intention of following her even to her bedchamber that night.

"No, your ladyship," he said. "But Huber said I should stay close."

"The corridor is close enough," Tuny said and shut the door on him.

Roth was evident when she came downstairs Monday morning. He appeared to be testing the strength of the lock on the front door by the way he kept snicking it closed and yanking on the latch. As Tuny passed him, he even rammed a shoulder against the wood.

"Stop that immediately," she ordered him. "I won't have you damaging Matty's house."

He straightened with a nod, but, as she turned for the dining room, he surreptitiously rubbed his shoulder. Apparently, Matty knew the value of a solid door too.

Roth made several tours through the house and in and out of the front and rear door during the morning, but he never reported seeing anything unusual. Still, Tuny's nerves were on edge by the time Ash arrived for their drive.

"I take it there were no incidents last evening?" he

asked after she was seated across from him in the carriage.

"None," she said. "Is that absolutely necessary, Mr. Roth?"

The dark-haired guardsman had been closing the shutters on the windows, plunging them into twilight.

"Possibly," he said.

"That might make it difficult to enjoy the park," Ash pointed out.

"I will open them when we reach the park," the guardsman replied.

"We're having a difference of opinion, the Imperial Guards and I," Tuny explained as Ash frowned at him. "They feel it important that I be closed up in as tight a space as possible. I like to breathe."

"Do you have reason to believe Lady Moselle is in imminent danger?" Ash asked the guardsman.

"I always suspect everyone is in imminent danger," Roth replied.

Tuny snorted. "Difficult life."

"But I am alive to appreciate it," he said, gaze stoically forward.

The carriage must have turned into the park, for he pressed an eye to the crack in the shutters, then leaned back to open them. The plane trees waved friendly fingers in the breeze, and she even spotted a rabbit hopping for cover among the shrubs as ladies and gentlemen strolled past.

"Lower the windows as well," Tuny instructed. "The breeze is lovely today."

She thought Roth might argue, but Ash began to lower the window on his side, and the guardsman followed suit.

The clean, fresh scent of the park drifted through the carriage. Soon Ash was nodding to acquaintances, and Tuny found a person or two she recognized. Then another carriage drew alongside. The open landau held a matron with perfectly coiled hair, what were likely two daughters by the resemblance in chin and eyes, and an older gentleman heavy of girth and broad of smile.

"Ah, Ashforde, well met, well met!" he caroled, hands settled complacently over his silver-shot waistcoat. "Dorothea, girls, you remember his lordship."

"Lady Wellmanton, Miss Wellmanton, Miss Araminta Wellmanton," Ash greeted them.

The young ladies giggled, and their mother inclined her head, but Tuny's hands tightened in her lap. Wellmanton's son, Robert, was the villain who had threatened Fritz earlier this summer, going so far as to challenge him to a duel and then claiming Fritz was the challenger. Fritz would have been imprisoned for threatening the life of a British subject, if Callie's testimony at his trial hadn't cleared him. Robert Wellmanton had dropped out of Society altogether, and Callie had heard he had been sent to rusticate at the family estate.

"Allow me to present Lady Moselle," Ash said. That smile to her seemed proud, as if her presence meant the world to him.

"Ah, yes, *Lady* Moselle," Lady Wellmanton said with a condescending smile. "Elevated for services to His Royal Highness, wasn't it?"

"Lady Moselle helped capture a dangerous foreign spy," Roth put in. "England should be grateful."

Lady Wellmanton regarded him with a puzzled frown, as if she couldn't understand why the furniture had decided to speak to her.

"A valiant lady, no doubt," Lord Wellmanton said genially. "I can understand your interest, Ashforde. Just don't forget there are many English ladies as valiant and as interested in catching your eye."

As if to prove as much, his two daughters batted their thin lashes at him.

"I may have a Batavarian title, my lord," Tuny told him, "but I was born and raised in England. Enough that I can tell English lace pretending to be French when I see it."

The older Miss Wellmanton clutched at her chest.

"Ah, I believe that's Lady Lilith and Mr. Villers just ahead," Lady Wellmanton said. "I must have a word. You will excuse us."

Her driver sent their horses forward at a pace that flattened the daughters against the well-padded seats.

"They are of no consequence," Ash said as his driver began moving their coach forward at a more leisurely pace.

"Clearly," Tuny drawled. "But you should be warned. Persist in your suit of me, and you will face that sort of thing everywhere you go. 'Oh, Lady Ashforde. You know her father was in trade, and by trade I mean he worked in a mill. Can you imagine?'"

"'Oh, the former Lord Ashforde,'" he countered in a high falsetto. "'Favored in every gambling hell in the city, to lose. And haven't you noticed how many street urchins bear an uncanny resemblance?'" He clacked his tongue.

"That wicked, was he?" Tuny asked, heart hurting for him.

"Not wicked so much as hedonistic." His voice had deepened with apparent sorrow. "He couldn't say no, to anyone or anything that promised to amuse him. I have a trust set aside to see to his other children. They will be cared for and educated. Like me, they had no choice in their father."

She couldn't imagine having a half-sibling and never interacting. "Do you ever think of bringing them home to live with you?"

"I did. But their mothers were rather adamant about keeping them, and I couldn't have a dozen or so women of no relation living with me, so I was forced to make other arrangements." He shrugged, but she saw what the movement cost him. "The oldest is my age. He's a rector in Kent and appears to enjoy it. The youngest is about

Rose's age. I receive reports from his school. They tell me he is very bright."

If the oldest was his age, his father had been dallying while his wife was still alive. Small wonder Ash was so careful in his emotions.

But surely he realized that a wife would expect more. Certainly *she* expected more. She saw how Charlotte and Matty worked together—in their investigations, in the running of the household, in the care of Rose and Daphne—and Ivy and Kendall were devoted to each other. How could she settle for a man who wasn't willing to give his heart fully?

CHAPTER FIFTEEN

ASH MIGHT STILL be considering what to do about Batavaria, but Tuny had just as big a matter to consider as he continued to court her: his ability to share his heart. He was an attentive suitor; that, she could not deny. Tuesday, he took her to Gunter's Confectionary. Though August had given way to September, the weather continued unseasonably warm, and the pineapple ice was particularly welcome. Huber quite enjoyed the blueberry flavor.

Afterward, they stopped by Hatchards. She had visited the famous bookseller with Charlotte on occasion, so she was used to the tall stacks, the hushed, almost reverent tone of the customers. Huber was clearly gawking, but at the magnificence of the collection or the number of hiding places, she couldn't know. Nevertheless, a clerk was happy to go scurrying off after a book Ash wanted.

"What do you think of Hatchards?" Ash asked, leaning one elbow on the wooden counter.

Tuny glanced around. "It is always impressive, but your library is better. I could be so fortunate as to have so many books."

He smiled at her. She liked to think he was smiling more often. In fact, he looked relaxed and happy in his single-breasted navy coat with small gold buttons and fawn-colored trousers. "In that case, I know somewhere else we should go."

Was that a challenge?

"Oh?" Tuny asked, but the clerk returned with the volume just then, and Ash tucked it under one arm before offering her the other. Once they were standing at the carriage, Huber just behind, Ash beckoned to his driver, who leaned over so Ash could murmur something up to him. The fellow glanced at Tuny, then Ash, and grinned for a moment before nodding respectfully.

"Very good, my lord."

"Where are we going?" Tuny asked as Ash settled next to her on the seat. Across from them, Huber looked just as interested in the answer.

"Allow me to surprise you," Ash said.

Huber sank against the squabs, reminding her of Daphne denied a treat. "I do not like surprises."

"I do," Tuny said, and she smiled approvingly at Ash.

She had seldom traveled east from Covent Garden for more than a mile, but she recognized the route to Lincoln's Inn Fields: out Piccadilly, skirting the dangerous area of Seven Dials. She shuddered at a glimpse of the dark streets, buildings crowding so close together it would be hard to see the sky, or a better future. If Matty hadn't pulled himself up by his fists, would they have ended up in the squalor, resorting to crime to pay their way?

"Are you chilly?" Ash asked, reaching for the padded wall behind them. A moment later, and he'd settled a blanket over her skirts.

Tuny twisted to look into the hidden compartment he'd opened. "What else do you have in there?"

"I'm not entirely sure," he admitted, twisting as well. His face was so close, she could see the sweep of his dark lashes against his cheeks. "Looks like another blanket or two and a pillow—did Griffiths think I intended to sleep in here? And a flask." He pulled out the silver bottle and uncorked it, then reared back. "This has obviously seen better days."

Huber held out his hand. "I will take it."

Ash stashed it back in the compartment and slid shut the door. "No, thank you. I've spent a good portion of my life dealing with my father's indiscretions. What's one more?"

"You think your father left that there?" Tuny asked, fingering the warm wool on her lap.

"The flask at any rate. Griffiths, my coachman, will have had the blankets cleaned recently, so you need have no concerns there." His smile was looking strained again.

Tuny glanced out the window, hoping to draw his attention to something better than memories of his father. "And what's that we're approaching, with the wall and towers?"

He leaned closer, and once again she was all too aware of his body next to hers, the easy grace, the strength.

"St. Bartholomew's Hospital," he said. "You can see the courtyard through the gates, there."

She caught a glimpse of a tall, multistoried white building with windows staring out on the stone courtyard before the coach carried them past.

He leaned back, and she wished she could think of something else to do or say to pull him closer again.

"I take it you haven't come this way before," he mused.

Tuny shook her head. "Until I was ten, I lived in Birmingham with my sisters and stepmother. Matty brought Ivy, Daisy, and me to London, then, to live with him. I haven't gone much beyond Mayfair and Covent Garden."

"Your father and stepmother must have passed, then."

"My father when I was six. The other Mrs. Bateman will probably outlive us all, spiteful thing that she is. She moved to Ireland and remarried. Make no mistake— none of us miss her."

There, she'd said it. Best he know what he was getting into.

"My father never remarried after my mother died," he said, gaze going out the window. "At the time, I wondered whether it was because he didn't want to love again. Now I realize he ever only loved himself."

"Well, that's dark," Tuny said. "Are we trying to outdo each other in heartache, then? I could tell you stories."

"I'm sorry to hear that," he said, gaze returning to hers. "Here I hoped to be unique in that regard."

"No chance there. Everyone has a sad story somewhere. But we have happy ones too. The day Charlotte came to be our etiquette teacher because Matty was being elevated and stayed to become part of the family." She looked to him expectantly.

"The day I discovered books could do more than instruct," he offered, "opening whole new worlds."

She nodded. "When Daphne and Rose came into our lives."

"When I knew the estate was solvent again."

They were veering back into sad territory. "When I became friends with Larissa, Callie, and Belle," she put in doggedly.

"When I met you," he said.

Oh, my! He'd set her to blushing again.

"I believe we may have reached our destination," her guard said.

She could have wished Huber to perdition.

They had pulled into a neat square with a large, grassy park in the center and buildings all along the eastern side. On the southeast corner, at Number 32, sat a large stone building with a glass cupola at the top.

Ash had recovered his usual polite demeanor, for he nodded toward the building. "Behold," he said as the carriage came to a stop in front. "The Temple of the Muses."

"I know the Muses!" Tuny cried. "They were in the book you loaned me. Nine women who personified the arts." She frowned at the building. "I didn't know they had a temple to them in London."

"Indeed," he assured her. "And I am one of their most devoted acolytes."

Tuny regarded him from the corners of her eyes as Mr. Huber opened the door and jumped out. "You're bamming me."

"I'm not entirely sure what that means," Ash admitted, "but I take it you think I've misspoken. I assure you every word is the truth. Come along if you'd like to meet them."

Bemused, she allowed him to hand her out of the coach.

The building held several businesses, but Ash led her and Huber up a flight of stairs to a wide set of doors.

"The Temple of the Muses," Tuny read in the gold-lettered sign over the door. "Being the largest bookstore in London." She turned to stare at Ash. "The *largest!*"

"See for yourself." He pushed open the door to give her entrance.

Inside was a long chamber with arched windows running along one wall that sent golden rays of light into the space. But every other wall, from the polished wood floor to the high ceiling, was filled with bookshelves, and each shelf groaned with books packed so closely together she wondered anyone could pull one out. In the center was a massive circular counter under the same-sized hole in the ceiling, through which she saw another floor filled with books. More books were piled on pallets by the windows or tucked into boxes in a corner, and everywhere, ladies and gentlemen strolled about examining, exclaiming.

She was fairly certain she was gaping, despite all of Charlotte's admonitions.

Ash moved to the counter. Even though a number of others stood near the glossy wood, a clerk immediately came to face him.

"Lord Ashforde, a pleasure to have you with us again. How might we be of service?"

"Lady Moselle would like to start a library," he told the fellow. "What do you have available?"

The clerk, whose long, thoughtful face seemed perfectly suited to his profession, looked from Tuny to Ash. "We have not had the delight of serving her ladyship before, and we are honored to help. I dislike mentioning financial matters, but you are aware of our policy?"

"Rest assured the matter will be resolved to the satisfaction of all," Ash said.

The clerk smiled. "Give me a moment." He hurried to the other side of the circle.

Tuny tugged on Ash's arm. "I can't start a library. Where would I put it?"

Ash looked a bit like a hawk that had noticed a choice rabbit hopping across the grass as he watched the clerk. "You'll no doubt have your own home one day. Consider this an investment in the future."

She wrapped the strings of her reticule around her fingers. "I didn't come prepared to invest."

"Leave that to me."

The clerk returned just then. "I am pleased to report that we recently purchased the library of a gentleman of some means from Yorkshire. The bindings have already been removed. Does her ladyship have a preference for the color of the leather?"

Tuny blinked. "You'd bind them all the same color?"

"But of course, your ladyship. To provide a more pleasing arrangement on the shelves. Many prefer a stately black but perhaps we might be bolder." He looked her up and down again. "Scarlet perhaps?"

"A nice Moroccan brown would be more suitable," Ash said, in such a quelling tone that the color climbed in the clerk's cheeks.

"Of course."

This made no sense. "See here, I don't want any old books in my library. Do you have the list of this fellow's holdings?"

"At once, your ladyship." The clerk hurried away again.

"Is there something in particular you want to see?" Ash asked.

Was that a tinge of concern now in his voice?

"Yes," Tuny said. "I don't know about you, but books are treasures in my house, like old friends. You don't just invite strangers to share your house with you."

Huber huffed as if he was quite in agreement.

The clerk returned with the list, and Tuny scanned down it. "Treatises in the art of war? Histories of great battles? Was this fellow a general?"

"He plotted many grand strategies from his armchair," the clerk assured her. "No doubt these titles inspired him."

"Well, they don't inspire me in the slightest," Tuny said. "Where are the adventure novels? The histories of England? Books on art and music and poetry?"

"Ah, yes," the clerk said, as if she'd given him insight into her character. "A lady of discriminating tastes. I would be happy to curate a selection for your ladyship, say, a thousand titles to start?"

Tuny choked.

"That would be excellent," Ash said, taking her elbow. "Prepare a list. I'll send someone to collect it later in the week, and Lady Moselle can make her selections from there."

"Very good, my lord." The clerk bowed to them both.

"I can't pay for a thousand books," Tuny hissed to Ash as they made way for the next customer.

"I am fully prepared to bear the cost," Ash said.

Once more she nearly choked. "And I can't accept such a gift. Charlotte taught us never to accept anything more substantial than a handkerchief or a flower from a gentleman. I'm fairly sure a thousand books are considered significantly more substantial in most households."

"Think about it," he urged. "Nothing would make me happier than to start your library for you. Who knows, it might someday come to reside near mine."

He was hinting of marriage. She wasn't sure whether to pretend she didn't know or order him to speak his mind. She settled on responding to his comment. "Very well, my lord. I will consider the matter."

Ash could only be pleased with how the day had gone. How all the days with Petunia had gone, if truth be told. She had had every opportunity to rebuff him, and she hadn't. Indeed, she seemed to enjoy his company. What had the Imperial Guards advised? He had learned what she liked, and he didn't have to learn to like it himself. They had far more in common than he'd thought. Perhaps, one day soon, he might speak to her brother about a proposal.

Sir Matthew and Charlotte were in the sitting room when Ash escorted Petunia into the little house. Her brother immediately waved him in.

"Ashforde, a word, if you please."

Petunia followed him into the room. Charlotte scooted over to give her space to sit on the sofa. Ash went to sit on the chair opposite.

"How might I be of assistance, Sir Matthew?" he asked.

The burly fellow rubbed his solid chin. "Charlotte and I were the ones hoping to be of service."

"And we think we may have been," his wife put in with a smile. "We spoke to Mr. Hollingsworth on your behalf. He was well aware that the rubies had been sold and to whom they had been sold: Lord Trelawney."

Ash held himself still. Trelawney? How had the man sat across from him in deliberations and said nothing? Or was he laughing on the inside for having beggared Ash's father?

"Lord Trelawney and I are acquainted," he said. "I will speak to him."

Charlotte nodded, obviously pleased to have been of help. He excused himself to go.

Petunia followed him to the door. "Is he a reasonable sort, this Trelawney?"

"I had considered him so," Ash allowed, all too aware of Huber watching from the sitting room. "But he's another of the king's advisors, and someone who has recently risen in standing at court. I cannot help wondering whether there is a connection between his rise and the rubies."

She lay a hand on his arm. "Be careful."

"I will," he promised. Then, Huber or no, he bent forward and brushed his lips against hers.

That. Always that. Emotions swirled and sang inside him. Difficult to keep them contained.

Difficult? Nearly impossible. He would have to work harder.

She lay a hand on his cheek as they separated. He only hoped he did not appear to be dashing out the door, even if his feet moved rather more quickly than usual.

He stopped beside the coach and drew in a breath. She was worth the challenge. He was still the master of his emotions.

"My lord?" Griffiths asked, voice laced with concern.

"White's," he told his coachman before climbing in.

The carriage moved away from Covent Garden, pressing him back against the squabs. But some part of himself seemed to have been left behind.

He hadn't been certain where to find Lord Trelawney, but his guess proved right, for he located the viscount at the card tables. Ash waited patiently while the fellow finished two more hands. The only sign that Trelawney had noticed him was the occasional flicker of his sharp eyes.

Finally, pulling the markers and coins he'd won toward himself, Trelawney stood. "I believe I'll have a spot of tea."

Several of his cronies groaned.

"I take it you'd like a word," the viscount said as Ash fell in beside him. "What's on your mind?"

"Let's sit," Ash said.

Together, they crossed the main room and found two chairs in a corner. Trelawney signaled to one of the staff for tea.

"It has been drawn to my attention that you have my family jewels," Ash said as the viscount made himself comfortable on the leather upholstered chair.

Trelawney raised a golden brow. "Who told you that?"

"The origin doesn't matter," Ash insisted. "The truth does. Do you have the Ashforde rubies?"

Trelawney crossed his legs. "No."

Ash regarded him.

Trelawney attempted his usual charming smile. "I had them for a time. A matter of honor between myself and the gentleman to whom your father sold them. You understand."

He was afraid he did. "What happened to them?"

Trelawney shifted on the chair as if finding it uncomfortable. "Another matter of honor, I fear. A hazard in my position."

"So you gambled them away too."

"In a manner of speaking." He nodded to the staff member who was removing a pot of tea, two cups, and various necessities onto the table between them.

Ash waited until they were alone again. "Where are they now?"

"Sorry," Trelawney said, look regretful. "I am not at liberty to say. And he may have sold them in any event.

You might want to speak to a chap off New Bond Street, very discrete. Name of Hollingsworth."

Ash rose. "If you should find your way clear to letting me know more details, my door is always open to you."

Trelawney inclined his head, and Ash left him to his tea. He stopped by the betting book, just to see if the fellow had cleared any debts recently, but found nothing.

He was still seething as he settled into the coach for the trip home. A gentleman would have realized the significance of those gems. His father might have lost them fairly, but Trelawney might have offered to sell them back to Ash. Then again, perhaps Trelawney was new enough to Society that he had no idea that a family's jewels were more important than their mere cost.

The carriage swerved, throwing him against the door. Never had he been more thankful for the padding his mother had found so delightful. A moment more, and Griffiths was bringing the vehicle to a stop. He yanked open the panel and peered down at Ash, face white.

"Are you all right, my lord?"

Ash righted himself. "Fine. What happened?"

"Someone had the temerity to throw a rock at me!" He bent and hefted what appeared to be a chunk of macadam rapped in paper.

Ash reached up a hand. "Give that to me."

His coachman was so quick to obey Ash might have thought the chunk of pebbled granite had burned him.

The paper unpeeled easily. The words had been written in pencil, in crude letters even Daphne might have managed.

The good of England is at stake. Do your duty. Tell the king to ignore the Batavarians.

He had done his duty since the day he was born.

And he would not be swayed.

CHAPTER SIXTEEN

GRIFFITHS MUST HAVE mentioned the stone to Peaves, for Ash's butler puttered about the library for most of the evening, as if he thought he should be on hand in case he was needed to administer smelling salts and soothe Ash's delicate sensibilities.

"You mentioned you served in the army," Ash told him at one point, after his butler had wiped the same bookshelf three times. "Perhaps I should ask Prince Otto Leopold whether he needs another member of the Imperial Guard. They seem to stand about for endless periods as well."

"Simply doing my duty, my lord," Peaves said. Nose in the air, he took himself off. But Ash caught him sauntering past the open door more than once.

Theban also had an opinion on the matter. The next morning, he outfitted Ash in a heavy wool coat and handed him a tricorn hat in blocked wool for his head.

"A bit behind the times," Ash commented. "Was it my father's?"

"I believe it belonged to your grandfather, my lord," Theban said. "But it is the sturdiest piece of headgear you own. Best to be prepared."

"The miscreant chucked the rock at Griffiths' head, not mine," Ash reminded him. "My normal top hat will do."

Theban tightened his lips in disapproval, but he fetched the hat and handed it to Ash.

Griffiths was similarly wary as Ash came down the steps to the waiting carriage late that morning. "Are you certain you want to go to Covent Garden, my lord? Perhaps a nice drive in the park."

The clerk from the Temple of the Muses had sent Ash the list of books for Petunia. He was not going to wait to give it to her.

"Covent Garden," Ash said as Jarls opened the door for him. "And be quick about it."

If he hadn't given the order himself, he might have thought Griffiths was trying to outrun a gang of highwaymen.

After all that, the Bateman residence was surprisingly quiet when Ash climbed down in front of it. Mindful of Griffiths glancing left and right, as if expecting to be set upon at any moment, he ordered his coachman to return for him in an hour. Though calls were generally supposed to last between a quarter and a half hour, he hoped Petunia might be willing to extend the time, for him.

Unfortunately, she was out.

"Tuny, Charlotte, and the girls are at the market," Sir Matthew confided when he let Ash in. "Roth is escorting them. But I'd be glad for a word while you wait."

He stalked into the sitting room, apparently assuming Ash would follow.

Which he did.

The chairs had always seemed a reasonable size to him, but Sir Matthew made them look as if they had been designed for a child. Leaning back and setting the wood to creaking, he rested both meaty hands on his thighs.

"Any news from Trelawney?" he asked as Ash took his seat.

"No good news," Ash allowed, leaning back on his chair as well, without so much as a whisper from the wood. "He had the gems, as you surmised. But he claims to have lost them recently and would not divulge the name of the new owner. A matter of honor, he said."

He snorted. "Convenient excuse."

"I thought the same, but I cannot force him to tell me."

He flexed his fingers. "Perhaps I should have a word with him."

Ash had an image of Sir Matthew pummeling the upstart lord to the ground. It wasn't entirely abhorrent.

"No, thank you," Ash said. "I'll make other inquiries. Someone else may be willing to relay the tale."

"Check the betting book at White's," Sir Matthew suggested. "That's where you found a mention of them the first time. You might see whether he paid off a debt recently."

"I had the same thought," Ash said. "No luck there either."

He nodded, then studied Ash for a few moments. Ash refused to squirm.

"It seems you are pursuing my sister," he said at last.

"I am," Ash said. Something thrummed through him, as if an expert musician had plucked the right string on a melody. "With honorable intentions, I assure you."

He nodded again, more slowly this time. "I've heard a few rumors about your father."

He would not stiffen. "Only a few?"

Sir Matthew shrugged, like a mountain quaking. "You are not your father. I'm certainly not *my* father. But I'd like to know where you stand on gambling."

"I don't gamble," Ash said. "On anything."

Sir Matthew cocked his head. "Marrying Tuny seems like a bit of a gamble to me."

It had to him once too. "I have come to appreciate your sister's sterling qualities. Loyalty, practicality…"

"And a punishing right," Sir Matthew added.

Ash stared at him. "Your sister boxes?"

He laughed. "Well, I tried to dissuade her, but she was

the littlest, and she always did like following me around. She used to sit on my back while I exercised, better than any set of weights. Mind you, she hasn't sparred with me in years. Too much a lady now, I suppose." He sounded genuinely saddened by the fact.

"Still," he continued, "I am her brother, and I want to know the fellow marrying her will be able to support her, in all the ways that matter."

Did her brother think Ash should challenge her to a match? His mind boggled. "I have sufficient income to support a home here in London as well as an estate just to the north in Herefordshire. I tithe twenty-eight percent of my income to the church and other charities as they are brought to my attention."

Sir Matthew smiled. "I remember your generous donation to the Society for the Prevention of Cruelty to Animals. One thousand pounds for a painting that likely wouldn't have gone for more than a few quid. I hope you found a place for it."

"It is hanging in the unused ballroom of my estate," Ash told him.

"Then it seems you have your financial house in order, my lord." He leaned forward, gaze drilling into Ash. "What about you? Are you ready for a wife?"

"It is a gentleman's duty to see to the next generation," Ash said.

He snorted again. "Spoken like a nob. She isn't a painting you can hang in a little used room and forget. She'll expect to be part of your life, all of your life. If you'll forgive me saying so, Ashforde, you seem to hold yourself from the world at a distance. Some might call it arrogance."

"Some have," he said, and even he heard the chill in his voice.

"And some might say you're hiding," Sir Matthew countered. "I'm in the latter camp. I put a few barriers around myself before I met Charlotte. I nearly killed a man in the boxing square, and I had convinced myself no woman would want such a husband. Why are you hiding?"

The question was intrusive. No one else would have dared to ask it. Even Petunia hadn't broached the subject. He knew just what to say to quell such presumption. But if he wanted to join this family, he had to be willing to share.

"My father was a thoughtless pleasure-seeker," he said. "I vowed to be nothing like him."

"And so you refuse to take pleasure in anything?" Sir Matthew asked, brows up.

"I refuse to allow any emotion to rule me—fear, sorrow, anger, worry, jealousy."

"And what of the more positive emotions? Hope, amusement, love?"

"In moderation," he allowed.

Sir Matthew chuckled. "Oh, that will never work, my lad. Tuny loves with every fiber of her being. I can't imagine her being happy with less from her husband."

Fear tiptoed closer. He could almost hear the insidious whisper: *This was why you decided against pursuing her.* She raised that longing within him, and he knew where it might lead. Was a middle ground not possible after all?

Sir Matthew pushed himself to his feet. "What you need is to prove to yourself that strong emotions won't be your undoing. I had to learn a similar lesson. Come with me."

Mystified, Ash rose and followed him from the room.

Sir Matthew led him through the kitchen, under the curious gazes of the cook and the maid, and out into the rear garden. High stone walls enclosed the space, and a graveled path ran the length, with a swath of grass on one side surrounded by flower beds and a kitchen garden on the other, teaming with herbs. He caught the scents of lavender and sage.

Petunia's brother took down two sets of thick leather gloves from a hook on the wall of the house and handed one to Ash. He recognized them from their counterparts at Jackson's Boxing Salon.

"Mufflers?" he asked.

In answer, Sir Matthew began to shuck off his coat. "Have you been trained in the art of boxing, then?"

"I've taken lessons from the Gentleman," Ash acknowledged.

"Good." Petunia's brother rolled up a sleeve, displaying a muscled arm. "Forget everything he taught you."

Ash blinked. "What?"

"Coat off, sleeves up, mufflers on," he ordered.

Bemused, Ash did as he bid, draping his coat over a bench by the garden before rolling up his sleeves. "Are you challenging me to a match?"

"Nothing so formal," the Beast of Birmingham assured him. He'd already pulled on the gloves and now struck his knuckles together as if to test the padding. The dull thud still sounded deadly.

So why was Ash so eager to try his luck?

Sir Matthew waited until he had pulled on the gloves as well before circling to the left. Ash mimicked him.

"Jackson says never fight from emotion," the former pugilist said. "Keep a cool head. Calculate your punches. I want you to let loose."

Ash kept moving around the little patch of grass, making sure he remained out of reach of those long arms. "Why? As you noted, it's a sure way to lose."

"And you don't like losing," he mused. "That won't do. To fall in love, to stay in love, you have to be willing to lose, if it means the one you love wins."

"That makes no sense," Ash protested.

With a roar, the Beast rushed him, fists swinging. Ash

barely managed to scramble under the punches and out the other side.

"Coward too, I see," Sir Matthew taunted.

Anger clawed its way up inside him. Logic shoved it aside. "It isn't cowardice to avoid your fists. It's prudence."

"Self protection, you mean." He swung again, and again Ash darted back, his boot heels crunching against the gravel of the path.

"You think only of yourself," his opponent jeered. "Tuny could do better."

Now fear joined the anger, but loathing was on its coattails. His father had done this, made him afraid to care, afraid to love, lest it devour him whole. His father had made choices that had cost them both. But he could make choices too.

"Petunia could only do better if she could find someone who loves her more than I do."

Once again, he stopped, blinking. Love? Yes! He was in love with Petunia Bateman, Lady Moselle.

The Beast of Birmingham's sister.

"Prove it!" Sir Matthew challenged, and he rushed Ash again.

Ash sidestepped and caught the man on the shoulder as he passed. As Sir Matthew turned to face him, a light gleamed in his dark eyes.

"Ready to give it your all, then?" he demanded.

Ash positioned his feet and raised his fists. "I am. Do your worst."

"No, Daphne, you must walk beside me," Tuny scolded as her niece once more attempted to wiggle out of her hold. It was the sixth time since she and Charlotte had taken the girls to Covent Garden market, Roth accompanying them in watchful silence. They had hoped to tire the pair out again, and Rose was certainly ambling along contentedly at her mother's side as they started for home. But Daphne had as much energy as when they had set out earlier that morning.

And Tuny didn't.

"Will there be candy?" Daphne asked, gazing up at her with hope shining from her dark brown eyes.

"Only for girls who walk quietly," Charlotte answered for Tuny. "And only when we reach home."

Daphne heaved such a sigh her little shoulders slumped. But she pressed her lips together as if to prevent another word from slipping out.

"I'm walking quietly, Mama," Rose pointed out.

"You certainly are," Charlotte agreed with a smile. "I'm very proud of both my girls."

Daphne's head came up, smile broadening.

They were both good as gold as Roth stopped traffic so that Tuny and Charlotte could cross the busy street in front of the market. Charlotte leaned closer to Tuny, voice a murmur. "Lord Ashforde seems to be proving up nicely."

Tuny's cheeks heated as Roth positioned himself behind them once more. "He does indeed. I begin to hope."

Charlotte beamed. "And the Batavarian question?"

She hadn't meant to speak louder, Tuny was sure. But she could almost sense Roth's attention shift to their conversation.

"He has yet to decide," she admitted. "And I cannot bring myself to push him. I don't know how he'd respond."

"You're afraid of losing him," Charlotte said.

Tuny nodded, unwilling to say the words aloud.

Roth moved ahead of them again as they reached the house. He opened the door, then scanned the entry hall and sitting room before allowing them to enter. The stillness pulsed at her. Well, that wouldn't last long now that the girls were home. Daphne was already turning to her mother.

"Remember the candy, Mama?"

"Let's take the vegetables to Mrs. Prescott, and then we can see about a treat," Charlotte told her daughters.

"I will check the house," Roth said, and he strode off down the corridor.

Tuny helped the girls off with their bonnets, then removed her own as Charlotte took them to the kitchen. Odd that Matty hadn't come down from his study to greet them. He must have heard the girls' voices. They echoed down the corridor even now.

"Ooh, Papa hit him!"

Hit him?

Roth came striding back to her, face tight. "You should know that your brother is in the rear garden, beating Lord Ashforde to a pulp."

Tuny shoved past him at a run, her blood roaring and his boots thudding behind her.

They *were* in the rear garden—a space barely twenty feet by twenty with grass, flowers, and Charlotte's garden—but Ash was hardly a pulp. His dark hair was tumbling over his forehead, and his normally polished boots were scuffed. He and Matthew had shed their coats and rolled up their sleeves, and her brother must have offered mufflers, for a thick glove covered each fist. As she watched, her brother swung at Ash, who managed a jab before dancing back out of reach.

"What are you doing!" she cried.

Ash glanced her way, and her brother landed a punch that set him to swaying. Tuny rushed forward and steadied him.

"That's enough!" she told her brother. "What were you thinking? You outweigh him by two stone!"

"And he's more than a decade younger," her brother countered. "What's your point?"

Tuny scowled at him. "My point is that someone could have been hurt!"

Ash disengaged from her with wounded dignity. "It was only a friendly match, Petunia. You needn't be concerned."

She glanced from his face, where a bruise stood out on one cheekbone and his lower lip was beginning to swell. "Certainly not. Apparently you don't value your teeth."

"I didn't break his teeth," Matty protested, holding up his fists.

Tuny pressed both hands to her brother's chest and shoved him back a step. "You've done enough. Go inside, and help your wife."

He nodded at Ash over her head. "Another time, my lord."

"Delighted," Ash said before spitting blood on the ground.

Fury barely made it possible for her to keep her mouth closed until her brother ambled into the house, tugging at the gloves as he went. Roth took up a position near the rear door.

Tuny glowered at him as well. "And you go inside too."

Roth frowned. "I cannot protect you if I cannot see you."

"Lord Ashforde just proved he is perfectly capable of fighting on my behalf," Tuny told him.

Now Roth eyed him. "He lost."

"I did not," Ash said, words coming out slurred. "I could have won if you hadn't arrived."

"I'd like to see *you* go a round with my brother," Tuny told the guardsman.

Roth's eyes brightened, as if he'd have enjoyed that as well.

"Go!" she commanded, pointing at the door.

He suffered himself to retreat to the house, but he

didn't close the door, and she knew he was still watching from just inside.

She turned on Ash. "Why?"

He shrugged, then grimaced as if the movement hurt. "Your brother invited me to fight. It seemed the sensible thing to do."

"Sensible!"

"Quite sensible," he insisted. He fumbled with the gloves.

Tuny took one of his hands and began pulling off the leather. "He was considered the bare knuckles champion of England for a time. He nearly killed a man in the square!"

"So he told me," he said, offering her the other hand. "Was it the Giant of Lancaster?"

She nodded. "It broke him up. He took care of Cassidy, the giant, until the day he died." She glanced up. "But if you knew he was dangerous, why did you agree to fight him?"

"He was trying to show me that one can commit to an endeavor with the entire heart," he explained as the glove came free. He had long fingers, capable hands. She wanted to cling to them and never let go.

She smashed the gloves between her hands instead. "And he thought a fight would prove commitment? We really must find a governess. My brother's gone mad from the work."

He cupped her hands with his. "Petunia, it's all right. I'm fine. Never better."

She gazed up at him. The eye that wasn't swelling was bright and clear, and the corner of his mouth that wasn't swelling was turning up.

"You didn't have to fight my brother to impress me," she told him. "You already impress me."

"I didn't fight your brother for you," he said gently, giving her hands a squeeze. "I fought him for me."

"I don't understand," she told him.

He released her to run a finger down her cheek, sending a tremor through her. "You said I impress you. You terrify me. And I can't get enough of you. Your brother was trying to show me that it's possible to give your best, all of yourself. To take a risk without fear."

"So, I'm a risk, am I?" she murmured. "As if you aren't."

He dropped his hand. "If I fail to come up to scratch, I have no doubt there will be other gentlemen clamoring to take my place."

"Dozens," she declared. "And I don't want any of them."

Then, shocked by what she'd just admitted, she turned and followed her brother into the house at a rather faster pace.

CHAPTER SEVENTEEN

HIS LIP STUNG, his cheek ached, and he was fairly sure he'd bruised a rib, but Ash had never felt better in his life. He'd gone toe-to-toe with one of the most talented pugilists in England and survived. More than that, he had proven he was stronger than his father. He'd been so afraid emotions would be his downfall. He'd felt those emotions surging through him, yet he hadn't compromised his honor.

Petunia was no danger to him. His own choices were the danger, and those he could control. He would never let her down.

Just as wonderful a revelation? She cared.

The agitated swish of her skirts and her high, proud carriage as she returned to the house said she was still entirely miffed with him. She'd worried her brother might hurt him. She had no idea that the greater hurt would come from losing her. He picked up his coat to follow her inside.

Roth stepped into Ash's path.

"Lady Moselle cares for you," he said.

Ash couldn't help his grin, even though his lip protested. "So it would appear."

Roth tipped his head so that his gaze met Ash's. "You will treat her with the respect due her station and her person."

"It would be my honor," Ash assured him.

Roth nodded, but he didn't step aside. "Do you intend to offer?"

"Shouldn't the lady know the answer to that question before her guard?" Ash countered.

Roth eyed him a moment more, then stepped aside. "I expect to be notified."

"I'll send an engraved announcement." Ash passed him, and Roth fell into step behind him.

The cook was busy with the fire when he entered the kitchen, but through the open door to the dining room he spotted Petunia in the sitting room beyond. The rest of her family members seemed to have found other ways to occupy themselves. Voices echoed from up the stairs, along with a deep growl. He frowned.

"The Great Bear," Tuny explained as he came into the sitting room. "It's a family game."

"Ah," Ash said, joining her. "Forgive me for concerning you in the garden. There truly was method in my madness."

"So you say," she allowed.

He started shrugging into his coat, and his shoulder informed him that was a poor idea. He must have winced, for she rose to help him.

"And you're certain it was worth it?" she asked as she eased the garment up his arm.

With her standing so close, it had been worth every moment. "Absolutely," he said.

She brushed something off his sleeve and stepped back. "Well, I hope you don't intend to make a habit of it."

"If it allows me to be part of your family, I cannot make that promise."

She frowned. "Do you want to be part of my family?"

"Very much," Ash assured her. "I never had brothers or sisters, much less nieces. I envy you yours."

Pink climbed in her cheeks. "They could be yours too."

The longing crested like a wave, leaving him floating.

"I would like that. Perhaps I should go speak to your brother."

Upstairs came shrieks of laughter.

"You've talked with Matty entirely enough for one day," she said. "Let me see if our cook has any ice. That lip is going to swell."

Not nearly as much as his heart when she brushed his cheek with a kiss before heading for the kitchen.

What was she to do with him? Very likely she could have coaxed a proposal from his lips—even with one fat from her brother's pounding—that very moment. She'd once dreamed of hearing words of love from him. Why was she hesitating to encourage him now?

Because he hadn't said words of love. He'd said he'd found his balance when it came to emotions. He'd said he enjoyed her family. Was it too much to ask that he claim undying devotion?

With him, very likely. But without that declaration, could she really trust that things would turn out differently this time?

Their cook, Mrs. Prescott, hadn't any ice, but she wet a towel and sent it back with Tuny for Ash to apply to his lip. Roth watched from the entry hall. That, at least, gave her and Ash a modicum of privacy.

It also gave her a moment to peruse the list of books the Temple of the Muses had sent to Ash. Much smaller than the thousand the clerk had originally suggested, and she spotted some favorite authors and titles among the set as well as a few she was eager to try.

"A very nice collection," she said, trying not to sigh. "But I still think it's too much to accept for a gift." Before he could argue, she met his gaze where he sat beside her on the sofa. "Better?"

He lowered the towel. "Yes, thank you. And please

think about the books. They could be a gift for the whole family."

Matty would be pleased, but Charlotte might wonder at the gesture and where to put the books. "I'll let you know," she promised.

"Perhaps on Sunday?" he suggested. "I should be sufficiently healed for services. Would you join me at St. George's Hanover Square this time?"

And have every nob in the city staring at her? "You didn't like St. Paul's?" Tuny asked.

"It was just as inspiring," he told her. "But I am a member of the parish of St. George's."

And so would she be, if she married him. The implication was clear.

Perhaps it was time she tried the notion on for size.

"Very well," she said. "Will you come by around nine? That should give us sufficient time to return to Mayfair for services."

"Perfect," he said. He handed her back the towel and rose. "I will say my farewells to your brother and sister-in-law." He bowed. "Until Sunday."

She nodded, and he took himself off. She picked up the towel, still warm from his skin.

Lady Ashforde.

She snorted. She couldn't accustom herself to being called Lady Moselle, and it was a title with no history behind it. How could she accustom herself to being the wife of a baron with a family lineage longer than her brother's arm?

Ash paused in the doorway of Sir Matthew's study. Charlotte and the girls were bundled in one of the chairs, and Petunia's brother was sitting on the floor in front of them, leaning against his wife's skirts, as she read from a book. Rose was twisting a reddish lock around one finger, and Daphne was trying hard not to suck a thumb, by the way the digit kept creeping toward her pursed lips. That longing engulfed him again. This time, he let it linger.

In his mind, he saw him and Petunia on a sofa at Lamote, his estate, a little boy with her warm brown eyes beside him, perhaps a little girl with Ash's dark hair beside her, listening, absorbing. Knowing they were loved and cherished.

He swallowed the lump in his throat.

He didn't think he'd made a sound, but Sir Matthew glanced up. Then he patted his wife's skirts, and she looked up as well.

"Lord Ashforde!" Daphne clarioned, starting to wiggle.

Charlotte visibly tightened her grip on both her daughters. "Ash. What can we do for you?"

"I wanted to take my leave of you," he said. "If I might have a word with Sir Matthew before I go?"

Petunia's brother hauled himself to his feet. "I'll be right back, girls."

Both Rose and Daphne were watching him as their father drew him back into the corridor.

"Something wrong?" he asked.

"No," Ash assured him. "And I cannot thank you enough for that bout in the garden."

He clapped Ash on the shoulder, and Ash did his best to stand his ground.

"It was good exercise," Sir Matthew allowed. "Tell your cook to put a raw beef steak on that lip."

He'd gag if she did. "I appreciate the advice. I would also like your permission to ask Petunia to marry me."

His sable brows shot up. "So soon? Good. She doesn't talk about it much, but I can tell she's been wondering. When will you go down on bended knee?"

"Monday, after I speak to the king," Ash told him. "However, I've asked her to join me for services on

Sunday. Afterward, I'd hoped to take her out to see my estate. It's about an hour and a half north of London, near Cheshunt."

He nodded. "Not so far we couldn't come for a visit now and again. And I expect you'll be in town for the sessions of Parliament."

"Of course. Make no mistake, Sir Matthew. When I marry your sister, I will be joining our families. I hope we may spend many happy occasions with you and your girls."

He grinned. "Wouldn't have it any other way. I'd welcome you to the family now, but the decision is Tuny's. We'll have to abide by her wishes."

"Of course." Ash inclined his head, and the baronet went back to his family. He could not doubt that his impending offer would be the topic of conversation between Petunia's brother and his wife as soon as their daughters were safely occupied. And, as Petunia had said, her nieces seemed to like him.

If only she would be as receptive to the idea of marrying him.

"You will accept when he offers," Roth said, entering the sitting room.

Tuny crushed the towel in her fist. "I don't take orders, especially not about that."

"Forgive me." He pressed his fist to his chest. "I did not intend that as an order, merely a statement of fact. You care about him, and he cares for you. It will be a good match."

"So everyone tells me," Tuny said, starting for the kitchen.

Roth followed her into the dining room. "You do not see the advantages?"

"For me? Certainly. I gain a title, lands, wealth, maybe even standing."

He opened the kitchen door for her, and she went through to wring out the towel and drape it over the wash basket to dry.

"Thank you, Mrs. Prescott," she told their cook. "The towel helped a great deal."

"Anything for your young man, miss," Mrs. Prescott said, beaming. Then she straightened. "That is, Lady Moselle."

Tuny smiled at her, then led Roth back to the sitting room.

"You see?" she said as he took up a spot along the wall. "Even Mrs. Prescott, who's known me for years, cannot bring herself to use a title for me."

"Perhaps *because* she has known you for years," Roth argued, a dark shadow against the wainscotting. "Count Montalban was the Captain of the Imperial Guard for years before the king gave him that title. He seems to have accustomed himself to the change."

"He was the son of a king," Tuny reminded him, going to sit on the chair nearest the window. The sun slipped past the tall buildings to warm her. "It wasn't all that big a change."

"And you are the sister of a baronet," he returned, moving alongside her. "That shouldn't be such a large change either."

He bent to peer out onto the street. He must have been satisfied with what he saw, for he straightened and pointed his gaze off across the room.

"You could sit," Tuny suggested.

"I will stand."

She rolled her eyes. "Your folly, then. Just don't expect me to look up at you. I have no wish to crick my neck."

His gaze remained in the distance. "You have no need to look up at me. Pretend I am a chair."

"You," Tuny said, "are no chair."

"A dresser, then."

"A bookshelf," she said, cocking her head. "Full of all sorts of knowledge. What tales would I find if I looked deeper?"

Still his gaze did not waver. "Not one you would wish to read."

She puffed out a breath. "You have a singularly dark view of the world, sir."

"You might as well, had you seen what I've seen."

"What have you seen?" Tuny asked with a frown.

He regarded her a moment before returning his gaze to the middle distance. "It matters not."

"Of course it matters, or you wouldn't have gone to the trouble of bringing it up. Out with it."

"I am on duty."

"You could at least be entertaining if you're going to stand there."

"I am not entertaining."

"That's true enough." Tuny sighed. "You know I could go to Lady Callie. She's probably heard all sorts of things about you from Count Montalban."

A nerve ticked in his cheek. "He would not betray me."

"Oh, he wouldn't mean to," Tuny said, foot swinging under her skirts, "but Callie hears everything, and remembers."

"I was once a criminal," he said.

Tuny blinked. "What?"

His shoulders came down, as if the words, once spoken aloud, had relieved a burden.

"My mother died birthing me," he explained. "And my father died fighting Napoleon when I was Rose's age. The only family who would take me in was a great aunt, and she was married to a man who managed one of the silver mines before King Frederick shut them down. I was small enough in those days that my great uncle could send me through the narrowest, darkest holes, where no man could reach."

"That's terrible!" Tuny cried. "Shame on him!"

"The shame was on me," he said. "I could have kept working as so many others did, through the heat of summer and the cold of winter. But when I was sixteen, I saw an opportunity to leave the mines behind. I noticed where the foreman stored the week's wages for the workers, and I stole them. I stole money meant for workers who struggled, like me. When another miner caught me as I was trying to escape, I struck him down. It took four men to subdue me. I was turned over to the authorities and spent the next three months in prison."

Tuny's fingers tightened in her lap, as if they would seize the bars even now. "How did you get out?"

"Captain Wyss of the Imperial Guard was recruiting for the Batavarian army. Napoleon was on the rise, and the king feared the French would overrun the country. Even a criminal like me could serve his king. If I died in the process, who would care?"

She could feel the pain in the memory. "But you didn't die."

"No. I served with distinction." His head was higher now, and pride lightened his voice. "And when the war was over, Wyss suggested to Count Montalban that I would make an excellent member of the Imperial Guard."

"They believed in you," Tuny said, drawing a breath. "That's good."

"Very good." His gaze met hers. "But if Lord Ashforde convinces your king to see the prince's side of things, His Royal Highness and Count Montalban will return to Batavaria. So will the Imperial Guard. Unlike some of the others, my memories of Batavaria are not kind."

"Plenty of room in England," Tuny said with a nod. "You've made friends here. I'm sure something could be done."

He cocked his head. "What could a man like me do in your country?"

"Matty was a bodyguard," she offered. "Some of the other pugilists have opened schools for boxing. You could teach fencing and shooting. I'm sure people would be delighted to learn from you. The Imperial Guard is very popular."

He straightened. "Perhaps. But any future we have will depend on what Lord Ashforde tells the king."

And any future she had would depend on what Ash told her about his intentions.

He seemed ready to offer, but she'd thought that before. Yet something felt different. Instead of the usual balls and rides, they'd shared interests: the girls, books, their pasts. He'd spent more time with her family. He'd even claimed he wanted to join it. Oh, how she wanted to believe that!

She was a bit of a mess by Sunday morning, though not, at least, in matters of dress. She doubted her heavenly Father cared what she wore to worship, but those who would be watching Ash would. He'd already seen her bronze silk with the figured overskirt, which she often wore to services. The other members of St. George's wouldn't know it. She made sure to add a bonnet lined with bronze-colored silk to cover her hair and the pearls Ivy had given her to adorn her neck and ears. By the appreciative look in Ash's eyes, she'd chosen well indeed.

He looked less pleased to find Tanner on her heels.

"I can protect Lady Moselle at St. George's," he informed the guard.

Tanner offered him a conciliatory smile. "I am certain you can, my lord. But have pity on a poor soldier. I must do my duty, as you must do yours."

The guardsman handed Tuny into the carriage, then made a show of jumping up beside the coachman.

"Not a bad sort," Ash mused as he took his seat beside her.

"I like them all," she confessed. "But a moment to myself would be appreciated."

"No other incidents, I take it?" he asked as the coach set off for Mayfair.

"None," she assured him. "And I have a feeling the first wasn't an incident either. They must grow bored following me about. Chasing after a potential threat, even an imagined one, gives them something to do."

"So long as you are protected," he said. "I cannot gainsay them there."

She knew the route to Mayfair by heart, but the closer they came to the church, the more her fingers tightened around each other in her lap. She had walked past the church any number of times crossing the area, so she knew the exterior wasn't any grander than that of St. Paul's. Of course, at St. George's, the grand pediment did indeed cover the front door.

The interior, however, was surprisingly plain. High boxed pews ran on either side of a center aisle, with galleries above them on three sides. The two spots that looked more impressive were the curved canopy over the pulpit and the massive reading desk, which rose fully an additional story above the altar and was enclosed with carved wood.

Tanner seemed content to sit near the back, where he could no doubt survey the surroundings, but Ash led her to a pew about in the middle of the chapel. That gave the gawkers plenty of time to take a look at her. She kept her smile pleasant and focused her gaze on the altar.

"Hst!" The sharp whisper brought her head around. Belle waved at her from the duke's family pew, and Callie and Larissa were smiling.

Tuny smiled back.

As she settled into place beside Ash, she recognized a few other gazes directed her way. Lord and Lady Carrolton were in town; the countess also sent her a wave from a few rows ahead and to one side before turning so that her gorgeous, plumed hat blocked the view of her mother-in-law. Tuny couldn't mind. The dowager countess seldom had a kind word for anyone. When Charlotte's brother and his wife Lydia returned from Scotland, they'd be in attendance as well.

Perhaps she wasn't so different here after all. Perhaps she and Ash had a chance. If she just had faith.

CHAPTER EIGHTEEN

"VERY INSIGHTFUL," TUNY told Ash as they exited the service at St. George's Hanover Square and Tanner fell in behind them. "I thought the rector's point was well taken, though it seemed to shock a few of his parishioners. Giving to the church doesn't mean just tithing. It means giving of your time and talents as well."

"Indeed," Ash agreed. "I have served on the Vestry in the past. Perhaps I should ask what needs doing now." He tucked her arm a little closer, as if to keep her safe in the considerable crowd exiting the building. She couldn't mind. There was something very fine about strolling along beside him, her skirts brushing his trousers.

"And what talents would you share?" Tuny asked him with a smile. "Would you embroider the vestments or tend to the grounds?"

He returned her smile. "Perhaps I can read to the lonely."

And didn't that sound lovely? She could see him at a bedside, leaning closer, face earnest, as he shared some story he'd found inspiring. He didn't look the least arrogant in her imagination.

"Ah, Lord Ashforde." Lady Wellmanton and her daughters materialized out of the crowd. All three ladies wore bright lustring, with plenty of frills and embroidery at the hem, cuffs, and neckline, and their bonnets were covered in a profusion of flowers and lace. Tuny felt like a hint of late autumn daring to intrude on the middle of spring.

"How delightful to see you here," the viscountess declared. "We had so little time to chat when we met in the park last week. Perhaps you could join us for tea, say tomorrow afternoon?"

She pointedly did not look at Petunia or Tanner. Neither did her daughters, whose gazes seemed to be latched onto Ash as if he were their last chance for a meal in the next month.

"I regret that I will be engaged tomorrow for a good part of the day," Ash told them. "As will your husband. We are scheduled to present our advice to the king on the Batavarian question."

Tuny would have sworn every breath caught, the breeze stilled, and even the earth stopped turning for a moment.

"Ah, of course," Lady Wellmanton said. "I am certain His Majesty will appreciate the amount of consideration you've given the matter. My husband tells me you are leaning toward advising against restoration."

He was? Tanner stiffened, and Tuny glanced to Ash, but his attention was fixed on the viscountess.

"I cannot say how Lord Wellmanton came to that conclusion," he said. "I have made it clear that I am considering the matter from all sides. Rest assured, I will have my case prepared to present to the king tomorrow."

"Well, certainly. We can have tea another time. I will send round an invitation. Come, girls."

Both daughters tittered at Ash before following their mother toward the waiting carriages.

"I'm glad to hear you haven't decided against the prince," Tuny said, as Ash turned toward his own carriage, Tanner going ahead to open the door for them.

"Will you refuse my suit if I do?" Ash asked.

Tuny stopped, forcing him to stop as well. "I told you from the beginning that courtship and your decision were not connected, sir. If I have given any other impression…"

"Peace," he said, giving her arm a squeeze. "You were very clear as well. But I know the matter is important to you. I would not want my decision to affect our courtship."

"It won't," Tuny said. Then she grinned at him. "So long as you come to see things my way."

As Tanner climbed up beside the coachman, Ash handed her in. His face was once more solemn.

"That was a joke," she informed him.

He settled beside her. "So I had hoped. Yet it is a difficult situation."

"Me, or the Batavarians?" she asked.

Finally his smile hinted. "Both. Though I would call our situation more challenge than problem. I like to think I'm up for a challenge."

She certainly hoped so. She glanced away from the warmth in his eyes to the scenery passing, then frowned. "This isn't the way back to Covent Garden."

"No," he agreed. "I had in mind another destination. Lamote Manor near Cheshunt, my family's country estate."

Her face swung toward him, and her eyes widened, until she looked a bit like Daphne seeking a biscuit. "Your estate?" She even sounded breathless.

"Yes," he said, trying to keep the pride from his voice. "It would seem the appropriate thing to do, considering."

She cocked her head. "Considering what?"

She was going to make him speak the words aloud.

"Considering what we are considering," he said.

She started laughing. "You cannot say it."

"It would be premature," he said. "You must understand the whole."

Now her brows went up. "Secret wife hidden away in the garret? Massive hound stalking the grounds? Monsters hunting the moor?"

"I fear my family history isn't nearly so entertaining," he said. "And Lamote Manor is situated in a fertile valley, not a moor."

She spread her hands. "Well, then, I suppose I will have to consider further."

He would have been dismayed if he hadn't seen the light in her eyes. "Please do. I know I am not the easiest fellow to have around."

She shook her head. "Compared to Matty, you're a paragon. Well, you're a paragon even if I don't compare you to Matty, truth be told. But there's always the Imperial Guards." She went so far as to wink at him.

Ash laughed. It felt good. Right.

So did the conversation as the coach veered north past the green of Regent's Park, then northeast along the River Lea. They talked about the books the clerk at the Temple of the Muses had suggested, debating authors and topics. They weighed the best composition of a library, fiction and nonfiction, and varieties of each. They even delved into which books should be read at which age and season of life.

From time to time, something outside the coach would catch her interest, so he shared about the narrow boats that plied the river, carrying people and goods to and from London; the fields growing flowers and crops for the markets; and the Royal Gunpowder Manufactory.

"Gunpowder?" she asked, peering at the long buildings and mill ponds before the coach swung toward the west.

"The army needs arms," he said with a shrug. "The site has operated for centuries."

She shrugged and returned to their discussion.

His shoulders tightened as Griffiths pulled through the tall, wrought-iron gates at the manor's front drive. He kept staff onsite even when he was in London, but he'd sent Peaves out the day before to make sure everything was in order. Set amid gently rolling fields, the square red brick house with its gothic white marble pediment over the front entrance was visible from every direction. Indeed, her gaze seemed fixed to the view as they swung onto the graveled drive.

Stable hands came running to take charge of the horses; a footman hurried down the steps to open the door for them. Peaves waited next to one of the three-story columns that edged the pediment. After seeing the warmth and energy of her home, he could only wonder if she saw the house as stilted.

He did at the moment.

"My lord, your ladyship," Peaves greeted them as Ash led her up the steps to the entrance. "Welcome to Lamote Manor."

Tanner had hopped down from the coach and was following at a respectful distance. Unlike his colleague, Roth, he did not seem to feel the need to survey every room before allowing Petunia entrance. Still, he stuck to her heels as they went through the door and into the entry hall.

She came to a stop in front of the stairs and turned slowly in a circle. He tried to imagine seeing the house for the first time: the saffron color of the upper walls, the white wainscotting and trim around each door. Bronze capped every pillar and the handrail on the crimson-carpeted stairs as they swept upward to bifurcate at the first landing. The parquet floor stretched to the right and left around the stairs, leading deeper into the house. He'd always considered the space stately.

"It's beautiful," she said reverently, and his shoulders came down at last.

Peaves looked particularly pleased with himself as he stepped forward. "May I take your bonnet, your ladyship?"

"Oh, yes, of course." She fumbled with the ribbons, then pulled off the fetching piece and handed it to him. A strand of hair had come loose in the process. Ash reached out and tucked it behind her ear.

She blushed.

"Would you like to see the house?" he asked.

She nodded, then latched onto his arm, and away they went.

She had never seen such a lovely house. Oh, Villa Romanesque, Ivy's home in Surrey, was pretty, but whoever had built it had been entirely too in love with marble, for it was visible everywhere, from the floors to the hearth to the pediments over the doors. And there was something very grand about Wey Castle, where Larissa, Callie, and Belle lived when not in London, even if the corridors wandered every which way, making it challenging to navigate.

But this? This was a home. Or at least, it could be.

The withdrawing room might have impossibly high arched ceilings in pink and blue and white, like a fancy cake, with matching frescos over the windows, but it had a deep bay walled with bookshelves, warm wood floors, and comfortable furnishings in deep red velvet. The dining room with its red and gold flocked wallpaper might have a massive sideboard topped by a gilt-edged mirror, and the table, when fully extended, probably sat thirty, but the cherry wood and padded seats seemed to encourage one to linger over a fine meal. The library was nearly as impressive as the one in London. And upstairs were plenty of bedchambers for visiting relatives and friends.

Or children.

As if he had followed the turn of her mind, he nodded

toward the stairs to the third story. "Would you like to see the nursery and schoolroom?"

"Very much," she said.

As they started up the graceful stair, she caught sight of a maid and a footman peering out from a doorway, faces alight with glee. Tanner seemed content to wait with them, though, for a moment, she thought he might have given Ash a thumbs up.

She knew a few families who had shoved their children into a forgotten corner of the house, but whoever had laid out the nursery and schoolroom at Lamote Manor had had other ideas. The wood-paneled walls were polished to a glow even though no child could have been in residence since Ash had left for school. Even here, bookshelves and books were plentiful, as were shelves filled with blocks, tin soldiers, and musical instruments like drums and pipes.

"You must have had fun here," she said, watching the sunlight sparkle on the windows.

"I likely would have had more fun if I had had a sister or brother," he allowed, leaning a hip on the worktable in the center of the room.

Tuny shifted her gaze to the map of England adorning one wall. "Then you'd like a larger family than you had."

"I would." The words held such longing her breath caught. "Would you?"

She nodded, afraid to look at him. "I didn't always agree with Daisy, my closest sister in age, but I wouldn't have traded her for the world. I like a big, messy, busy family. And dogs."

She gathered her courage and met his gaze. "Not hounds to ride to the horn. Family dogs. Maybe a cat too, if they get along. And what do you think of parrots?"

His brows climbed nearly to his hairline. "I hadn't thought of any of them. But I'd be willing to give them a try."

Tuny smiled. "What a refreshing attitude."

He cleared his throat, as if he wasn't used to praise. "What else would you like to see?"

"The kitchens," she said.

That seemed to surprise him as well, but he led her down the stairs, and Tanner fell in behind them. Peaves scurried out of sight, but not before Tuny caught a grin on his usually stern face.

"Good ovens, steady water supply, and plenty of light and space to work," she said after looking over the long room with its copper pots and pans hanging from racks. He had confided that his cook and her staff were in London. That was probably a good thing. The cooks and butlers in the great houses she'd visited seemed to have strong ideas on where the mistress of the house belonged.

"Mrs. Clowers seems satisfied with it," he said as she started past him again.

Another maid darted out of the way. Had she been listening at the door? She gave Tuny a timid nod before disappearing into the servants' hall.

They returned to the drawing room to find tea laid out for them.

"I thought your cook was in London," she said, setting out to pour for him and Tanner.

"She is. She packed a hamper for us, and Mr. Peaves set the kettle to boiling."

On the opposite wall from Tanner, the butler inclined his head at her.

"You thought of everything," Tuny told Ash.

And he had. They feasted on Scotch eggs, potted tongue, sharp cheese, and crusty bread, with apples for dessert. All too soon, it was time to start back for London. Two footmen escorted them to the carriage, where a groom was holding the horses. All three men eyed her expectantly, as if they thought she might fly up into the clouds like one of Viscount Worthington's balloons. She was so happy, she might have obliged them. She sent them a smile, and they all grinned and bowed.

"Your staff is certainly attentive," she said as the carriage rolled down the drive. "Here and in London."

"Most have known me since I was a boy," he explained. "More importantly, can you see yourself as their mistress?"

"Possibly," she said.

She felt the squabs give as he slumped.

Likely he'd been hoping for more enthusiasm. The truth was, it was all too easy to imagine herself in such fine surroundings. But it was so far from her family. She couldn't remember a time when they hadn't been just across the corridor, if not in the same room. Was she ready to let them go?

Yet, wasn't that what marriage entailed? The verse popped into her mind.

Therefore shall a man leave his father and his mother, and shall cleave unto his wife.

It wasn't just the husband. A wife left her father and mother too, or, in her case, her brother and sister-in-law, to cleave unto her husband. Instead of relying on Matty and Charlotte, she would have to rely on Ash.

She must have been quiet for too long, for he lay a hand on her arm.

"Penny for your thoughts," he said.

She offered him a smile. "Just thinking about what you asked. What it would mean to move here to Lamote Manor."

"I realize it would be a great change, but we would only be in residence when Parliament was not in session, and we could go down to London at any time." He seemed determined to paint a rosy picture. "There's even a horse-drawn railway that opened in June from the city center to the river. You could go by boat, if you'd like."

What a leisurely way to live! Floating down the river to see family, floating home to be with her husband.

"Daphne and Rose would love it," she told him. "Though I can't imagine what I'd do with them on a narrow boat."

"Perhaps just the railway," he suggested. "They can go by carriage the rest of the distance. I'd be happy to send a coach for them, whenever you like."

Tuny eyed him. "You are being remarkably accommodating for a man who was once so certain we would not suit."

He sobered. "That was the greatest mistake of my life, and I have regretted it ever since."

"Took you three years to come around," Tuny pointed out.

He grimaced. "You might have noticed it generally takes me time to reason things out to my satisfaction."

"Well," Tuny said, "if it's taken you weeks to come to terms with the Batavarian question, I suppose I should consider it an honor you needed three years to decide on me."

He took both her hands in his. "And I have decided, Tuny. There is no other woman for me except you. I am convinced I will never be truly happy unless you are at my side."

Goodness! That was plain speaking indeed. Tuny swallowed, but he hurried on as if he thought her silence stemmed from doubt.

"I know I hurt you when we parted three years ago. Please tell me how I can make that up to you."

She dropped her gaze to where his hands held hers so capably. "At first, I was angry that you couldn't seem to see me for myself. Lately, I've been more afraid you'll see me all too well and decide I'm not enough for you."

"Never!" he vowed.

She smiled at the fervency in his voice. "I'm glad to hear you say it." She glanced up and lay a hand to his cheek. "Because I long ago realized there's no other man for me except you."

He gathered her close, then, pressing kisses along her cheek, her jaw, her lips. She trembled in the joy of his embrace, returned his kisses one after the other. A man couldn't behave this way and not love, could he? Surely she'd finally touched his heart. Her own heart sang.

He drew back, then positioned himself with one arm about her shoulders. "Tomorrow, I have to see the king."

After the moments they'd just shared, she felt as if he'd draped a wet blanket about her instead of his arm. Shouldn't she be hearing a proposal after such a demonstration?

"Yes," she said, waiting.

"I'll stop by before I go, so you'll know what I plan to advise," he continued. "Afterward, I'll come tell you how it went. I imagine you and your family as well as Prince Otto Leopold and his brother will be anxious to hear."

"Very likely," she agreed, wondering how she'd mistaken him again.

"And I will be equally anxious to make my case as to why you might want to consider marrying me."

Ah! She grinned at him. "Make it a good one, then. I've been waiting for three years."

He lifted her hand and pressed a kiss against the knuckles. "I will never let you down again."

CHAPTER NINETEEN

ASH SAT IN his library, surrounded by books on every subject imaginable. A shame he could not believe they held the answer to the dilemma before him.

What was he to tell King George about the Batavarian problem?

For, despite everyone calling it a question, problem it was. He had vowed he would not be swayed in his opinion. He had stood up to Wellmanton's blandishments, an unknown assailant's bullying. But when he thought of disappointing Petunia, against his promise that very afternoon, his stomach shriveled.

So much for not allowing emotions to cloud his judgment.

He took a deep breath and focused on the paper before him, but a pretty face and laughing eyes kept interposing themselves between his quill and his arguments. She was more than he could have dreamed of in a wife, and he was ready to lay his heart at her feet. She said there was no connection between his decision and her affections, but he struggled to believe that.

How could she love a man who lacked the courage to tell her he loved her too?

For he did. Deeply. Forever. He'd tried to fight it, but the feeling only grew stronger with each passing day. She deserved to know. And he would tell her, as soon as this business was settled.

He felt a presence and glanced up to find Peaves hovering.

"Did you have need of anything, my lord?" his butler asked with his usual solicitation.

A new head, a new heart.

Petunia.

"I am sufficient, Peaves," he said. "Tell Mrs. Clowers I will be dining in tonight but not to go to any trouble. Something simple I can eat at the desk would suit me fine."

"Very good, my lord."

He hesitated.

Ash waited.

Peaves crept closer. "Forgive the impertinence, my lord, but there have been murmurs among the staff, here and at the manor, and I would not want your routine to be disturbed in any way."

Ash set down his quill. "What sorts of rumors?"

"The staff is very much hoping for a word about you and a certain lady. I told them it was inappropriate to ask, but…" He spread his hands as if he were helpless to deal with them.

As if he weren't the one most interested in the answer.

"I am planning on proposing to Lady Moselle tomorrow," he said. "Her brother has given his blessing, and I have every hope that she will agree."

Peaves lit up like a rocket at Vauxhall. "Oh, excellent news. Congratulations!" He must have remembered himself, for he immediately schooled his face. "That is, I will let the staff know their concerns are unfounded. Rest assured they will do their duty and welcome their new mistress warmly."

"I would expect nothing less," Ash told him.

His butler bowed himself out. Ash swore he heard a whistle of pleasure before the door shut behind the fellow.

At least someone was happy about all this. He would be

too, if he could just determine the right course of action.

The prince and his father wanted their kingdom back. King William and his court wanted to keep it. There was no middle ground.

Or was there?

He seized up the pen as inspiration struck. Yes, that. Oh, of course. And that. The king would be mad not to see the wisdom of the plan. This was what would keep the peace in Europe.

And the peace between him and Petunia.

A scratch let him know Peaves was back. It couldn't be dinner yet.

"Yes?" he asked. "Are the staff perhaps wanting to suggest how I should propose? Who to invite to the wedding?"

His butler grimaced and shuffled into the room. "No, my lord. Forgive the interruption. This came for you. The footman is awaiting an answer."

Ash took the vellum and broke the seal.

I have located the Ashford rubies. The owner will only be in London tonight. He leaves on a packet for Van Diemen's land tomorrow, to make his home among the colonies near Antarctica. If you have any hope of buying back the stones, come now. My footman will show you the way.

It was signed Wellmanton. It seemed the viscount had indeed located the rubies.

The rubies. The last piece of his inheritance, his life, to save from his father's destruction. The stones his mother had so loved would look well on Petunia. They were the very least he longed to give her.

Ash set his plan aside and rose. "I'm going out, Peaves, and I'm not certain what time I'll return. See that no one disturbs the desk. I am preparing something special to discuss with His Majesty tomorrow."

"Well?" Matty asked when Tuny returned home Sunday evening as the sky was purple with twilight. "What did you think?"

Tanner had been relieved by Roth, who was patrolling the house as if he thought brigands had broken in while she'd been out. Charlotte must have finished settling the girls to sleep, for she was sitting close to her husband on the sofa, fingers of one hand twined in his. Would that be her someday? Sitting beside Ash on one of the beautiful red velvet sofas in the lovely withdrawing room of Lamote Manor, holding hands and opening hearts?

She put on a smile. "I take it you knew where I was going."

Her brother nodded as she went to seat herself on one of the chairs. "He let me know he'd be escorting you out to his estate."

"Lamote Manor," Charlotte supplied. "The family seat for generations. I visited once with Worth, when Ash's father had expressed interest in funding a scientific endeavor."

Tuny blinked. "Ash's father was interested in natural philosophy?"

"Ash's father was interested in many things," Charlotte said with a rueful smile. "This particular fascination didn't last long, alas. But I remember being impressed with the elegance of the place."

"It *is* elegant," Tuny agreed. "Soaring ceilings, bric-a-brac everywhere, fancy furnishings."

Matty frowned. "You don't sound happy about that."

"Oh, I think I could be happy there," Tuny assured him. "I'm just waiting for him to ask."

Charlotte reached across and squeezed her hand. "He'll ask, Tuny. He cares. It shows in the way he looks at you."

"Well, he looked at me like that three years ago, and see where it led?"

"Has he done nothing to endear himself this time?"

Matty pulled away from Charlotte to crack his knuckles.

"Plenty," Tuny said. "So don't get any ideas about another match. You bloodied him quite enough last time."

Matty placed his hands on his thighs. "It was a friendly round, I tell you."

"At least in your mind," Charlotte told him with an affectionate smile. Then she turned to Tuny. "But he's right, Tuny. I see differences between then and now. Three years ago, he wasn't interested in becoming better acquainted with your family. Now he's happy to spend time with even Daphne and Rose! Three years ago, there was no mention of church or his home in Herefordshire. Now you've visited both with him."

She was right. He hadn't tried to kiss her three years ago either, and now she would never forget the warmth of his lips against hers, the caress of his fingers along her cheek, the reverent murmur of her name. It felt as if a stronger foundation had been laid, one on which she and Ash could build. Where she had feared he could not love her for herself, now she knew she didn't have to be anyone but herself.

"I know," she told Charlotte. "And I am hopeful."

"You should be," Matty said. "He asked for my blessing, and I gave it. I expect the fellow to follow through."

She sucked in a breath. "He asked for your blessing? When was this?"

Matty shrugged, as if it weren't a momentous occasion that might change the course of her life. "The other day. He seemed sure of himself."

Oh, but she hoped so!

"Good," Charlotte said. "For if he fails to come up to scratch this time, I don't think Matthew will be the only one who wants to take him out in the garden and pummel him flat."

That forced a laugh out of her.

Still, the day played out in her mind as she lay down

to sleep that night. His devoted attention to the service, the way he'd deflected Lady Wellmanton's barbs, their conversation that had wandered nearly as far as the coach in its topics, the look in his eyes—part pride, part hope—as he'd shared his home.

And the adorable way his staff had watched out for him, as if every bit as hopeful of a match.

A match with her.

If she wanted that, she had to trust him. She had to believe he truly cared. So, when he came tomorrow, if he asked to marry her—when he asked to marry her—she would say yes.

He didn't come.

She waited a good portion of the morning in the sitting room, and no fancy carriage pulled up before the door. Charlotte stopped by twice before returning to Daphne and Rose. Her nieces played quietly, as if they knew she was listening for the sound of horses being reined in. Matty seemed to think Ash's coachman had mistaken the way, for he went outside and looked up and down the street.

What time was Ash's meeting with the king? Surely he wouldn't neglect his duty. So was he neglecting his duty to her? Had he changed his mind after all?

Did she truly mean so little to him?

The doubts surrounded her, poking, prodding.

No! She would not think that way. He'd made her a promise, and she knew he would keep it. She believed in him and their future together.

She turned from her latest trip to the sitting room window to eye Keller, who had emboldened himself to join her instead of standing in the entry hall as he usually did.

"Something's wrong," she told him.

Immediately he drew himself up with a fearsome frown

that made his black uniform look entirely appropriate. "Is someone outside, your ladyship?"

"No one," she said. "And Lord Ashforde should have been here by now."

His frown cleared. "His lordship is on his way to see the English king."

"He said he'd stop here first." She started for the door. "We need to find him. You know as well as I do how much is depending on this meeting with the king today. We must make sure Ash isn't hindered from attending."

"But it is my duty to see to your protection," Keller protested. "Not his."

Tuny gave him a grim smile. "Then you had better keep up, for I intend to see that he's safe."

First, however, she located her brother. He and Charlotte had retired to the rear garden and were pointing out various species of plant to the girls. How Charlotte had experimented when she'd first married Matty, trying to find the perfect combination of flowers and herbs that would thrive in the small, north-facing space. Now Rose was doing her best to look interested. Daphne was already skipping from stone to stone up and down the path.

"Ash should have been here," Tuny told her brother without roundaboutation. "I want to make sure nothing's happened to him." As Matty frowned, she turned to her sister-in-law. "I'll hail a hack to Mayfair, but do you think we could borrow the Worthington coach if we need to go farther?"

"I'll write a note for you to take," Charlotte said. She hurried for the house.

"May I come too?" Rose asked. "I like riding in the coach."

"I know you do," Tuny said. "But we're not sure how long we'll be out. I need you and Daphne to do something very important, though."

Immediately the five-year-old came pelting back to their sides. "What?"

Tuny crouched on the path and met their wide-eyed gazes. "Someone must stay and watch for Lord Ashforde. I am counting on you to tell him where I've gone and wish him all good fortune on his meeting with the king."

Rose nodded solemnly.

"Where are you going?" Daphne asked.

"Good question," Matty put in, crossing his arms over his chest.

Tuny rose. "To his house to make sure everything is all right. But he might have already left and could come here while I'm on my way there."

Daphne shook her head. "That's confusing."

"Very," Tuny told her. "Thank you both, and I promise to bring you stories when I return." She dropped a kiss on each head.

Matty followed Tuny to the door even as Charlotte came back out.

"Here," her sister-in-law said. "Give this to whoever's on duty. With Worth and Lydia out, some of the staff will have been given a holiday. Betsy's gone to hail a hack. I expect it might take a few minutes."

"Do you mind staying with the girls while I go with Tuny?" Matty asked her.

Rose came up to them. "We have an important job, Mama. We are to tell Lord Ashforde where Aunt Tuny has gone."

"And say happy birthday," Daphne added, joining them.

"Say good luck," Rose corrected her.

Daphne pouted. "Birthdays are better."

"Much better," her mother said with a smile. "But we must tell him what Aunt Tuny asked, not what we wish."

"Why?" Daphne asked.

Charlotte turned to her husband. "I'll stay with the girls. But please, be careful."

He pecked her cheek before following Tuny into the house, leaving Charlotte to explain the importance of telling the truth.

By the time the hack arrived, Tuny had added a blue wool spencer to her muslin gown and topped the outfit with a simple straw bonnet that framed her face. Keller still did not look convinced of her quest, but he climbed up beside the coachman as Matty handed Tuny inside.

"You think he's in danger," her brother said as the coach took off.

"It may be nothing," Tuny demurred. "But Leo and Fritz thought it necessary to assign a guard to me. I can't help wondering whether they assigned him to the wrong person."

"That fellow Huber spotted following us after services," Matty mused. "Perhaps he was watching Lord Ashforde, not you."

She shivered, for all the day was warm. "Oh, I hope not. But there was a man in Hyde Park as well. I must be sure Ash is safe."

His townhouse did not look any less stately than the last time they had visited, but as they approached the front door, Tuny could hear what sounded like a woman wailing. Matty stepped around her to pound on the door.

"Open, in the name of the king!" he shouted.

Tuny stared at him.

Matty shrugged. "I didn't say which king. I imagine King Frederick wants to know how today goes as much as his sons."

A pale-faced footman yanked open the door. "Who's there?"

"Sir Matthew Bateman, appointed agent of the King of Batavaria," Matty said, shouldering him aside. "Take me to your master, immediately."

"He likes to be forceful," Tuny explained as she slipped

in behind her brother in time to see a lady who was likely the cook disappear down the stairs.

"I can't," the footman lamented.

Her brother drew himself up and widened his stance. "You will. Unless I find him first." He raised his voice. "Hoy, Ashforde! You're wanted."

"What is the meaning of this?" Peaves demanded, coming down the stairs at a clip that did not bode well for his safety. As his gaze met Tuny's, some of his usual starch leaked back in.

"That is, good day, Sir Matthew, Lady Moselle," he said, coming to a stop at the bottom of the stairs, head high and chin thrust out. "I regret that his lordship is not at home to visitors."

"That's a polite excuse," Tuny informed him. "If you tell him we're here, I'm sure he'll see us."

Peaves sighed. "That's just it, your ladyship. He isn't here. He received a note last night and left immediately in response. We haven't seen him since."

CHAPTER TWENTY

TUNY MUST HAVE swayed, for the butler put out a hand to steady her. Matty went one further.

"What note?" her brother barked. "Who brought it? What did it say?"

Peaves seemed to shrink in on himself further with each question. "A footman brought it," he finally squeaked out. "I didn't recognize him, nor did his lordship see fit to share the contents of the note."

Matty squared his shoulders, always an impressive sight. "Show me where he took possession of it."

What a blessing her brother knew what he was about, for her mind was whirling as she followed him and the butler down the corridor to the library. For once, even the sight of all those books failed to move her.

Something had happened to Ash.

Why? How? Who could have done such a thing?

More importantly, how could she save him?

Matty went to the desk and rummaged about in the documents on top.

"Now, see here," Peaves said, rallying. "Those are his lordship's private thoughts. You have no call to rifle through them."

"If I end up saving his life, I doubt he'll quibble," Matty said. He thrust a piece of parchment at Tuny. "Looks like he had some ideas on what to tell the king."

She forced herself to scan the words, and her heart

leaped. "Oh, my! This is brilliant! It will solve so many problems." She lowered the paper. "But, Matty, the fact that he found a resolution to the Batavarian question is all the more reason to suspect someone wanted to stop him from speaking with the king."

"Apparently so." He handed her another note.

This one stole her breath. But only for a moment.

"Wellmanton," she growled. "Thank you, Mr. Peaves. My brother and I will take matters from here."

The butler hesitated, hands wringing in front of his immaculate waistcoat. "You will bring him home, won't you, your ladyship?"

"I promise," Tuny said. "But you can help. Send word to Weyfarer House, the home of the Duke of Wey on Clarendon Square. Prince Otto Leopold and Count Montalban should have arrived by now, and with them a contingent of the Imperial Guards. Tell the guards we will be retrieving them shortly, and let them know that their future is at stake."

Peaves' head snapped back and up. "At once, your ladyship."

Keller also straightened as they all came back into the entry hall, then followed Tuny out the door. Matty called up directions to Clarendon Square to the waiting hack driver.

"Are we going to fight?" Keller asked her.

"Very likely," Tuny told him. "But we should probably start with a little diplomacy."

The hack deposited them in front of the double-townhouse the Worthingtons owned, and the footman on duty hurried to take word to the coachman in the mews behind. Leaving Matty to wait, Tuny and Keller walked the short distance up the square to Weyfarer House.

She was not surprised to find it in an uproar. Ash's footman had barely beat them to the door and was now huddled in the corner; Count Montalban was barking orders to the Imperial Guards while Prince Otto Leopold and Larissa debated strategy and Callie, Belle, and Aunt Meredith plotted staffing. Fortune wound her way through the melee. Tuny bent to pick her up.

"We could all use a little of your insights about now," she murmured.

Matty put two fingers in his mouth and blew a sharp whistle.

"Thank you, Sir Matthew," Underhill, the butler, said beside them, rubbing an ear. "Lady Moselle and Sir Matthew to see you, your ladyships."

Larissa came to join Tuny by the door, blue eyes soft. "I'm so sorry, Petunia. We will find him."

"Of course we will," Tuny said, though something inside still fretted like a bird tugging at a worm. "I know where to go. I'd just like a little extra support at my side."

Both Count Montalban and Prince Otto Leopold stood taller. Roth, who had been guarding them that day, stepped forward before they could, Huber and Tanner at his side. They all clapped fists to chests.

"We are at your command, Lady Moselle," Huber said.

"I knew you would be," Tuny assured them.

A short while later, they exited the Worthington coach in front of the Wellmanton townhouse. Her brother had known the way. Unfortunately, the Wellmanton butler took one look at Matty beside her and the four Imperial Guards behind and was even less inclined to allow them entrance than Peaves had been. Tuny intervened as Matty swelled up.

"My brother was once known as the Beast of Birmingham," she said apologetically. "We never could dissuade him that speech was preferable to fists. And

I'm afraid he's been tutoring Mr. Keller, Mr. Roth, Mr. Huber, and Mr. Tanner, here."

Matty cracked his knuckles for emphasis. Roth's smile had an edge to it. Tanner, Huber, and Keller stepped closer, hands on the hilts of their swords.

"I will see if Lord Wellmanton might be available," the butler said, moving off as quickly as dignity allowed.

"Stand ready," Tuny murmured, "but don't start a fight. That's how they nearly imprisoned Count Montalban early this Season, by claiming him the aggressor."

"Better aggressor than victim," Roth grumbled.

"Best to keep a level head," Tuny countered. Then she straightened as Lord Wellmanton himself came down the corridor to meet them.

"Lady Moselle, Sir Matthew," he greeted, "to what do I owe this honor?"

How convenient for him to ignore the guards at her back. "We're here because you kidnapped Lord Ashforde," Tuny said. "Release him to our custody now, and no one need know."

Lord Wellmanton put a hand to his heart and staggered. Keller rushed forward to support him. His butler goggled.

"Ashforde, kidnapped?" the viscount wheezed as the other guards exchanged glances. "This cannot be! And just when I managed to secure his family jewels to return to him."

This couldn't be an act. His face was pasty, his jowls quivered, and sweat stood out on his forehead.

"A footman came to his house last night," she told the viscount as Keller helped him regain his footing. "He brought a note claiming that the man who had the jewels was about to leave the country and Lord Ashforde must come now if he wished to save them. The note was signed with your name."

He shoved Keller away as if burned. "Scurrilous! I would never stoop so low!"

"Low enough," Matty muttered.

"I am innocent, I assure you," he protested. "Oh, what a shame his lordship will not be able to present his case to the king."

"He'll be there," Tuny told him. "I'll make sure of it. Just see that you keep the other advisers from closing the conversation with the king until Lord Ashforde arrives."

His smile wasn't in the least supportive. "Oh, certainly, certainly, and may I wish you every fortune in finding him."

Tuny glanced to her contingent. "Mr. Roth, I would hate for anything to happen to Lord Wellmanton the way it has Lord Ashforde. Please accompany him to the meeting."

"Oh, no need," Lord Wellmanton protested, but Roth inclined his head.

"Your servant, Lady Moselle. I will see that his lordship reaches the meeting and nowhere else."

One look at the guard's determined face, and Lord Wellmanton subsided.

Matty and the other three guards joined her in starting for the coach.

"You believe him?" her brother asked.

"I'm afraid I must," she replied. "But he won't be able to do more damage with Roth nipping at his heels."

"Where next?" Tanner asked as they reached the coach.

Tuny met their gazes in turn. Huber was frowning, Tanner was tense, and Keller was gripping his knife hilt as if he would never let go.

"Only one other person might have a reason to prevent Ash from presenting his thoughts to the king," she told them.

She looked up at the Worthington coachman, who was watching. "Take us to the home of the Envoy for Württemberg."

There! With a highly satisfying snap, the last of Ash's bonds separated. He shook his hands free of the rope and set to work on the hood that had been wrapped around his head.

What a fool! One word from Wellmanton, and he'd dashed off in a coach that had taken him to his doom. As soon as it had stopped in a dark corner of London, he'd been set upon by three men, bound, and hooded. He hadn't been able to tell where they'd taken him, but he'd heard first one, then another thank the third for payment right before being deposited in this cell. The last thing he'd heard from his remaining captor was the thud of the door closing.

How long had he been here? Hours? Days? There was no light to be had. As it was, he'd managed to sit, then scoot his way around until he'd bumped into enough pieces of wood to conclude he was in a storage room of some sort, surrounded by crates. Thankfully, one of those crates had had a loose nail, and he'd spent the last while working it against his bonds until he was free.

Now he climbed to his feet. Sleep would have been welcome; he felt his weariness to his bones. But not until he escaped.

He felt his way forward until his hands hit stone. The outer wall? Turning, he took several more cautious steps until he hit a solid wood surface again. Likely the inner wall. That meant his prison was about ten feet from side to side. His experiment in the other directions yielded the same result as well as a bruised shin from hitting the crates. He'd also located the door, which was made of stout wood with no latch on the inside. The air was becoming stale enough that he could almost guarantee there was no window and likely only the single door.

He rubbed his wrists, pondering possibilities.

Had he missed his appointment with the king? Would His Majesty listen to his excellent plan once others had offered options?

Would Tuny be forever disappointed in him?

No, not that. That he could not bear.

Overhead, something thumped.

Ash paused, listening. There it came again, almost as if something had been dragged. He wasn't alone, but was that a sign of friend or foe?

Only one way to find out.

"Help!" he shouted. "Help me! Below you! Help!"

He paused, listening. Were those voices?

"Release me at once!" he railed at the ceiling. "I am a peer of the realm!"

With a creak of little-used hinges, the door opened, spearing light into the space. Ash squinted against the brightness, making out a tall form, broad shoulders. The footman from last night?

"Quiet, you!" he ordered.

Was that an accent? A shame Peaves hadn't noticed. A shame Ash couldn't place it.

But he didn't wait for another word or movement. Last night, they'd surprised him. Today, Ash would surprise him. He rushed the fellow, fists up and at the ready. One good blow to the jaw, and his captor was stumbling. Ash shoved him deeper into the room, dashed out the door, and slammed it shut behind him.

He leaned against the panel, breath coming in pants. A light trickling through the soot-grimed window near the ceiling cast the space in twilight, but at least he could see that the door latch was solid. He glanced around, located another crate, and dragged it over just in case the footman knew a way to open the door. It might open inward, but at least the crate would slow up his assailant a moment.

He drew another breath, and elation surged through

him. He'd done it. He was free. He wanted to caper through the boxes, strut about the space in triumph. He shook off the feeling. The win would be short-lived if he didn't find a way out.

Another survey told him that he was indeed in a cellar, if the other crates and sacks lying about were any indication. The shadows were deep, but nothing moved among them, and he caught no sound nearby. Fewer items clustered to the right, so he edged along and was rewarded with the sight of stairs leading upward.

Back to the wall, he took one step at a time, watching, listening. He even put his ear to the door at the top, but it must have been thick, for he heard nothing but the pounding of his own heart.

He opened the latch and peered out.

He was in a corridor on the main floor of a house of some standing, for the wallpaper was flocked and the credenza against one wall was of walnut inlaid with ivory. There went any hope that he might be in the Wellmanton townhouse. He'd called on the viscount on occasion, so he had a general idea of how his home was decorated.

To his left, he made out a portion of a kitchen. As he watched, a lady in a mop cap passed on the way toward the sink. He slipped farther down the corridor.

Now he heard voices. As he drew closer to what must be the front door, he could even make out the words.

"I am sorry to hear of Lord Ashforde's disappearance, but I fail to understand why you think I might know anything about it."

That accent he recognized. It was from either Batavaria or Württemberg. He'd assumed the English investors had been the ones insisting he advise against Batavarian restoration. Württemberg investors must be as worried or more.

Best to escape while he could.

"I think you know something about it because you and

your country stand to benefit the most if he fails to speak to King George."

Petunia!

He froze, the door within feet of him. She was in danger! He would not leave this house without her. He didn't have to think, to weigh the pros and cons, to see all sides of the argument. He raised his fists once more, turned, and stormed into the room.

Envoy von Mandelsloh had just opened his mouth to respond to Tuny's statement when a madman stormed through the doorway. She'd left Huber and Tanner circling the house, but Keller came to full alert, and Matty climbed to his feet, even as Ash—hair wild, clothes disheveled, ropes trailing from his wrists—skidded to a stop between Tuny and the envoy.

"Get out, quickly," he said to her. "I'll hold him off."

Matty stepped up beside him. "We'll hold him off."

"We will all hold him off," Keller said on the other side.

Herr von Mandelsloh glanced from one to the other, then tilted his head to see around Ash and meet Tuny's gaze. "We seem to have found your missing baron."

Trembling, Tuny rose and lay a hand on Ash's shoulder. "Are you all right?"

He turned just enough to meet her gaze, as if loathe to let the envoy out of his sight. "I should ask you that question."

"I'm fine," Tuny said, barely resisting the urge to take him in her arms. "When you didn't come by the house this morning, I knew something was wrong."

"We've been following the trail ever since," her brother put in.

"A trail," the envoy said, "that appears to have led you here, I am sorry to say." von Mandelsloh shook his head. He'd been willing to receive them and surprised by her vehemence, but adamant that he had had nothing to do with the matter. What was she to think now?

He looked to Ash, brow up in question. "Where have you been, my lord?"

"Confined in your cellar," Ash said. "Where you'll find your footman in a locked room. He likely has a bruise on his jaw." He nodded to Matty. "Thanks to your tutelage, Sir Matthew."

Matty's smile hitched up.

"It may be Schmid," the envoy said. "My housekeeper informed me that he did not come down for breakfast this morning, and his room was empty. We assumed he had found other ways to occupy his time."

"And so he did," Ash allowed. "You will want to question him."

"Prince Otto Leopold will want to question him, too," Keller added.

The envoy's look was strained. "Always happy to assist another citizen of Württemberg."

The quiet Keller must have learned from Matty too, for his scowl was fearsome. "Prince Otto Leopold is not a citizen of your country, and neither is any loyal Batavarian. You will pay for your crimes."

"But I have committed no crimes," the envoy protested, spreading his hands. "I cannot be blamed for what one of my servants decides to do."

"No," Ash said. "But you can be blamed for allowing a traitor in your home. I wouldn't be surprised if he wasn't the one who hurled a rock at my coach the other day. Lord Canning, the Foreign Secretary, will likely want a word with him and you. For now, I'll settle for the use of your carriage."

"No need," Tuny said. "We came in the Worthington coach. We can take you straight to see the king."

Herr von Mandelsloh steepled his fingers. "Oh, was that meeting scheduled for today?"

As if inspired by his words, the clock on the mantel chimed eleven.

Ash groaned. "Yes, at this very moment."

"Go," Keller said, keeping his gaze on the envoy. "Huber and I will deal with the footman. You speak to your king so we may see this matter settled, once and for all."

Ash tipped his head, and Tuny joined him in backing from the room, Matty between them and the envoy.

As soon as they were ensconced inside the coach, Tanner on the bench with the coachman, Tuny threw herself into Ash's arms. "I was so worried!"

He held her, arms strong and breath a caress against her cheek. "I might have been killed, had you not come for me. How did you know?"

She pulled back. "We went to your house, and Matty found the note about the rubies."

His brow went up. "Peaves allowed the intrusion?"

Matty, seated across from them, shrugged. "Didn't give him much choice."

Tuny nodded. "And we found your plan as well. Oh, Ash, it's brilliant!"

His face sagged. "I thought so. But the king isn't kind to those who do not honor their appointments with him. He may not even allow me to speak."

"He will," Tuny said. "We'll think of something."

With him beside her, anything was possible.

CHAPTER TWENTY-ONE

THE COACHMAN PUSHED the horses from Mayfair down to St. James's, where the meeting with the king was to be held at the palace. Tuny did what she could to help put Ash together again, removing the ropes from his wrists and aching at the sight of the bruises and abrasions.

Her fingers shook as she retied his crushed cravat at his throat. What would have happened if they hadn't found him or he'd been caught escaping? Would his captor have been content to let him go once the king had made his decision? Or would he have been lost to her forever?

He reached up a finger and smoothed a tear from her cheek. "It's all right, Petunia. We're safe. I won't let anything harm you."

She nodded, emotions clogging her throat.

His gaze clung to hers. "I will do everything I can to convince the king to follow my plan. I don't want to let you down."

"You won't," she managed, forcing her hands to do no more than brush dust off his lapels.

"I did, once," he murmured.

"That," Tuny said, breath coming easier, "is behind us."

The red brick wall and tall tower of the palace reared up at the end of the street. The carriage stopped before the main double doors—thick, iron-bound, and painted black—and they all climbed down to be met by the stares of the guards on duty.

Which were only slightly stonier than that of the waiting Roth.

The dark-haired guardsman stepped forward and saluted Tuny. "I accompanied Lord Wellmanton to the palace, your ladyship, as you ordered, but I was denied entrance. He spoke to the guards before he went in. I could not hear what he said."

Tanner glanced at the palace guards. "I cannot like our odds."

Ash stepped forward. "I am Lord Ashforde, advisor to the king. I was expected."

"The meeting has started," one of the guards said. "All others must wait."

Ash drew himself up, until he was every inch the lord. "By whose orders?"

The guard drew himself up as well. "By order of the king."

Tuny slipped between them, causing Tanner and Roth to stiffen.

"Let me speak to the king," she said, fighting the tremble that threatened. "I have urgent news His Majesty must hear."

"No admittance without prior authorization," the guard said, looking through her.

Ash's eyes narrowed. "Do you know to whom you speak?" he demanded. "This is the acclaimed Lady Moselle. His Majesty will not be pleased to hear you kept her standing." He turned to Tuny. "My utmost apologies for this affront, your ladyship. Please do not allow their lack of foresight to dim your views of our kingdom. I assure you, His Majesty in no way wishes to be on poor terms with your illustrious monarch."

Tuny put her nose in the air. "I should think not. I fear what he might do when he hears I was turned away from even speaking with your king."

The guards exchanged glances, then one stepped back. "I will send word to the Lord of the Chamber."

Oh, that would never do! Whoever he was, he'd see through her in an instant.

"The Lord of the Chamber!" Tuny cried. "That is an insult worthy of death!"

Tanner and Roth drew their short swords. The remaining guard leveled his pike.

"You may enter," his comrade said. "But I will escort you."

Tuny kept her gaze haughty as she and Ash followed him into the palace.

She had never been inside St. James's before. Commoners were seldom invited to visit the royal family. The corridors were long, lofty, and inlaid with dark wood. Massive paintings of previous members of the aristocracy lined the walls, their baleful stares following her progress. The thick carpet muffled every step.

She would have loved to have asked Ash about the origins of the suits of armor and the bronze and marble busts on pedestals, but that would have given away the game.

Another guard was on duty at the firmly closed door of the chamber. The guard who had accompanied them spoke quietly to him, then withdrew. This fellow appeared to be more reasonable, for he looked Tuny up and down, then inclined his head.

"I will announce you, my lord, my lady," he said. He opened the door.

She wanted to peer around him, but that was not the mark of an acclaimed lady of Batavaria, or any other kingdom. So, she waited impatiently while their sovereign granted him his attention.

"Lady Moselle and Lord Ashforde, Your Majesty."

He stepped aside, and Ash escorted Tuny through the door.

This room had creamy walls with tapestries hung from the high ceiling. In the center was a long, polished wood table that could seat twenty comfortably. Now it seated only five, and she recognized Lord Trelawney and Lord Wellmanton. But all of them were gazing at her and Ash with varying degrees of amusement or annoyance.

She had only seen King George's likeness in the newspapers, but she had no difficulty identifying him with his greying blond hair and perfectly tailored coat. Seated at the head of the table, he peered myopically at them. "Lady Moselle? What is this?"

Tuny broke away from Ash to dart forward and drop a deep curtsey. "Your Majesty, forgive the intrusion, but I wanted to plead with you to hear Lord Ashforde. He was delayed from attending this auspicious meeting because of a cruel attempt at kidnapping and only just now wrested himself free to fly to your side."

"Indeed." The king's tone was frosty. "And who are you that I should believe you? I know of no title of Moselle in my peerage."

Tuny dared to straighten. "But I'm sure you remember the Beast of Birmingham. I am his sister."

The king's stern face broke into a grin. "The Beast of Birmingham! Excellent chap! Saved my life once. *Him*, I distinctly remember elevating. How is your brother?"

"Your Majesty," Lord Trelawney drawled, "perhaps we could return to the business at hand? I'm sure the Beast's sister wouldn't mind waiting."

The king wagged a finger at him. "Never keep a lady waiting, Trelawney. Clever fellow like you should know that." He focused back on Tuny. "Tell me how your brother does. Still winning fights for England?"

"Of course," Tuny said. "In fact, he's even now fighting to ensure Your Majesty has the best advice possible on this thorny issue of Batavarian restoration. That's why he sent me with Lord Ashforde."

She stepped aside and looked to Ash, who was gazing at her in such awe her cheeks heated.

She was a wonder. Ash could not have handled the king better. He took the opportunity she had presented, stepped forward, and bowed. "Thank you, Your Majesty, for entrusting me to advise you. I'm sure you've heard from the others the many considerations that might lead you to favor one decision over another."

"He has," Trelawney put in. "And I fear you will weary him by adding others."

"Our king does not weary so easily," Petunia said, head up. "He bears the burdens of the crown with honor."

"Though it does grow heavy at times," the king lamented with a hand to his brow as if he could feel the weight of the crown of state even now. "Do get on with it, Ashforde."

"Of course, Your Majesty. The question, as I see it, is finding a solution that is fair for the former king of Batavaria, the current king of Württemberg, and the people of the land. Here is what I propose. First King Frederick shall be given control of his ancestral lands but as a vassal state to King William."

Wellmanton had opened his mouth as if to protest. Now he shut it and frowned thoughtfully.

"Second," Ash continued, "King Frederick will send a representative, elected by the people of Batavaria, to the Württemberg Parliament so that their concerns may be considered there, just as our people have representation before our king in our Parliament."

The king nodded. "It has worked well for generations."

"Third," Ash said, knowing this might be the sticking point, "Prince Otto Leopold will remain in England, as the first ambassador from Württemberg. The current envoy and all members of his staff must leave. They have not proven themselves allies to either their country or ours."

"Now, that is too harsh," Wellmanton said. "Envoy von Mandelsloh has been invaluable to our deliberations with Württemberg."

"So invaluable that King William has never petitioned to have him promoted to a full ambassador," Ash pointed out. "Having an ambassador the king can trust, who is connected to England by marriage, will make the union between our kingdoms stronger."

"Prince Otto Leopold is marrying the eldest daughter of the Duke of Wey, if memory serves," the king mused.

"And his brother, Count Montalban, is marrying the second daughter," Ash offered.

The king nodded. "I can see the wisdom. Anything else?"

"Your citizens and our distinguished visitors have continually been plagued by certain men associated with Württemberg, including Alonzo Mercutio, alleged spy for King William, and Gruber von Grub, once secretary to the envoy. All must be imprisoned."

The king hitched himself up in his seat. "Quite right. Entirely too much of that spying business going around. And King Frederick and his son must stop ennobling British citizens. It's becoming an epidemic." He leaned toward Ash. "Frankly, I don't know how he does it. You should have heard the complaints when I elevated the Beast of Birmingham, and the fellow had saved my life!"

Ash was fairly certain Petunia was trying not to grin.

The king leaned back. "I like this plan. What say my other advisors?"

Canning spoke for the first time, like a flute intruding on a bass solo. "It seems logical to me, Your Majesty. King William remains in control, but King Frederick may see to the welfare of his people."

"Our aims are well served," Trelawny agreed.

"And what if King Frederick should enact laws that run contrary to King William's desires?" Wellmanton ventured.

"No duke in England is allowed to make laws, only Parliament, with His gracious Majesty's consent," Ash said. "The same would be true of Württemberg and Batavaria."

"I see it as the best of all worlds," Greville put in genially. "I should be happy to draft the agreement."

The king waved a hand. "Ask Julian Mayes, Lord Belfort. He's a clever fellow. And the Batavarians trust him." He brought both hands together to rub them eagerly. "It seems we are finished here. Miss Bateman, you will join me for tea. I want to hear all about your brother's triumphs."

They'd done it. Tuny wanted to crow it from the rooftops. Larissa, Callie, Leo, and Fritz would be so pleased.

But first, it appeared, she had to attend tea with the king.

And so she found herself seated in a room decorated in entirely too much scarlet and gilt, presiding over a tea service with so much silver she might have bought out every seller at Covent Garden. Lord Wellmanton had managed to include himself in the invitation, as if he did not trust what Tuny and Ash might say to the king. At least he sat quietly on one of the upholstered chairs, glancing about at them all. It was only after the king had been called to other duties and Lord Wellmanton, Tuny, and Ash were walking out of the palace that the viscount cleared his throat.

"Good of you not to mention my name to the king in association with this kidnapping affair," he said as they strolled down the long corridor again. "Nasty business. You can be assured I had no part in that."

"I would like to believe you," Ash said. "But the note mentioned the Ashforde rubies, and I cannot think how the Envoy for Württemberg could have known about them. You, on the other hand, have been rather pointed in your references."

"And now he's gone and found them," Tuny put in to Ash before looking to the older lord. "You did mention that when we dropped by your home, Lord Wellmanton."

His smile was sickly. "Yes, I have located them. I would be delighted to return them to you, Ashforde, for a consideration against my time and trouble, of course."

"Not having it," Tuny said. "I doubt you spent all that much time and trouble. And seeing how Lord Ashforde is keeping your neck from the noose, I'd think you'd be happy to hand him those rubies, free of charge."

He tugged at his cravat. "As you say, Lady Moselle."

"Be advised," Ash said, smile amused, as they came out into the sunlight, "that if I learn you had more to do with this business than it appears, your name may still come up in my discussions with the king."

As if they agreed with every word, Tanner and Roth marched forward and aimed their glares his way.

"Of course," Lord Wellmanton said, voice once more wheezy. He bowed to them both and took himself off in the general direction of White's.

Matty and the carriage were waiting. "Well?" her brother asked.

"The king heartily endorsed Ash's plan," Tuny said, pride in him nearly popping the buttons from her spencer. "They're going to enlist Uncle Julian to draft the agreement."

"He'll make it right and tight," Matty predicted. "I'll stop to let the prince and count know when we return this lot to Weyfarer House. Can we drop you home, Ashforde?"

"I would appreciate cleaning up," he allowed. "May I call on you this evening, Petunia? There is much we must discuss."

She could only think of one thing now that the Batavarian question had finally been settled. "Of course."

Matty eyed the two of them but said nothing. Tanner climbed up on the bench with the coachman, and Roth rode inside next to Matty. It might have been her brother's considered look or Roth's hard gaze, but Ash remained silent.

The afternoon passed in a whirlwind. They set Ash down at his house, and Tuny had to force herself to allow him out of her sight. But there was no longer a reason for anyone to harm him. Indeed, Peaves looked so relieved to see him she thought the butler might burst into tears.

There was even more relief at Weyfarer House, where they ventured next to tell Leo and Fritz the good news. Uncle Julian and Owen Canady had joined the group. Leo hugged Larissa, Fritz kissed Callie, and Owen hugged Belle.

Belle released him to clap her hands. "The perfect ending!" she declared. "Rights returned, everyone staying in England, and weddings all around." She looked pointedly to Tuny, who blushed. For all she hoped, she wasn't ready to claim victory just yet.

As voices rang over each other with questions and laughter, she sidled in next to Roth, Huber, Keller, and Tanner, who were standing against the wall. Keller and Huber had returned to Weyfarer House after depositing Ash's kidnapper with Bow Street to be brought before the magistrate on charges.

"And are you pleased with the news?" she asked the men who had become like brothers to her.

Huber smiled, teeth showing white against the bronze

of his skin. "I am very happy for the prince, the count, and their father, as well as the people of Batavaria. Justice has been served."

"Your baron is very wise," Keller agreed with a touch of envy in this voice.

"Even if he took his time making his decision," Tanner added with a grin.

Roth nodded. "The right decision in the end."

Tuny eyed them all. "And what's your verdict on location? Will you be returning to Batavaria to serve the king or staying in England and starting a new life?"

Roth's dark head inched up. "I will stay in England. Tanner and Keller tell me they feel the same way."

Now Tanner and Keller nodded.

She felt Huber's sigh. "As do I. My duty has not changed, it has just expanded to those for whom I care."

"Including Miss Winchester?" Tuny teased.

His jaw tightened. "I am, of course, at her disposal. Employment, however, will be another issue."

Tuny glanced to where Aunt Meredith was smiling at Uncle Julian. Fortune was watching the guardsmen with her great copper eyes as if she knew something.

"Perhaps Lady Belfort and Fortune might have a say in the matter," Tuny said.

As if she'd heard her name, the cat slipped down from her mistress's lap and padded closer. She went from guardsman to guardsman, baptizing them with a rub of her cheek against their boots.

Huber bent and ran a hand along her back. "Sweet kitty."

Fortune stalked off into the fray again.

"I don't think she likes being called kitty," Tuny told him. "But I must say, you four made a good impression. There's hope for you yet."

CHAPTER TWENTY-TWO

IT FELT ODD to be going home with no Imperial Guardsman at her side. For now, Roth, Keller, Huber, and Tanner would be returning to the Chelsea Palace until the prince started for Württemberg to have Ash's brilliant agreement ratified by all sides. So, no one stood watching from the entry hall or sitting room. Life could return to normal.

As if to prove as much, Matty and Charlotte presided over a quiet family dinner, or at least as quiet as was possible with Rose and Daphne at the table.

"I finally heard from the employment agency this afternoon," Charlotte told them all. "They apologized for misplacing Miss Winchester but highly recommended a Miss Archer, who will come by on Wednesday for an interview. I've seen her credentials. Quite impressive."

Rose frowned. "But why can't Aunt Tuny be our governess, Mama?"

"Yes, why?" Daphne put in, as if refusing to forego the opportunity to use her favorite word.

Charlotte winked at Tuny before answering her daughters. "Because I expect your aunt may be moving out of the house shortly."

"Why?' Daphne asked.

"I'll explain once I know my plans," Tuny promised her.

Charlotte and Matty certainly thought they knew her

plans, for they made sure dinner was over and the girls safely upstairs before the knocker sounded.

Stomach fluttering, hands trembling, Tuny answered the door herself. After all, it was her future calling.

Ash stood on the step, hair once more carefully combed about his handsome face, cravat perfectly tied. Instead of evening black, however, he wore his dove grey coat and trousers and a waistcoat shot with silver. In his hands was a large black velvet box. Beyond him, his coachman and footman grinned at her before the coach moved off.

Ash bowed. "Lady Moselle."

So it was to be formal. She curtsied. "Lord Ashforde. Do come in."

She led him to the sitting room and made a point of perching on one end of the sofa, so he could sit beside her. But instead of joining her, he stood with the box so firmly gripped in his hands she might have thought he'd leave finger impressions on the velvet.

He licked his lips, as if struggling to find the words.

Perhaps she should make this easier for him.

"Peaves seemed delighted to have you back," she said.

A smile appeared. "*All* my staff seemed delighted to have me back. Peaves went so far as to give me the thumbs up as I was leaving this evening."

Her heart started beating faster again. "Oh? Did he have reason to wish you luck?"

"The greatest reason I have ever had," he said. Their conversation seemed to have emboldened him, for he went down on bended knee before her. "Petunia Bateman, Lady Moselle, I adore you."

Breath was suddenly hard to find, but she managed to speak. "Adore? That's a strong word for you."

"I'll give you another. I love you. I want to spend the rest of my life making you happy. Like my ancestor, I want to give you every piece of my heart." He opened the box and held it out to her.

Inside, deep red in silver, the Ashforde rubies gleamed at her. They were nothing to the light shining in his eyes.

"Darling Petunia, would you do me the honor of…"

"Aunt Tuny!" Daphne dashed into the room. "I can count to ten. Want to hear?" She spotted the rubies, and her eyes widened. "Oh, sparkles!"

Charlotte was hard on her heels. "Sorry. Aunt Tuny can listen to you count another time. Wait, do you hear that sound? I think it might be the great bear. Help me escape."

She ushered her youngest daughter out of the room.

"You were saying?" Tuny prompted.

He set the rubies aside and took her hands in his, his grip now sure, warm. "Would you do me the honor of…"

"Aunt Tuny!" Rose scrambled into the room and dived behind the sofa. "The great bear is coming! Hide!"

Ash smiled at Tuny, then stood. "Quick, Rose!" he called. "The dining room. He'll never find you there!"

Rose ran for the other room. Ash followed her and quietly shut the door. Just to be certain, Tuny went to shut the sitting room door too.

"Alone?" Ash asked as she met him in the middle of the carpet.

"Likely not for long," Tuny predicted. "So, yes. I will marry you. I've been in love with you since the day we met three years ago. Now, kiss me, quick, before a member of the Imperial Guard or another member of my family shows up!"

By Michaelmas, widely recognized as the end of harvest, London was witness to no less than four weddings that fueled discussions around every Society table for weeks afterward. The first, held at Westminster Cathedral with all pomp and circumstance, united Prince Otto Leopold of the Principality of Batavaria in the Kingdom of

Württemberg with Lady Larissa, oldest daughter of the Duke of Wey. The happy couple would be accompanying the delegation to Württemberg to sign what the papers were calling the Batavarian Doctrine, then returning to England to take up their roles as ambassadors to the Court of St. James's.

The second, a select affair for family and friends, was held at the Chelsea Palace, where Frederick, Count Montalban, married Lady Calantha, middle daughter of the Duke of Wey. The pair, whose starry-eyed vows left many a lady sighing in envy, would be settling on an estate in Surrey, near Wey Castle, where they planned to raise *Sennenhunds*.

The third, celebrated at St. George's Hanover Square, was a sumptuous event with flowers and ribbons decorating the pews and no less than a dozen attendants for the bride and groom when horse breeder Owen Canady wed Lady Abelona, youngest daughter of the Duke of Wey. The two were planning a lengthy honeymoon in the north of England before retiring to their new home of Primrose Cottage in Weyton, across the bridge from the castle.

The fourth filled the pews of St. Paul's Covent Garden with perhaps the widest assortment of attendees London had ever seen. A duke and duchess sat side by side with pugilists. A marquess and marchioness were shoulder to shoulder with former Batavarian Imperial Guards. And servants from both the bride's and groom's households crowded the back of the church as Petunia Bateman, Lady Moselle, married Thomas, Lord Ashforde.

"We did it!" Belle crowed at the reception that followed at the Ashforde home in Mayfair. Somehow, she managed to wrap her arms around both her sisters and Tuny.

"And by harvest, I'm told," Tuny agreed. "Never thought I'd see the day."

"At times I did wonder whether we could fulfill our wedding vow," Larissa admitted.

"Me too," Callie said.

"I knew we'd to it," Belle said smugly. She glanced to where their aunt and uncle were speaking with her mother and father. "And so did Fortune."

"I wonder who's next," Larissa mused.

"I think I know," Tuny said, and she motioned them closer.

That evening, Meredith poured Julian a cup of tea as they sat in their withdrawing room, well satisfied. He had a travel desk on his lap, a fact that seemed to annoy Fortune no end, and was at work polishing the Batavarian Doctrine. Even critics of King Frederick were hailing it as a mastery of political maneuvering. Of course, King George was taking full credit.

"Though I'm glad you'll be available to help Larissa and Leo, I'm not sure I like that you must travel with the delegation to present this to King William," she said, handing him the cup, sweetened with sugar, as he liked it.

He smiled as he accepted it. "We have remarkably fast ships these days, and travel on the Continent is safe. The entire trip can be accomplished in a matter of weeks."

"Weeks." She sighed. "The days will be endless."

"I am persuaded you will keep busy," he said.

As if to prove as much, Fortune jumped up into her lap and peered into her face.

"The guards, yes, I know," Meredith said. "I've already been giving it some thought. There are families that require bodyguards for various reasons, and others who wish swordmasters to train their heirs. I suppose a gentle man like Mr. Huber might serve as tutor. But first, I'd like a word with Miss Winchester."

Julian frowned. "Miss Winchester, the governess from

Alaric and Jane's house party? I thought she'd disappeared."

"She has," Meredith said. "And I know just the man to find her."

Fortune settled down on her lap, apparently quite satisfied as well.

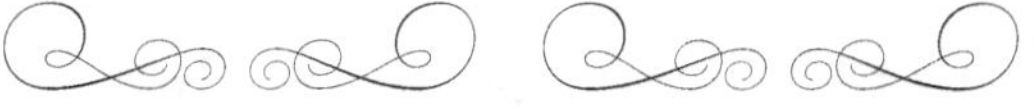

THANK YOU FOR choosing Tuny and Ash's story! They make quite a pair. Though King Frederick has his kingdom back, I'm glad that Larissa, Callie, and Belle will all be settled in England. If you missed any of their stories, look for *Never Pursue a Prince* (Larissa and Leo), *Never Court a Count* (Callie and Fritz), and *Never Romance a Rogue* (Belle and Owen). And you can begin the original Fortune's Brides series with *Always Kiss at Christmas*, when Meredith and Julian first decided to wed, and *Never Doubt a Duke*, when Larissa, Callie, and Belle's parents fell in love.

Look for a new Fortune's Brides series coming in 2023: Guarding Her Heart. Meredith and Fortune will have their hands full with the four former Imperial Guardsmen who decided to stay in England. So will Miss Winchester, who, as it turns out, has been having some adventures of her own.

Learn more at
www.reginascott.com/bodyguard.html.

OTHER BOOKS BY REGINA SCOTT

Fortune's Brides Series

Never Doubt a Duke
Never Borrow a Baronet
Never Envy an Earl
Never Vie for a Viscount
Never Kneel to a Knight
Never Marry a Marquess
Always Kiss at Christmas
Never Pursue a Prince
Never Court a Count
Never Romance a Rogue
Never Love a Lord

Grace-by-the-Sea Series

The Matchmaker's Rogue
The Heiress's Convenient Husband
The Artist's Healer
The Governess's Earl
The Lady's Second-Chance Suitor
The Siren's Captain

Uncommon Courtships Series

The Unflappable Miss Fairchild
The Incomparable Miss Compton
The Irredeemable Miss Renfield
The Unwilling Miss Watkin
An Uncommon Christmas

Lady Emily Capers

Secrets and Sensibilities
Art and Artifice
Ballrooms and Blackmail
Eloquence and Espionage
Love and Larceny

Marvelous Munroes Series

My True Love Gave to Me
The Rogue Next Door
The Marquis' Kiss
A Match for Mother

Spy Matchmaker Series

The Husband Mission
The June Bride Conspiracy
The Heiress Objective

The Regent's Devices Trilogy (writing as R.E. Scott with Shelley Adina)

The Emperor's Aeronaut
The Prince's Pilot
The Lady's Triumph

Frontier Matches

The Perfect Mail-Order Bride
Her Frontier Sweethearts

And other books from
Harper Collins, Mirror Press, and Revell.

ABOUT THE AUTHOR

REGINA SCOTT STARTED writing novels in the third grade. Thankfully for literature as we know it, she didn't sell her first novel until she learned a bit more about writing. Since her first book was published, her stories have traveled the globe, with translations in many languages including Dutch, German, Italian, and Portuguese. She now has more than 60 published works of warm, witty romance, and more than one million copies of her books are in reader hands.

Alas, she cannot have a cat of her own, as her husband is allergic to them. Fortune the cat belongs to her critique partner and dear friend Kristy J. Manhattan, who supports pet rescue groups and spoils her four-footed family members. If Fortune resembles any cat you know, credit Kristy.

Regina Scott and her husband of 30 years reside in the Puget Sound area of Washington State. She has dressed as a Regency dandy, driven four-in-hand, learned to fence, and sailed on a tall ship, all in the name of research, of course. Learn more about her at her website at www.reginascott.com.